I0676512

Butterfly Kisses

LULU HART

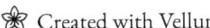 Created with Vellum

Content Warning

Graphic Sex

Playlist

"Glad You Came" by The Wanted
"DIg It" by Bring Me The Horizon
"Hymn for the Weekend" by Coldplay
"Drunk Enough" by Bilmuri
"Vore" by Sleep Token
"One Last Song" by A1
"I'm Kissing You" by Des'ree
"Losing My Mind" by Falling In Reverse
"Forever" by Papa Roach
"Sith Mode" by Not A Toy
"Stargazing" by Myles Smith
"Lovely" by Billie Eilish & Khalid
"Concrete Jungle" by Bad Omens
"Sad Money" by Call Me Karizma
"Breakeven" by The Script

Playlist

ONE HIT WONDERS

"Butterfly" by Crazytown
"MMMBop" by Handon
"Wonderwall" by Oasis
"Ice Ice Baby" by Vanilla Ice
"Tubthumping" by Chumbawamba
"I Love You Always Forever" by Donna Lewis
"Baby, I Love Your Way" by Big Mountain
"Freak Like Me" Adina Howard
"Just a Friend" Biz Markie
"Epic" by Faith No More
"Far Behind" by Candlebox
"Better Days (And the Bottom Drops Out) by Citizen King
"Good" Better Than Ezra
"Teenage Dirtbag" by Wheatus
"Who Let the Dogs Out" by Baha Men
"Stacy's Mom" by Fountains of Wayne
"I Believe in a Thing Called Love" by The Darkness
"Your Beautiful" by James Blunt
"Handlebars" by Flobot
"Macarena" by Los Del Rio
"Barbie Girl" by Aqua
"Im too Sexy" by Right Said Fred

Contents

Chapter 1	1
Chapter 2	9
Chapter 3	17
Chapter 4	25
Chapter 5	33
Chapter 6	39
Chapter 7	47
Chapter 8	57
Chapter 9	67
Chapter 10	75
Chapter 11	83
Chapter 12	91
Chapter 13	99
Chapter 14	107
Chapter 15	117
Chapter 16	125
Chapter 17	131
Chapter 18	139
Chapter 19	147
Chapter 20	155
Chapter 21	165
Chapter 22	173
Chapter 23	179
Chapter 24	189
Chapter 25	197
Chapter 26	205
Chapter 27	215
Chapter 28	221
Chapter 29	227
Chapter 30	235

Chapter 31   243
Chapter 32   251
Chapter 33   259
Chapter 34   267
Chapter 35   275
Chapter 36   283
Chapter 37   291
Chapter 38   297
Chapter 39   303
Chapter 40   309
Chapter 41   313
Chapter 42   323
Chapter 43   331
Chapter 44   341
Chapter 45   347
Chapter 46   355
Chapter 47   363
Epilogue   369

About the Author   381
Also by Lulu Hart   383

Chapter One

CHASE

I GUESS the worst part isn't catching Ava naked with some guy I don't recognize—it's how little I feel about it.

The image should be seared into my brain: her pale skin flushed pink and sweaty, her mouth forming that perfect O of surprise, the guy scrambling to cover himself with her comforter. But as I close the door behind me, it's already fading like an overexposed photograph.

Three flights of stairs and I'm outside her dorm building, the fall air hitting my face. Students pass by laughing, completely unaware that my relationship just ended. The campus feels surreal, like I'm walking through someone else's life.

This makes four. Four girlfriends who've cheated. I should probably start a punch card. Ava broke the record for the shortest amount of time—three weeks. Maybe I should feel rage or heartbreak, but instead there's only this hollow space where those emotions should be.

My phone buzzes. Ava. Four texts in rapid succession:

Chase please

It's not what it looks like

Come back

We need to talk

I slide the phone into my pocket without responding. The campus coffee shop is just ahead, and I find myself walking toward it.

It's packed with students, but I barely notice them as I get in line. My mind keeps replaying the last four relationships like some kind of twisted highlight reel. Different faces, same ending.

"Next," calls the barista, a girl with purple hair.

Shay, according to her name tag—gives me a sympathetic smile as if she can read the disaster written all over my face.

"Rough day?" she asks.

"You could say that. Two iced coffees with almond milk."

I step outside, both cold cups in my hands. One for me, and one... well, I know exactly who the second is for, even if I won't admit it to myself.

The walk back to my off-campus house gives me too much time to think. *Why do I keep ending up with girls like Ava?* Girls who see someone convenient until something better comes along.

Maybe I'm the problem. Maybe I've been choosing women I know will eventually hurt me. Or maybe it's my type —pretty girls with secrets behind their smiles. Picking them

2

because deep down, I know they could never measure up to the person I want.

The one I've wanted since sophomore year who's completely off-limits.

I turn onto my street. *What am I doing?* This is pathetic, bringing her coffee like some lovesick puppy. Yet I can't seem to stop myself.

I unlock the front door, balancing the coffee cups as I push it open, then use my foot to close it behind me.

When I step inside the living room from the foyer, Bebe sits cross-legged on our worn leather couch, textbook balanced on her knees, neon yellow highlighter poised between her fingers. Her reddish-brown hair falls in a curtain around her face as she studies, completely absorbed. It's her—my brother's wife—and the girl I've been secretly in love with since the moment she moved in with us.

She looks up, her eyes brightening when she sees me.

"Chase! You're back early." She closes her textbook. "I thought you were hanging out with Ava today?"

I hand her one of the coffees.

"Yeah, about that..." I take a sip of my coffee, stalling. "I just caught her with a guy in her dorm room. So that's over."

"What?" Her eyes widen, the coffee in her grasp forgotten. "Are you serious? Chase, that's terrible!"

I shrug, trying to appear casual while cataloging every detail of her reaction—the way her brows knit together, the flash of anger in her eyes. She seems more upset than I am.

"God, what a complete bitch," she mutters, setting her coffee on the table with unnecessary force. "I never liked her, you know. I mean, I tried because you did, but there was always something off about her."

"Was there?" I ask.

Bebe pats the cushion next to her. "Sit. Are you okay? Obviously you're not okay, but... how are you holding up?"

I sink onto the couch beside her. "I'm fine, actually. That's the weirdest part."

"You're probably in shock," she says, her hand resting on my arm.

"Possibly," I say, though I don't think it's that. It's resignation.

She shifts closer, her side pressing against mine. Then she's leaning into me, her head finding that perfect spot between my shoulder and chest. I freeze, afraid to move, to breathe, to do anything that might make her pull away. This is torture of the sweetest kind.

"You deserve so much better than her," she murmurs. "You'll find someone who sees how amazing you are, Chase. Someone worthy of you."

I swallow hard. This isn't unusual—Bebe's always been affectionate with me. It's just how we are together, these casual touches that mean nothing to her and everything to me. She's being a friend, offering comfort without realizing she's both the cure and the disease.

"I'm not sure that person exists," I say, trying to keep my voice light.

"She does." She insists. "Trust me."

"Thanks," I manage to utter. "But I might be the problem. Four for four isn't exactly a great batting average."

She pulls back enough to look at me, her eyes fierce. "Don't you dare blame yourself. Some people don't know a good thing when they've got it."

The front door swings open and closes suddenly, and my

brother Luke stands there in the archway, keys dangling from his finger. His eyes take in the scene—his wife curled against me on the couch—and his mouth quirks up into an amused smile.

"What's going on here?" he asks, eyebrows raised as he drops his backpack by the door.

Bebe immediately straightens, though she doesn't move away from me completely. Her bottom lip juts out in a pout.

"He caught Ava cheating on him," she announces, her voice tight with indignation on my behalf.

Luke's face falls for a second before he winces. "Another one? Seriously?"

I let out a long sigh and gesture helplessly with my free hand. "See? That's exactly how everyone is going to associate me now. Chase Sullivan: the guy who gets cheated on."

"You've just had a string of bad luck," She insists, squeezing my arm. She looks at Luke with earnest eyes. "The right girl for him is definitely out there. Someone who'll actually appreciate him."

"Yeah," I say, feeling a sudden reckless urge to blurt out something stupid. Something to break the tension. "So, Bebe, are you volunteering for the job?" I throw my brother a mischievous grin. "Luke, maybe I'll just steal your girlfriend. She clearly has good taste in Sullivan men."

She gasps and playfully slaps my arm. "Chase! You're terrible!" But she's laughing.

She thinks I'm joking... okay, I am.

I am joking—sort of. Except there's a part of me that isn't, and I wonder if that shows on my face.

Luke shakes his head, amused rather than offended. "Nice

5

try, little brother." He reaches down and pulls her up from the couch.

The way she melts into him makes my chest ache. That easy affection, the way they fit together—it's like they were designed as matching pieces. I watch as she tilts her head to him, the adoration in her eyes unmistakable when she looks at my brother. They really are perfect for each other.

And I mean it. I'm genuinely happy for them. Luke deserves someone amazing, and Bebe—well, she deserves the world. My brother can give her that.

Before she can say anything, he's kissing her—not the quick hello I'm used to seeing, but something deeper, more possessive.

I avert my eyes, but I'm still able to hear the wet sounds of their tongues meeting. The hollow feeling in my chest expands, threatening to swallow me whole.

"And that's my cue to leave," I announce, standing so quickly I almost knock over my coffee.

"Chase, wait," Bebe calls after me as I head for the stairs. "Where are you going?"

"Upstairs," I mutter, one foot already on the bottom step. "Might as well study."

And by study, I mean smoke weed.

"Are you going to the Kappa party tonight?" she asks. "The one everyone's been talking about?"

I turn back slightly. "I wasn't planning on it."

"You should go," Luke chimes in, his arm still loosely draped around her waist. "I've got an early day at the office with dad tomorrow, but Bebe wants to check it out. She could be your wing-woman. Help you find a rebound."

6

Her eyes light up. "Yes! That's exactly what you need. Come on, Chase. It'll be fun, I promise."

I look between them—his encouraging smile, Bebe's hopeful expression. The thought of spending the evening with her, even at a crowded party where I'll have to watch guys hit on her all night, is still better than the alternative—sitting alone in my room.

"Fine," I say. "A party might be exactly what I need."

"Yes!" She claps her hands together. "I'll come get you at nine."

Chapter Two

CHASE

I RELUCTANTLY AGREE and get to my bedroom—closing it behind me. I grab a small wooden box out of my dresser that holds my weed and light a joint. The first hit burns my lungs in that familiar way, and I hold the smoke before exhaling toward my open window.

But in my calmness all I can think about is Bebe. Specifically, the time I came home early to find her and my brother having sex. It was two weeks ago—I'd cut my last class —I just didn't feel like going. The house had seemed empty, but then I heard sounds coming from their bedroom. I should have known. I should have walked away. But something made me look through the cracked door that was open just enough to see.

She was on top of him—head thrown back, her reddish-brown hair cascading down her bare back. I stood there frozen, unable to look away from the sight of her riding my brother with slow, deliberate movements. The angle gave me a clear view of her profile—lips parted, eyes closed in ecstasy. Her breasts swayed with each motion, catching the afternoon light that filtered through the half-drawn blinds.

I remember thinking how beautiful she looked in that moment, and hating myself for the thought. She had no idea I was watching—neither of them. Luke's hands gripped her hips, guiding her rhythm as she whispered something I couldn't quite hear.

Every second I stood there was another betrayal—of Luke, of myself, of whatever screwed-up boundaries we were supposed to have in this house. But I remained there for what felt like hours, watching the girl I'd been crushing on with my brother.

When I finally tore myself away, I slipped out of the house without making a sound. Spent the rest of the afternoon walking aimlessly around town, trying to burn the image from my mind. But it's still there, crystal clear, playing on repeat every time I close my eyes.

I take another hit. The weed is dulling the edges of my thoughts, making the memory of Bebe and Luke a little less sharp, a little more distant. *Thank God.*

It has become my ritual now—getting high whenever I need to escape. None of my brothers know about it. Not Luke nor Wes. They'd lose their minds if they found out about this —about the pills in my sock drawer too. Mr. Perfect Law student using drugs or the regular. What a joke.

I lean against the windowsill and stare at the darkening sky. *When did I become this person? This... shell who needs chemicals to feel normal?* Six months ago, I was acing my criminal justice classes, had a clear path to law school, and was fully invested in our family's Keeper society obligations.

Now I can barely drag myself to class. The Keeper meetings seem like elaborate playacting—grown men with their secret handshakes and ancient oaths. *What's the point of it?*

I take a third hit and hold the smoke deep in my lungs when my cellphone vibrates against my desk. Dad's name and photo flash on the screen. I exhale sharply and silence it with my thumb. I already know what he wants. The Keepers' monthly meeting is tomorrow night, and he's probably calling to remind me about Celeste Astor.

She just moved to town with her family—another legacy Keeper household with generations of "honorable service." Dad introduced us last year. She'd smiled politely, tucked her perfect dark hair behind her ear, and made small talk about law because that is also her major. The ideal Keeper daughter for the youngest son. Dad's been not-so-subtly pushing us together ever since.

Not interested. Not even a little.

The phone lights up again, but this time it's Jason's name on the screen. I swipe to answer.

"What's up?" I say, my voice coming out raspier than I expected.

"Dude, are you smoking right now?" He laughs. "It's like four in the afternoon."

"Time is a social construct," I mutter, taking another hit. "What do you want?"

"I heard about Ava," he says. "Tough break, man."

I almost drop the joint. "How the hell—" I pause, looking at the time on my phone. It has been literally an hour since it happened. Who told you?"

He chuckles on the other end of the line. "Small campus, smaller friend circle. You know how it goes."

"Fantastic." The weed is definitely hitting now, making everything seem slightly ridiculous. "So, my personal life is already public knowledge."

"Silver lining though," he continues, his voice brightening. "Now you can come camping with us this weekend. Two nights in Blackridge Forest, no cell service, just beer and campfires."

I lean against my headboard, remembering Ava had shot down this camping trip; therefore, I declined too.

"I don't know, man," I sigh, staring at the burning joint between my fingers. "I kind of want to wallow in self-pity for a while."

"Exactly why you need this," he pushes.

I take a final drag, feeling the smoke fill my lungs. Maybe he's right. Maybe I need to distance myself from campus, from this house, from the constant reminder of what I can't have. That both of my brothers have found love while I'm here left behind.

"Fine," I mutter. "I'll come."

"Yes!" Jason's victory whoop is so loud I have to pull the phone away from my ear. "That's what I'm talking about!"

It hits me I've now been talked into two things today—the party tonight and camping tomorrow. My life is suddenly filling up with plans I didn't make.

"We're leaving at 9 AM sharp," he states. "Pack light, but bring your good sleeping bag. The forecast says it might get cold at night, possibly some rain."

"Yeah, yeah," I mumble, feeling exhausted all of a sudden. "I'll be ready."

I hang up and set my phone on the nightstand, stubbing out what's left of my joint in the empty soda can I keep by my bed. My eyelids feel heavy as I sink back against my pillows. Just a quick nap before the party...

Someone's shaking my shoulder. I crack one eye open to see Bebe leaning over me, her face half in shadow from the dim light of my bedside lamp.

"Chase? Are you alive?" Her words cut through the fog in my brain.

I blink, trying to orient myself in the darkness of my room. I have no memory of falling asleep, just the lingering haziness of the weed clouding my thoughts.

"What time is it?" My voice sounds as if I've been gargling gravel.

"It's almost nine." She perches on the edge of my bed. She's changed into a tank top and jeans, her hair falling in loose waves around her shoulders. "Do you still want to go to the party? You look pretty out of it."

I push myself into a sitting position, running a hand through my hair. "Yeah, yeah. Give me a minute to wake up."

She studies my face. "Are you sure? We don't have to go if you're not feeling it."

"I want to," I insist, suddenly desperate not to disappoint her. "Just need to change."

She nods and stands. "I'll wait downstairs. Don't fall back asleep!"

As soon as she closes the door behind her, I swing my legs

over the side of the bed. My head is pounding uncomfortably, the weed hangover already settling in. I'm not going to be much fun at this party unless I do something about it.

I rifle through my dresser for a clean shirt, deciding on a dark blue button-down that Bebe once said brought out my eyes. As I change, my fingers brush against the tiny plastic bag hidden beneath my socks—tiny colored pills inside.

What the hell, why not? I fish one out—a small blue tablet with a dolphin stamped on it. I've taken E twice before, both times at music festivals where the pulsing lights and thrumming bass called for chemical enhancement. But tonight feels like it needs something extra.

I swallow the pill dry, grimacing at the bitter taste that lingers on my tongue. It'll take about an hour to kick in, which means I'll be feeling it right when the party gets going.

I give myself a quick once-over in the mirror, passing my hand through my disheveled hair in a halfhearted attempt to tame it. My pupils are already slightly dilated from the weed, but otherwise I look normal enough. No one would suspect that beneath this façade of the respectable law student is a mess of contradictions and bad decisions.

I head downstairs, bracing myself for a night of with Bebe while pretending I'm there for any other reason.

As soon as my foot hits the bottom step, she spots me and practically leaps off the couch. She's bouncing on her toes, clapping her hands together with a childlike enthusiasm that makes my chest ache.

"Finally!" she squeals, grabbing my wrist. "You look great! This will be so fun!"

Her excitement is infectious, radiating off her in waves as she twirls in a little circle, her hair fanning out around her. For a moment, I forget about Ava, about Luke, about all the reasons I shouldn't be alone with Bebe tonight.

"We're going to dance and drink terrible beer and find you a hot rebound," she continues, tugging me toward the door.

I can't help but smile at her enthusiasm. "You seem more excited about this party than I am."

"Because I know exactly what you need right now," she says.

You?

Chapter Three

DAISY

I'M three sips into my coffee and halfway through convincing myself that "not leaving my bed" counts as a productive Thursday night when Olivia kicks my dorm door open as though she's in an action movie.

No knock. No hello. Just—*bang*—and now my heart rate is double what my Fitbit thinks is possible.

"Emergency!" she yells, storming in like she is running from the paparazzi and tosses her oversized purse onto my bed.

"Did someone die, or is Starbucks out of pumpkin spice again?"

She grins—too wide, too smug. "Better. Guess who's single?"

My stomach drops. Not from dread. From the violent, almost embarrassing hope clawing its way up my throat. "You can't just start a conversation like that without naming names—"

"Chase Sullivan," she says, drawing out each syllable as if she were announcing the winner of a game show.

I nearly choke on my coffee. *Chase Sullivan*. The same Chase who's been my secret crush since I moved to Ambrose and started at Dalton U last year. Tall, stupidly handsome, and —most importantly—utterly unaware I exist. The same Chase who'd been in a relationship off and on for... forever. I try to play it cool. "Oh. Huh. That's... interesting."

"Interesting? That's all you've got?"

I roll my eyes but can't help asking, "So what happened? They didn't last that long."

"According to Becca, who heard from Joey—" She pauses for dramatic effect, leaning forward, "—Ava cheated on him. With a guy from her statistics class."

"Seriously?" My heart does this weird flip-flop thing. Not because I'm happy about it—okay, maybe a tiny part of me is —but mostly I feel... awful for him. "That's terrible."

"I know, right? Apparently, he walked in on them this afternoon."

I wrap my hands around my coffee mug, feeling the warmth seep into my palms. "Poor Chase."

"Poor Chase?" Olivia raises an eyebrow. "This is your chance, Daisy. The guy you've been crushing on forever is finally available."

"I barely know him," I protest, though my cheeks flush hot. "We've been in the same room maybe four times total?"

"But you've never actually talked to him," she finishes for me.

"Right." I shrug, trying to seem casual.

The truth is, I've spent more time watching him from

across rooms than I care to admit. The way he leans forward when he's really listening to someone. I've watched him help drunk strangers find their friends at parties. I've seen him debate passionately in political science, but never in that aggressive style some pre-law guys do, like they're trying to crush their opponents. He argues ideas, not people."

"You're thinking about him right now, aren't you?" she asks, snapping her fingers in front of my face.

"Maybe I am." I tuck my legs under me. "But it's not just that he's cute. He's funny, and he likes to have intellectual conversations."

"Brains and beauty. A rare combination," she says with a wink.

I sigh, resting my chin on my hand. "But have you noticed he seems... different lately? Even before this Ava thing?"

"Different how?"

I sigh. "You know, less... I don't know, sparkly?"

She snorts. "Sparkly? What is he, a vampire?"

"You know what I mean. When I first saw him last year, he was always laughing, always the center of attention naturally. Now he's quieter."

"Of course I haven't noticed, but you would, wouldn't you? Tracking his emotional state like you're writing his unauthorized biography."

I throw a pillow at her, which she catches with annoying grace. "I just pay attention to people."

"You pay attention to one person in particular." She tosses the pillow back, then suddenly jumps up as if she's been electrocuted. "Oh my God! I can't believe I almost forgot the best part!"

"What?" I sit straighter, my coffee sloshing dangerously close to the rim of my mug.

Her eyes are practically gleaming. "Chase's going on the camping trip tomorrow."

"The one *we're* going on?"

She beams. "Jason convinced him. You, me, my boyfriend, s'mores, and the man you've been secretly planning your wedding to."

I groan, shoving a throw pillow over my face. "This is a disaster."

"Correction," Olivia says, plucking the pillow away. "This is fate. And fate says you'd better pack something cuter than your butterfly pajama pants."

I glanced down at my pajamas. The cartoon butterflies have little sunglasses on. *What's not cute about them?*

I groan, pulling my blanket over my head. "He doesn't even know my name."

"Then you'll just have to make sure he learns it," Liv says, yanking the blanket down. "Starting with the right outfit."

Before I can protest, she's already halfway across the room, flinging open my closet doors with the kind of determination usually reserved for FBI raids.

"Let's see..." She grabs my oversized hoodie. "No." My favorite ripped jeans. "Too casual." A sweater I wear to literally everything. "You look like a kindergarten teacher in this."

I scowl. "A *cool* kindergarten teacher."

She ignores me, pulling out a floral dress. "Too innocent. We need him to think you know how to pitch a tent and break a man's heart."

"That's... specific," I mutter.

Liv tosses the dress onto my bed and goes deeper,

emerging with my old high school track hoodie. "Absolutely not."

She pauses, holding up a pair of cargo shorts I wore on actual hikes. "If I ever see you in these again, I will burn them myself."

By the time she's done, my closet looks like a crime scene, and I have a sad little pile of maybe four outfits that had survived her judgment.

She steps back, hands on her waist. "Alright, now, when you see him at the campsite, here's the move: you walk up," she takes a step back, spreads her arms wide, and says, "Like this."

I watch as Olivia transforms before my eyes. Her shoulders drop, her hips sway with each deliberate step as she glides across my dorm room floor like it's a runway in Milan. There's a confidence in each movement that makes me both jealous and terrified.

"That's your sultry walk," she announces.

"I can't do that."

"You absolutely can," she insists. "Now, when he's looking at you—and trust me, he will be—you need to toss your hair."

Before I can argue, she demonstrates with a dramatic flourish, her dark curls cascading through the air in slow motion like she's filming a shampoo commercial. The move is so perfect I half expect to hear wind chimes.

"I don't have the hair you do," I point out. Mine is straighter, and generally less cooperative.

"Doesn't matter. It's all in the attitude." She grabs my shoulders. "And then—this is crucial—you ask him if he can help you start your fire."

I blink. "That sounds like an innuendo."

Her grin widens. "Exactly. Men love feeling useful. It's like catnip to them. Or, if you want to play it mysterious, just lean on something and say, 'Do you know much about bears?'"

I gawk. "*Do you know much about bears?* What does that even mean?"

"It doesn't matter! He'll be intrigued! Boom— conversation starter," she says, shoving the pile of "acceptable" clothes at me. "Pack these. Leave the butterfly pajamas here."

I grab the clothes from her hands, then set them back on the bed.

"Liv, stop." I take a deep breath, feeling a sudden surge of confidence that honestly surprises me. "I love you. You're my favorite cousin, and I appreciate your complete honesty, but I'm going to be myself—butterfly pajamas and all."

Her mouth drops open like I've suggested we invite aliens to our campsite.

"But—"

"No buts. Chase Sullivan might be single, but he's never going to notice me, but if he did, he should like the real me. The one who thinks sunglasses on butterflies is peak fashion."

Liv stares at me for a long moment, then lets out a dramatic sigh. "Fine. But when you're single at thirty with fifteen cats, don't come crying to me."

"I'm allergic to cats," I remind her. "And I like who I am."

She sighs, but there's a hint of a smile. "You're impossible."

"But at least I'm happy," I add.

Her face shifts, her playful expression melting into something more serious. She sits beside me on the bed, gently tucking a strand of hair behind my ear with a tenderness that makes me pause.

"That's just it," she says softly. "I want you to be happy. Really happy."

I frown. "What makes you think I'm not?"

She looks at me with those big brown eyes that have always seen right through me, ever since we were kids sharing popsicles on her parents' back porch.

"You hide in this room every weekend. You've been at Dalton U for a year and your closest friend is still your cousin." She squeezes my hand. "Having Jason in my life has made everything better—brighter somehow. I want the same for you."

The fact is, I've gotten comfortable in my little bubble of solitude, butterfly pajamas, and Netflix marathons.

"I am happy," I insist, but even I can hear the lie. Something is missing from my life.

I swallow hard, not sure what to say. I've watched her and Jason together. The way they laugh at inside jokes, the casual way they touch each other—like it's the most natural thing in the world. And yes, sometimes I wish I had the same.

"It's just... hard for me," I admit finally, my voice barely above a whisper. "Getting attached to people. Finding someone who'll understand."

Her expression softens. She's the only one at Dalton U who knows about my hemochromatosis. The lack of energy, general weakness, brain fog and the occasional joint pain that sometimes makes it impossible to get out of bed, the constant fatigue that makes me choose Netflix over parties.

"Hey," she says gently, "the right person will understand."

I shrug, not convinced. My last relationship ended when Brandon got tired of canceled dates and my "constant excuses."

Olivia squeezes my hand. "Did you do your treatment today?"

I nod. "Yeah. I should be good for the weekend."

Chapter Four

CHASE

THE BASS HITS me before we even reach the house—a physical force vibrating through my chest as we walk up the driveway. The pill is starting to take effect, making everything sharper, brighter, more intense.

"Holy shit," Bebe whispers, eyes wide as we approach the sprawling two-story colonial. The Kappa house is practically pulsing with energy, silhouettes of dancing bodies visible through every window, red cups dotting the yard like plastic flowers.

I feel a strange disconnect as we step through the front door, like I'm watching myself from a slight distance. The crowd parts as we enter, and I notice several glances in our direction. A girl I vaguely recognize from my constitutional law class catches my eye and waves enthusiastically.

"Baby Sullivan!" she calls out, her voice cutting through the music. "I didn't know you were coming tonight!"

I force a smile, that familiar weight settling in my stomach.

Baby Sullivan. Not Chase Sullivan. Not even Chase. Just the youngest Sullivan brother—a footnote to Wes and Luke's legacy.

"Who was that?" Bebe asks, leaning close enough that I can smell her perfume. The scent hits me harder now, the MDMA heightening all my senses.

"No idea," I lie, taking her elbow gently. "Come on, let's get drinks."

I navigate through the throng of bodies, creating a path for her to follow. The music pounds through me, each beat sending pleasant waves of warmth down my spine. I keep my hand lightly on the small of her back as we push deeper into the house, trying to ignore how it feels to touch her.

The kitchen is slightly less crowded, though still packed with people filling cups from kegs and mixing questionable concoctions. I grab two clean cups from the stack on the counter.

"What's your poison?" I ask, gesturing to the makeshift bar spread across the kitchen island.

Bebe's eyes scan the bottles. "Surprise me?"

I mix us both vodka cranberries—simple but effective. As I hand her the cup, our fingers brush, and electricity shoots up my arm. The pill is definitely working now.

"Thanks," she says, taking a sip. "Oh! That's good."

As she drinks, her attention shifts to something happening at the dining table.

"What are they doing?" she asks, pointing to where a group of about ten people are seated around the table, passing what looks like a playing card from person to person—using only their lips.

A girl in a tight red dress is sucking the card against her

mouth, then leans toward the guy next to her who's trying to "blow" it off her lips and onto his. Their mouths come dangerously close to touching, which is clearly the point of the game.

"It's called Suck and Blow," I explain, feeling the drug making me hyper-aware of Bebe's fingers still wrapped around my arm. "You pass the card around without using your hands. If you drop it..."

Right on cue, the card falls between a couple, and their lips meet in what quickly becomes a full-on make-out session. The table erupts in cheers.

"... that happens," I finish.

She watches, fascinated. "I've never seen that before."

It hits me again how different her upbringing was from mine. Homeschooled until college.

Someone at the table waves us over, but I shake my head and take Bebe's hand instead.

"Come on, let's dance," I say, feeling bold as the MDMA fully takes hold. "Much more fun than watching people swap spit."

The music wraps around us as we push through bodies toward the living room. Everything feels heightened—the brush of strangers against my arms, the kaleidoscope of colored lights, and especially her hand in mine.

The room has been transformed into a makeshift dance floor, furniture pushed against walls to create space. Bodies move in rhythm to some EDM track I don't recognize, but my body responds to it instinctively.

Bebe turns to face me, her eyes bright with excitement. "So," she says, leaning close to be heard over the music, "see anyone you like? Any potential rebounds?"

I'd completely forgotten that was the point of tonight—her playing matchmaker. The thought of kissing another person while she's standing right here seems absurd.

"I'll let you know," I say, having absolutely no intention of doing so.

She nods and finishes her drink, setting the empty cup on a nearby speaker. Her body sways to the beat, and I feel my own responding in kind.

"Dance with me," she says, not a question but a command.

The music shifts to something with a deeper bass, and I let the rhythm take over. The pill has me feeling weightless, amplifying everything—the bass feels like it's inside me, my body moving with a confidence I rarely possess. And Bebe... God, Bebe is glowing. I'm not sure if it's the MDMA or just her, but she looks ethereal. She raises her arms above her head, her top riding up to reveal a sliver of tanned stomach that catches the pulsing lights.

I can't take my eyes off her. The way she moves is mesmerizing—uninhibited, joyful, like she's completely surrendered to the music. She spins around, her hair fanning out, and finds me watching. Instead of looking away, she smiles and dances closer, until we're moving together in our own little bubble amid the crowd.

I let myself go, also surrendering to the music and the high. For once, I'm not overthinking every movement, every word. I'm just... here. Dancing with the girl I can't have, pretending for just one night that she could be mine.

She throws her head back laughing, and the moment feels perfect until a guy stumbles backward, knocking into her hard. She falls forward with a surprised gasp, crashing against my chest. My arms instinctively wrap around her waist to steady her as I glare at the drunk guy who's still oblivious to what he's done.

"Hey, watch it!" I call out, tightening my grip on Bebe. The guy turns, sees us, and raises his hands in a half-hearted apology before disappearing back into the crowd.

I should let go now. That's what a friend would do—make sure she's okay, then step back to a respectable distance. But the E is coursing through my system, making every point of contact between us feel like tiny electrical currents.

"You okay?" I ask.

She nods, looking at me with those wide mismatched eyes. "Yeah. Thanks for catching me."

This is the moment I really should drop my hands. Step back. But I don't. Instead, I loosen my hold slightly, resting my hand on her hip. She doesn't pull away.

And then we're dancing again.

The music transitions to something slower, more sensual. Our bodies find a new rhythm together, swaying in sync. She remains, and I'm hyper-aware of every inch where we connect—her hands on my shoulders, my fingers lingering at her hip, the occasional brush of her thigh against mine.

To anyone watching, we must look like a couple. The thought sends a thrill through me, heightened by the drug circulating in my system. My heart pounds in time with the bass, and everything about Bebe seems impossibly vivid—the flush on her cheeks, the slight sheen of sweat on her collarbones.

I know she's just being nice. This is Bebe being Bebe—comfortable, friendly, completely unaware of the effect she has on me. To her, this is just dancing with her husband's brother, helping him get over a bad breakup. Nothing more.

But the MDMA is making it impossible to maintain that rational thought. The music swells, and a wave of exhilaration washes over me. In that moment of chemical-induced courage, I slide both hands to her waist. She doesn't flinch or step back. Instead, she meets my gaze with a soft smile. The drug heightens everything—the warmth of her skin under my palms, the scent of her perfume, the curve of her lips.

The rational part of my brain is screaming at me to stop, but it's drowned out by the music and the chemical euphoria flooding my system. In this moment, with her body pressed against me and her eyes locked on mine, I can almost believe she feels it too.

I dip my head closer, closing the distance between us. She blinks in surprise, but she doesn't pull away, and that's all the permission my drug-addled brain needs.

I press my lips to hers. For one suspended heartbeat, time stops. Then reality crashes back as her body goes rigid. Her hands push against my chest, breaking the connection. When I open my eyes her face is a portrait of shock.

The look on her face is like a knife in my chest. Everything inside me crumbles as I watch shock transform into hurt, her eyes wide with disbelief. *What have I done?*

"Chase..." Her voice breaks on my name. She steps back, creating a chasm between us that feels miles wide.

"Bebe, I'm sorry, I—" The words catch in my throat as the magnitude of my mistake hits me. The high that had made everything seem possible just moments ago now makes the pain sharper, more vivid.

"How could you?" she whispers, barely audible over the music. A tear spills down her cheek.

I reach for her, desperate to fix what I've broken, but she flinches away from my touch. The rejection is physical, a blow to my already aching chest.

"Please let me explain—" But there's nothing to explain. No excuse that could possibly make this okay.

Before I can say anything else, she turns and pushes through the crowd. The sea of bodies swallows her, and just like that, she's gone.

I stand frozen, the music suddenly too loud, the lights too bright. People continue dancing around me, oblivious to the catastrophe that just occurred.

Luke is going to kill me.

Chapter Five

CHASE

THE TASTE of tequila is still bitter in my mouth when I stumble through the front door. My head spins, a carousel of poor decisions and worse consequences. After Bebe ran off, I found some guy selling weed and spent the last few hours getting high on the back porch of the Kappa house, staring at nothing.

It's 2 AM according to my phone—seventeen missed calls from Luke. Each one a promise of what's waiting for me. I considered not even coming home.

The house is quiet, though. Too quiet. Maybe Luke's asleep.

I climb the stairs carefully, each creak of the old wood sounding like a gunshot in the silence. My room is dark when I push the door open, and I don't bother with the light. The weed has mellowed the MDMA crash, leaving me numb and disconnected as I pull my wallet from my back pocket and move to place it on my dresser.

The door behind me slams open.

I barely have time to turn before Luke's fist connects with my face. The impact sends me sprawling backward, crashing into my dresser. Before I'm able to regain my balance, he is on me, tackling me to the floor with a force that knocks the wind from my lungs.

"You fucking piece of shit!"

His weight pins me as blow after blow rains down. I taste blood as his fist collides with my mouth. Another punch lands squarely in my eye, sending white-hot pain through my skull. I don't raise my hands to block. Don't push him off. *I deserve this.*

Each impact feels like penance. For wanting what wasn't mine. For betraying my brother. For hurting Bebe. My head rocks back against the hardwood floor with each hit, but the physical pain is nothing compared to the look in Luke's eyes— pure betrayal illuminated in the hallway light spilling through the doorway.

When he finally stops, his chest heaves with exertion. He pushes himself off me, standing over my crumpled form like an avenging angel.

"What the fuck is wrong with you?" he snarls, his voice raw with rage. "Bebe came home crying. Thirty fucking minutes, Chase. That's how long it took to calm her down before she could tell me what happened." His voice cracks on the last word. "She couldn't even speak. My wife couldn't even tell me what my brother had done."

"I'm sorry," I mumble, tasting copper. "Luke, I'm so fucking sorry."

He laughs, a hollow sound that holds no humor. "Sorry?

You think 'sorry' fixes this? You kissed my wife, Chase. *My wife.*"

I try to push myself up, my arms shaking with the effort. "I was rolling," I confess, unable to meet his eyes. "I took E before the party. Got carried away with the feeling."

He goes still above me. In the dim light from the hallway, I can see his expression shift from rage to disbelief.

"Since when do you do drugs?" The question hangs between us, heavy with accusation and something else— disappointment that cuts deeper than his fists ever could.

"A few months," I admit, finally managing to sit up, my back against the dresser. "Started with weed. Then, sometimes pills."

Luke moves backward as if I've struck him. "Jesus, I don't even know who you are anymore." He runs a hand through his hair, exhaustion settling over his features. "What happened to you?"

I let out a hollow laugh that turns into a wince as pain shoots through my semi-split lip. "I've been asking myself the same question." I taste blood as I speak; metallic and warm. "Wish I knew."

He stares at me for a long moment, his eyes searching mine like he's looking for something—some remnant of the brother he thought he knew.

"How long?" he finally asks, his voice quieter now.

"A few months, like I said—" I mumble.

"No." He cuts me off, his jaw tight. "How long have you been in love with my wife?"

The question hits me like another punch. I freeze, mouth half-open, no words coming out. The room suddenly feels airless, as though all the oxygen has been sucked away in an instant.

"What?" I croak out, but it's a weak denial, and we both know it. "I'm not—"

"Don't." His voice is deadly quiet.

I look at my brother, feeling the weight of his question crushing me. But I can't answer it. Not directly. The truth is too raw, too shameful.

"I'm fucking lonely, Luke," I say instead, my voice breaking. "You and Wes... you both found someone. And I'm just... here. Left behind."

His expression shifts, confusion replacing some of the anger.

"What are you talking about?"

I wipe blood from my lip with the back of my hand. "Every girlfriend I've had has cheated on me. Why can't I find what you have? What Wes has?"

He takes a step back, leaning against my doorframe.

"I'm drowning," I admit, tasting blood as I speak. "I can't focus on classes. My grades are slipping. I don't give a shit about The Keepers anymore. All those meetings, all that legacy bullshit dad keeps pushing—it feels meaningless."

My body aches as I push myself up straighter against the dresser. "I wake up every morning and can't remember why any of it matters. Law school. Being a Keeper. It's like I'm just going through the motions while everyone else moves forward —happily."

Luke takes a step back, processing. The rage is still there, but something else too—uncertainty.

"Nothing you're saying excuses what you did," he says, shaking his head. His anger has tempered but not disappeared.

"You can be lonely, confused, whatever—but you crossed a line tonight. A serious fucking line."

"I know." My voice sounds small, even to my own ears.

"You need to get your shit together," he continues, and there's something like concern mixed with the disappointment in his tone. "The drugs... whatever this was tonight. It needs to stop. Before you destroy yourself. Before you destroy this family."

I nod, wincing as the movement sends pain shooting through my battered face. He's right. I'm spiraling, and tonight I took Bebe and Luke down with me.

"Where's Bebe?" I ask, needing to face the full consequences of what I've done. "I need to apologize to her."

His expression hardens immediately. "You're not going anywhere near her." His voice leaves no room for argument. "We're staying at Amelia's place tonight—maybe for a while. I don't trust you."

His words sting worse than my split lip. Him not trusting me—his own brother—is a knife twisting in my gut. And the worst part is he's right not to.

"Luke..." I start, but I don't know what to say. *What can I possibly say to make this better?*

He watches me, his face a mask of emotions I can't fully read in the dim light. Anger, yes, but something else—disappointment, betrayal, confusion.

"I never thought you could do something like this," he finally says, his voice quieter now, which somehow hurts more than his shouting. "You would be the last person I'd expect to hurt me. We're brothers, Chase."

He shakes his head slowly, as if he's trying to dislodge the image of me kissing Bebe from his mind, then turns and walks out, pulling the door closed behind him with a quiet click that feels more final than if he'd slammed it.

I don't call after him. Don't try to explain again. There's nothing left to say.

I sit there on my bedroom floor, feeling hollow—like something vital has been scooped out of me, leaving an empty shell. The high from earlier has completely evaporated, replaced by a crushing sobriety that makes everything painfully clear.

Chapter Six

DAISY

I'm MENTALLY COUNTING the trees we pass to avoid thinking about the fact that in exactly forty-seven seconds, Chase Sullivan will get into this car. *With me.*

Olivia giggles as we turn onto his street, the sound making my stomach flip like I've swallowed a live fish. She's been like this the entire drive—practically vibrating with excitement that isn't even for her own benefit. It's exhausting being the subject of someone else's matchmaking fantasy.

"What's so funny?" Jason asks from the driver's seat, glancing at his girlfriend with a mix of amusement and suspicion.

"Nothing," she replies too quickly, then catches my eye in the rearview mirror with a look that says we're sharing some delicious secret.

We're not. Well, she thinks we are, but the "secret" is just my embarrassing crush that she's determined to transform into a wilderness romance.

"It's definitely something," he persists, slowing the car as we approach Chase's house. "You've been giggling all morning like you're plotting a bank heist," he finishes, just as he pulls up to the curb.

My heart jumps to my throat as Jason honks the horn. *This is it.* The moment I've been simultaneously dreading and looking forward to since Olivia burst into my dorm room last night.

I smooth my hair nervously, grateful I chose my favorite blue sweater instead of the crop top Olivia tried to force on me. The seconds tick by like hours. No movement from the house.

"Maybe he changed his mind," I whisper, equal parts disappointed and relieved.

Jason honks again, longer this time, more insistent. I wince at the sound. Nothing says "we're totally cool and casual" like aggressively honking outside someone's home.

"He's coming," Olivia says, twisting in her seat to look at me.

The front door finally swings open, and there he is. Chase is carrying a duffel backpack and a rolled-up sleeping bag under his arm. He's wearing a faded gray t-shirt and dark jeans, his hair slightly messy, like he just got out of bed—but don't let that fool you—he's still sexy.

Olivia gasps.

I see it too. He has a black eye. And is that... a cut lip?

I stare, forgetting all my anxiety about seeing him in the shock of his injury.

"Holy shit, man," Jason says. "What happened to your face?"

Chase shrugs, the movement casual despite the violent evidence painted across his features. "You should see the other guy."

Olivia turns to me with wide eyes, her expression a mixture of shock and something else—fascination, maybe? Like she's watching a soap opera unfold in real time. I stare back at her, my jaw slightly open.

My stomach twists with a weird blend of concern and—I hate to admit it—a tiny flicker of attraction. *Why is it that a black eye makes him look even more intriguing?*

Chase walks around the SUV to the driver-side passenger door. When he opens it, he glances over and notices me sitting in the back seat. His good eye widens a little in recognition, and despite the bruising, he's still devastatingly handsome. He manages a polite smile that induces my heart to stutter.

"Oh," Olivia says, suddenly remembering her manners, "Chase, you remember my cousin Daisy, right?"

I raise my hand in an awkward little wave, feeling my cheeks heat and immediately regret it. *Who waves at someone who is two feet away?*

He just nods, his expression unreadable as he slides into the back seat beside me, bringing with him the faint scent of mint and something woodsy.

Jason climbs into the driver's seat and starts the engine. "Everyone good?" he asks, adjusting the rearview mirror. "Got about two hours to the campsite."

Two hours. Next to Chase Sullivan. In this tiny space.

"This is our spot," Jason announces, matching the campsite number to his online reservation on his phone. "Let's set up."

I survey our campsite—a flat area surrounded by trees, with a small fire pit already built from stones with logs around it. It's peaceful, the kind of quiet you never get in the city or even the suburbs.

"Daisy, you can assemble your tent over there," Olivia points to a spot near the edge of the clearing. "Chase, you're next to her."

Of course I am. I shoot her a look that she pretends not to notice. I trudge over to my designated spot, dragging my tent bag behind me. As I unpack, I glance over at Chase, who's already got his tent halfway set up.

I turn back to my mess of nylon and metal rods spread across the ground. The instructions might as well be written in hieroglyphics. I fumble with the poles, trying to thread them through the proper sleeves, but my fingers feel clumsy and uncooperative.

After ten minutes, I've made embarrassingly little progress. My hands are shaking slightly—a familiar tremor that tells me I've been pushing myself too hard. I pause, taking a deep breath, attempting to center myself as my heart beats a tad too fast from the exertion.

"Need help?"

Chase's voice cuts through my concentration, flat and emotionless. I look up to find him standing over me, his face unreadable except for that impressive black eye. His tent is already perfectly assembled behind him.

"Please," I say, trying not to sound as desperate as I feel. "I have no idea what I'm doing with this thing."

He kneels beside me, taking the tangled mess of poles from

my hands. His fingers brush against mine for just a second, but it's enough to send a ridiculous flutter through my chest.

"These go here first," he says, connecting two poles with a snap. "Then you thread them through these sleeves."

I watch as he assembles my tent with swift, practiced movements. It's almost hypnotic how quickly the jumble of parts transforms into an actual structure under his hands. In minutes, he accomplished what would have taken me an hour of frustrated swearing.

When I glance over my shoulder, I catch Olivia staring at us with a smile so wide it threatens to split her face in half. As soon as Chase's back is turned, she makes exaggerated gestures at me—pointing at Chase, then making talking motions with her hand. She mouths something that looks like, "Say it!"

I shake my head frantically, trying to convey "absolutely not" with my eyes.

Liv's not having it. She points more insistently, then pretends to be writing in the air. When I still don't respond, she makes a motion with her hands, curling them like claws. *Bears, right?* She wants me to use that ridiculous conversation starter about bears.

"Um," I say, turning back to Chase as he hammers the final stake into the ground. "Thanks for helping with my tent."

He nods, not looking at me directly. "No problem."

My mind races for an idea of something to say before he walks away. *What was her stupid line again?* Something about... oh, right...

"Hey," My voice comes out higher than I intended. "do you, um, know much about bears?"

He freezes. When he turns to look at me, his expression is a mixture of confusion and something else.

"Bears?" he repeats.

"Yeah, um..." I trail off, realizing how weird this must sound. "I was just wondering if we might see any out here. You know, while camping." I laugh nervously, wishing the ground would open up and swallow me whole.

"I don't know," he says flatly. His face closes off completely, any hint of warmth vanishing.

I panic at his indifferent response and suddenly my mouth is moving faster than my brain. "It's just—I saw this nature show where they said if you encounter a bear in the wild, you're supposed to make yourself look big and clap your hands and yell 'yo bear' really loud to scare them off."

His eyebrow rises, his good eye studying me with growing confusion.

And then, because apparently I've lost all control of my limbs, I find myself standing straight, stretching my arms wide above my head, and clapping my hands together. "YO BEAR!" I shout, my voice echoing through the clearing.

The forest goes silent. Even the birds stop chirping.

What possessed me to do that?

Behind me, I hear Jason burst into laughter. Olivia makes a strangled noise that sounds like she's either dying or trying not to laugh.

Chase stares at me, his mouth ajar. For one horrifying second, I think he's going to walk away. But then—miracle of miracles—the corner of his lip twitches. It's not quite a smile, but it's something.

I stand there, mortified, feeling my cheeks burn hot

44

enough to start a forest fire. The silence between us stretches painfully as he stares at me like I've sprouted a second head.

"The rest of the crew should be here in about twenty minutes!" Jason calls from across the clearing, breaking the excruciating moment. He holds up a cooler. "Chase, want a beer while we wait?"

Chase doesn't even look at me again. He just turns and walks toward Jason without another word, leaving me standing alone next to my newly erected tent.

I whip my head at Olivia, who's suddenly very interested in organizing something in her backpack. When she finally meets my gaze, she shrugs her shoulders with an innocent expression that makes me want to scream.

"Bears?" I hiss when I reach her side. "I sounded like a complete idiot!"

"I thought it was cute," she whispers back, not looking nearly apologetic enough.

"He looked at me as if I were insane. I just did a bear impression in front of Chase Sullivan. I'm never going to recover from this. I hate you," I tell her, dropping my voice to a harsh whisper. "I genuinely, truly hate you right now."

Olivia plops down beside me, throwing an arm around my shoulders. "No, you don't. You love me." She squeezes me tight. "And you should thank me, because now he definitely knows who you are."

I put my hands on my head and groan. "Yeah, he knows me as the crazy bear girl. That's so much better than being invisible."

"At least it's memorable," she says, bumping her shoulder against mine. "Trust me, he's intrigued."

I peek through my fingers at Chase across the clearing. He's talking to Jason, beer in hand, not even glancing in my direction. "He looks really intrigued. He can't keep his eyes off me."

"Give it time," she says with maddening confidence.

Chapter Seven

CHASE

"Sorry about Ava," Jason says.

I shrug, glancing at my beer. "Not exactly heartbroken about it."

"No?" he raises an eyebrow, taking a swig from his own bottle.

"Nah." I run my thumb along the bottle's edge.

He nods slowly, his eyes lingering on my face. "So that's not how you got the shiner? Catching her with some guy?"

I let out a dry laugh. "No, man. I have no idea who she was with, and he can have her. Seriously." I take another pull from my beer, the cold liquid numbing my throat. "I'm done with that whole situation."

"Then what happened to your face?" he presses, lowering his voice as he glances toward the girls across the clearing.

"It's nothing," I say, looking away. "Just a stupid fight last night after a party."

The truth sits heavy on my tongue, but I can't bring

myself to speak it. Luke and Bebe deserve better than having their business spread around like gossip at a campfire. I've already hurt them enough.

He studies me for a moment, then nods slowly. "Alright, man. I get it."

"Get what?"

"That you don't want to talk about it." He takes another sip of his beer.

Relief washes over me. "Thanks," I say quietly. "I appreciate that."

"No problem." He claps me on the shoulder. "Just know I'm here if you need anything."

I nod, grateful for his understanding. Our conversation drifts to safer topics—classes, sports, the weekend ahead—but my attention keeps wandering across the clearing to where the girls are sitting.

Daisy is talking animatedly to Olivia, her hands moving as she speaks. She's pulled her long blonde hair back now, revealing more of her face. I find myself watching her longer than I mean to. There's something different about her— something genuine that stands out against the backdrop of sorority girls and business majors.

She's wearing these high-waisted mom jeans that somehow work on her, paired with a blue cardigan covered in little yellow butterflies. It's not trying too hard—it's just genuinely her.

I suddenly remember where I first met Daisy. It was Jason's birthday party last fall. She'd been standing in the corner with a red cup, wearing this pink t-shirt. I'd noticed her right away—something about the way she seemed completely comfortable being on the periphery of the party, observing everything with those big, blue eyes.

I thought she was cute then. Not in that obvious, Instagram-filtered way most girls at Dalton try for, but in a way that was real. A little geeky, yeah. But there was something about her quiet presence that made me want to talk to her.

I'd meant to go over, talk to her. But then Brittany, my girlfriend at the time, had shown up, already tipsy and demanding attention. By the time I'd managed to extract myself, Daisy had disappeared.

Since then, I've spotted her around campus a few times, always with Olivia, always hanging back, never saying much.

The sun catches in her hair when she turns her head, laughing at something Olivia said. That bear thing she did earlier... I'm still not sure what to make of it. Most girls I know would rather die than allow themselves to appear silly like that, especially in front of someone they barely know. There was something refreshing about how unguarded she was, even if it was bizarre.

I smile again at the thought of her standing there with her arms raised, shouting "YO BEAR!" into the empty forest. She looked mortified afterward, her cheeks turning a deep shade of pink that spread all the way to her ears. I shouldn't have walked away so quickly, but I wasn't expecting to feel anything close to amusement today. Not after everything with Luke and Bebe.

I should've known better than to come here. I should be at home, facing my brother, taking whatever else he needs to dish out. But instead I'm here in the woods, watching a girl I barely know, finding comfort in her awkwardness.

She catches me looking and offers a small, hesitant smile.

Something inside me loosens, just a fraction. I smirk back, despite everything. Despite the guilt that's been crushing me. Despite the throbbing pain in my face that serves as a constant reminder of what I did.

I needed her smile. More than I realized.

The sound of engines breaks the moment. Two more SUVs pull up to our campsite, tires crunching over fallen leaves and twigs. Music blares from one of them—some beat that pounds in time with my headache.

"Finally!" Jason yells, raising his beer in greeting as people pile out of the vehicles. "The party has arrived!"

As everyone sets up camp and the coolers get unloaded, I drift between conversations, nursing the same beer. I help Carrie pitch her tent, listen to David's story about a crazy party at his fraternity house, and unload a cooler full of White Claws from his truck. Meanwhile, I find myself constantly looking at Daisy.

She's been moving through the growing crowd too, helping set up the food table, laughing at someone's joke, ducking away when a frisbee flies too close to her head. I'm not trying to watch her, but my eyes keep finding her.

The campfire roars to life as the sun sets, casting long shadows across our makeshift village of tents. Someone plugs their phone into a portable speaker, and music fills the clearing. Beers are passed around, and the atmosphere shifts as day turns to night.

I scan the crowd, searching for the blue cardigan with the

yellow butterflies. My eyes sweep past the grill where I last saw her helping Jason arrange burgers. She was there a few minutes ago, the firelight catching in her hair.

Now she's gone.

I glance toward the fire pit where Olivia sits comfortably on Jason's lap, her arm draped around his shoulders. The rest of the group clusters near the fire, faces illuminated by the dancing flames, voices rising and falling with laughter and conversation. No sign of Daisy.

I set my beer down, suddenly needing to know where she is. Maybe she's grabbing something from her tent. I make my way across the campsite, nodding at a few people as I pass but not stopping to chat. When I reach her tent, I hesitate, then call out softly.

"Daisy? Are you there?"

Silence. The flap is tied shut, and there's no light inside.

I turn, scanning the darkened edges of our campsite, and notice the narrow trail that leads to the lake. Something tugs at me—intuition, maybe—and I follow the path without really deciding to. The further I get from camp, the quieter it becomes, until all I hear is the soft crunch of pine needles under my feet and the distant hooting of an owl.

The trees part, revealing the water spread out before me, its surface a perfect mirror for the night sky. And there she is, perched on a large flat rock at the water's edge, her back toward me. The moonlight catches her blonde hair, turning it silver. She's staring up at the stars, so still she might be part of the landscape.

"Mind some company?" I call out, but she doesn't move or acknowledge me.

I step closer, careful not to slip on the rocks. She hasn't

turned around yet. Maybe she's ignoring me, which would be fair after how I reacted to her bear impression.

"Daisy?" I try again, louder this time, close enough now that I could reach out and touch her shoulder. "Want some company?"

She jumps, startled, whirling around with wide eyes. For a second, she looks almost frightened before recognition crosses her face. She pulls something from her ears—earbuds; I realize —and offer a sheepish smile.

"Sorry," she says, tucking the earbuds into her pocket. "I didn't hear you."

"I wasn't trying to scare you," I say, feeling awkward now that I have her attention.

"Did Liv send you?"

"No, why?"

She hesitates for a moment, then slides over on the rock, making space for me. I settle next to her, careful to leave a respectful distance between us. The stone is still warm from the day's sun, a pleasant contrast to the cool night air.

"What are you listening to?" I ask, genuinely curious about what pulled her away from the group.

Instead of answering, she hands me her phone. The screen glows, displaying her playlist. I scroll through the songs, a smile slowly spreading across my face.

"'MMMBop'? 'Ice Ice Baby'? 'I'm Gonna Be (500 Miles)'?" I can't help but laugh, scrolling further. "These are all one-hit wonders."

"Don't judge," she says, but there's no defensiveness in her voice. "They're perfect. All that creative energy channeled into one perfect moment of musical brilliance, and then..." She snaps her fingers. "Gone."

"I'm not judging," I say while scrolling. "'Teenage Dirtbag,' 'Barbie Girl'... this is actually a pretty cool playlist." I hand her phone back. "Most people I know just listen to whatever's trending."

The water is perfectly still, mirroring the stars above like a second sky beneath us.

"Thank you." Her voice is soft as she takes the phone, and when she smiles, something catches in my chest. There's a quiet genuineness to it I hadn't noticed before—the way her eyes crinkle slightly at the corners, how the moonlight illuminates the curve of her lips. It's not the practiced, camera-ready smile I'm used to seeing. It's real. Beautiful in its simplicity.

I clear my throat, suddenly aware I've been staring. "So why'd you escape the party?"

She looks back toward the distant glow of the campfire, where shouts and laughter echo through the trees. "I'm not really a social person. Too many people. I needed a break from..." She waves her hand vaguely at camp. "All of that."

"Me too," I say, surprised by my honesty. "I probably shouldn't have come this weekend at all."

Her eyes flicker to my battered face, but she doesn't ask. Instead, she says, "I get that. Olivia practically dragged me here."

"Jason didn't exactly give me a choice either," I confess.

"Friends," she sighs.

"Actually," I say, looking out at the moonlight reflecting on the water, "I'm glad I came. Despite..." I gesture vaguely at my bruised face.

She turns to me, surprise flickering across her features. "Yeah?"

"Yeah." The admission feels strange on my lips, but true. "Something about being out here... it helps clear my head."

"Me too," she says, pulling her knees to her chest. "Still beats being alone in my dorm staring at the ceiling, overthinking everything."

"What would you be overthinking?"

She shrugs, her shoulder brushing against mine briefly. "Oh, you know. The usual existential college crisis stuff. Whether I'm in the right major. If I'm wasting my parents' money. How will I support myself?"

"What's your major?"

"Entomology," she says, and I can hear a shift in her voice —a warmth that wasn't there before. "Or at least, that's what I want to do."

"Bugs?" I ask, trying to keep the surprise from my voice.

"Specifically, butterflies," she comments. The moonlight catches something in her eyes—a spark of genuine excitement that makes her seem to glow from within. She sits straighter, her hands animated as she continues. "Did you know monarch butterflies migrate thousands of miles each year? Their brains are smaller than a pinhead, but they navigate across continents with precision that puts our GPS to shame."

I smile at her passion. It's infectious, the way she lights up talking about something she clearly loves. Her entire demeanor has shifted—the shy, awkward girl from earlier replaced by someone confident and alive. She tugs at the sleeve of her cardigan, drawing my attention to the tiny yellow butterflies embroidered there. *Ah, makes sense now.*

"I've got a small collection of specimens back home. Nothing fancy, but I've been cataloging different species since high school." She pauses, her expression falling as quickly as it had brightened. "But it's not exactly practical. I'm spending a lot of money and this education, and I don't even know if I'll gradu—"

"Graduate?" I ask when she suddenly stops talking, observing her face.

She looks away, turning back to the lake. "Never mind," she says softly.

I nod, not pushing it. I recognize that look—the same one I gave Jason when he asked about my black eye. Some things you're just not ready to talk about. We all have our secrets, our struggles.

"It's beautiful out here," I say instead, changing the subject.

She visibly relaxes, her shoulders dropping slightly. "Yeah, it is." She takes a deep breath, then releases it slowly. "Thanks for not asking."

"About what?" I give her a small smile, and she returns it, gratitude in her eyes.

Chapter Eight

DAISY

W E S I T in silence for a moment, the gentle lapping of water against the shore filling the space between us. In the distance, someone cranks up the music at camp, the bass line thumping faintly through the trees.

"Do you want to go back?" I ask, nodding toward the glow of the campfire.

He shakes his head. "Not yet. If that's okay?"

"More than okay," I say, surprising myself with how much I mean it. The idea of rejoining the party, with its forced laughter. "So what about you? What's your major?" I ask though I already know.

"Pre-law. At least I thought I was," he says after a moment, his voice quieter now. He stares out at the water. "Now, I'm not so sure."

"What do you mean?" I ask, turning to face him more fully.

Chase sighs, running a hand through his hair. "I don't know. When I started, it seemed like the right path. It piqued my interest and was something my dad could support."

"But you don't want that anymore?" I venture carefully.

"I'm unsure." He picks up a small stone and tosses it into the lake, watching the ripples spread. "That's the problem. I'm going through the motions, taking the classes, doing what I'm supposed to do, but there's nothing there. No drive. No passion." He glances at me. "Not like you with your butterflies."

The comparison catches me off guard. I hadn't realized he was actually listening when I rambled about monarchs.

"I see how your face changes when you talk about them," he continues. "Like you found something that lights you up inside," he says, his voice softening. "I want that again. I used to feel that way about things. Before..."

He trails off, staring at his hands. The moonlight catches the angles of his face, shadowing the bruise around his eye but highlighting the tension in his jaw.

"Everything's such a mess right now," he admits, so quietly I almost don't hear him. "My life is falling apart, and it's my own damn fault."

There's so much more he's not saying, pain lurking beneath the surface. I glance at his hand resting on his lap.

"I made some bad choices," he continues, not looking at me. "Hurt people I care about. And now I don't know how to fix any of it."

He doesn't elaborate, and I don't press him. The weight of whatever he's carrying seems too heavy for this fragile moment between us.

Before I can overthink, I take a breath, reach over and place my hand gently over his. His skin is warm against mine.

His fingers twitch slightly beneath mine, but he doesn't pull away.

"I wish I could take some of that pain away," I whisper, surprising myself with my boldness. "Whatever it is you're going through."

Chase turns to look at me, his expression unreadable in the moonlight. The bruising around his eye seems darker somehow against the paleness of his skin.

"I deserve it," he says finally, his voice low. "The pain. All of it."

I want to protest, but something on his face stops me. His hand moves beneath mine, turning his palm upward until our hands are pressed together. Slowly, deliberately, he intertwines our fingers, and my breath catches in my throat.

"That might be why awful shit keeps happening to me," he continues, staring at our joined hands. "The universe's way of making things even." His thumb traces small circles against my skin. "Like how every girlfriend I've ever had ends up cheating on me."

"Everyone?" I ask softly.

"Every single one." He lets out a humorless laugh. "Ava was just the latest in a long line."

"I'm sorry," I say, squeezing his hand gently. "You didn't deserve that."

He shrugs, his eyes still fixed on the lake. "Don't be. We were together for only a few weeks. I wasn't invested—not really. She was the one who asked me out," he adds, staring at a point somewhere in the distance. "I knew I should have said no, but I thought... maybe I should give it a chance. Maybe this time would be different."

"What happened?" I ask, my voice barely above a whisper.

He laughs again, but there's no humor in it. "What always happens. I caught her in bed with a guy. Classic, right? The worst part is, I wasn't even surprised."

I bite my lip, unsure what to say. His hand is still warm in mine, our fingers interlaced as if we've done this a hundred times before.

"It's not even that she cheated that hurt specifically. I barely knew her. It's just..." He trails off, searching for words.

"The pattern?" I offer softly.

"Yeah. That it happened again. That's what hurts. Makes me wonder what's wrong with me, you know? What am I doing that makes them cheat? Why not just break up with me before? Why even date me?"

I shake my head, feeling a surge of protectiveness I didn't expect. "Nothing's wrong with you. Some people just suck."

That pulls a genuine laugh from him—small, but real. The sound warms something inside me.

"Very scientific analysis," he says, the corner of his mouth lifting to a smirk.

"I'm serious," I insist. "It's like my butterflies. Some species migrate thousands of miles to find what they need, while others never leave the same flower patch their whole lives. People are the same way—some are loyal by nature, others are always looking for the next thing."

"So I just keep picking the migratory ones?"

"Exactly." I nod, feeling a strange boldness wash over me in the darkness. "At least you've had relationships. Real ones. People who actually see you." The words tumble out before I can stop them. "I'm basically invisible to guys. They don't even notice me."

Chase's eyebrows furrow. "That can't be true."

"Trust me, it is. In high school, I was just the quiet girl who knew too much about insects. At Dalton, I'm... well, nothing's changed. I've had no dates since moving here. Not even a chance to have bad ones."

"I noticed you," he whispers.

I snort. "Yeah, after I made a complete fool of myself with that ridiculous bear impression."

His mouth quirks up at one corner. "The bear thing was pretty memorable."

"Mortifying is the word you're looking for," I groan, but I'm smiling too. "But seriously, guys like you don't notice girls like me. That's just how the universe works."

"Guys like me?"

I shrug, suddenly feeling vulnerable under his gaze. "I don't know. I guess I'm not the type that stands out. I'm not loud or flirty or—" I gesture vaguely at nothing, "—whatever it is that makes tall, handsome and popular guys notice a girl."

His expression shifts, a playful light dancing in his eyes. He sits up a little straighter, and his lips curve into a smile.

"On behalf of all tall, handsome, and allegedly popular guys everywhere," he says with mock formality, placing his free hand over his heart, "I'd like to extend our sincerest apologies. We've clearly failed in our most basic duty of noticing incredible women who know fascinating butterfly facts."

A laugh bubbles from my chest, genuine and unrestrained. I cover my mouth, but it's too late—the sound has already escaped.

"There it is," Chase says softly, his playfulness giving way to something warmer. "Your laugh. It's beautiful."

My cheeks burn at the compliment, and I drop my gaze to our still-intertwined fingers. "Thanks," I mumble, suddenly aware of how close we're sitting.

He releases my hand, but before I can feel disappointed, I feel his touch on my face. His fingertips are gentle as they brush against my cheek, tucking a strand of hair behind my ear.

"For what it's worth," he starts, his voice dropping to a whisper, "I see you, Daisy."

The way he speaks my name makes something flutter inside my chest. His eyes—even the bruised one—are looking at me with a fervor that steals my breath. I can't look away.

He swallows hard, his Adam's apple bobs in his throat. He leans in closer, and suddenly the space between us feels charged with electricity. My heart hammers against my ribs so loudly I wonder if he can hear it. His face is inches from mine now. *Is this really happening? Is Chase Sullivan about to kiss me?*

Slowly, carefully, he rests his forehead against mine. The contact sends warmth spreading through me, and I close my eyes, savoring the closeness.

"I shouldn't be doing this," he whispers, his breath warm against my lips. "I don't deserve good things, Daisy. I destroy everything I touch. Everyone I care about gets hurt."

I open my eyes to find him watching me, vulnerability and desire warring in his gaze. Without thinking, I reach up and gently brush the edge of his bruise, feeling him flinch slightly.

I can feel the pain in his words, see it etched across his face, illuminated by moonlight. But at this moment, I don't care about his warnings or what might happen tomorrow. I care only about now, about the way he's looking at me like I'm something precious. Without breaking his gaze, I whisper words I never thought I'd have the courage to say.

"Then do your worst."

For a heartbeat, he looks shocked. Then something shifts in his expression—a flash of desire that makes my stomach flip. He leans in slowly, deliberately, and when his lips finally meet mine, it's like electricity coursing through my body.

His lips are softer than I expected, but firm as they brush against my own. One of his hands slides to the back of my neck, fingers tangling in my hair as he deepens the kiss. When his tongue teases against my lower lip, I part my mouth with a small gasp, letting him take the lead.

I've been kissed before, but never like this. Never with this much intensity, this much feeling. My hands find their way to his shoulders, gripping the fabric of his hoodie like I might float away if I let go.

There's a strange sensation—a light tickle against my cheekbone, so faint I almost miss it. Chase must feel it too because he pulls back, his eyes questioning. But then he's kissing me again, more insistent this time, his fingers threading through my hair.

I can't help it—a giggle escapes me, light and airy against his lips.

He pulls back, his expression a mix of confusion and amusement. "Are my kisses funny?" he asks, his voice husky.

"No, it's just..." I touch my cheek where I felt the tickle. "Your eyelashes. They brushed against my face."

"Yours did on mine too. And that's... funny?"

"It's called a butterfly kiss," I explain, feeling warmth

spread across my cheeks. "When someone's eyelashes flutter against your skin. Like butterfly wings."

His expression alters—surprise, then a softness I haven't seen before. "Of course you would know that," he states.

I smile. "Sorry for laughing. It just felt nice. I've heard of butterfly kisses before, but never had one until now."

"Don't apologize," he says, his thumb tracing my jawline. "I like your laugh."

The tenderness in his voice makes my heart stutter. This can't be real—Chase Sullivan kissing me under the stars. Things like this don't happen to girls like me.

He leans forward again, but this time he doesn't kiss my lips. Instead, he brings his face close to mine and deliberately flutters his long dark eyelashes against my cheek.

The delicate sensation of his lashes against my skin is so gentle, so intimate—carrying a weight that even a kiss doesn't.

"Did I do it right?" he whispers, his face still close to mine. "The butterfly kiss?"

My cheeks flush hot, suddenly shy under his intense gaze. I can only manage a nod, words escaping me completely.

His mouth forms a smile—not the guarded one I've seen all day, but something genuine that reaches his eyes. "Good," he murmurs, his hand sliding to cup my cheek. "Now let me try the regular kind again."

This time when his mouth meets mine, there's no hesitation. His lips are warm and certain as they move against mine, and I melt into him. My hands find his chest, feeling his heartbeat racing beneath my fingertips. He tastes like beer and mint, and something uniquely him I can't name but already crave.

The kiss deepens, his tongue sliding with mine as his hand

slips from my face to my waist, pulling me closer. I feel dizzy with want, with the impossible reality that this moment is real.

He pulls back just enough, his eyes searching mine with an intensity that makes my breath catch.

His lips find mine again, more urgent this time. One hand tangles in my hair while the other wraps around my middle, pulling me closer until I'm practically in his lap. The rock beneath us is hard and uncomfortable, but I barely notice, lost in the sensation of his mouth on mine, his hands exploring the curve of my waist, the small of my back.

I loop my arms around his neck, fingers threading through his hair. It's softer than I imagined, and I can't help but tug gently, drawing a low sound from his throat that sends heat spiraling through me. The night air is cool against my skin, but everywhere Chase touches me burns.

Time loses meaning as we kiss under the stars. The distant sounds of the party fade completely, replaced by the quiet wash of water upon the shore and our mingled breaths. His kisses slow eventually, becoming less desperate and more tender, like he's savoring every moment, memorizing every detail of my face with his fingertips and lips.

When we finally break apart, I'm breathless, my lips swollen and tingling. He presses his forehead to mine. Neither of us speaks for a long moment, as if words might shatter whatever magic has wrapped around us.

I can't believe this is happening. My heart feels like it might burst from my chest, overflowing with a happiness so intense it almost hurts. Chase Sullivan just kissed me—really kissed me—like I was something precious, something desired.

The rational part of my brain tries to temper my joy with caution. I've learned the hard way not to expect too much, not to build castles in the air from a single moment. People leave. Things change. Especially when it comes to guys like Chase—gorgeous, complicated guys who could have anyone they wanted.

But for now, in this perfect bubble of moonlight and quiet water, I let myself feel the happiness.

Chapter Nine

CHASE

I WAKE up hard as a rock, my cock straining against my boxers, and the first thought that floods my mind isn't Luke's wife—it's Daisy.

Huh. That's new.

For weeks now, I've been waking up with Bebe's face haunting my dreams—but this morning it's all blonde hair, butterfly kisses and a laugh that makes something warm unfold in my chest.

The guilt that's been my constant companion is still there, but muted somehow, pushed aside by memories of last night. Of *her*.

I lie back on my sleeping bag, staring at the canvas ceiling of my tent as sunlight filters through, casting everything in a soft orange glow. Outside, I hear the early risers moving around camp, the clink of a camp stove, low voices trying not to wake the others. But I'm not ready to join them yet. Not when I can still feel the phantom press of Daisy's lips against mine.

God, her kisses. I didn't expect it to hit me like that.

The bulge in my boxers demands attention, and I briefly palm myself, catching a groan before it can slip past my teeth.

I close my eyes and let myself remember how it felt when she whispered, "Do your worst," against my lips. The invitation was in her look. The way she melted into me, soft and warm and real. And those butterfly kisses. I'd never heard of them before, but the delicate flutter of her eyelashes against my skin sent something electric through me.

Butterfly kisses might be my new favorite thing in the world. Not just any butterfly kisses—hers specifically.

After we finally pulled apart last night, we sat there talking for what felt like hours, shoulders touching, fingers intertwined. She listened when I talked about the pressures of school from my dad. She didn't judge or offer advice—just nodded and squeezed my hand when my voice got tight.

When we walked back to camp, the party was in full swing. Music thumping, people dancing around the fire, and Jason doing a ridiculous keg stand while everyone cheered. Daisy hesitated at the edge before joining Olivia and the other girls.

I didn't sleep with her. I wanted to though—*fuck*; I wanted to.

Now I'm lying here, hard and aching, trying to be a better man. I press the heels of my hands against my eyes, willing my body to calm down, when I hear it—her laugh, floating across the campsite. Bright and unrestrained, like sunshine breaking through clouds.

Fuck.

I. Want. Her.
I don't deserve her.

Before I can think too much about it, I roll out of my sleeping bag and pull on a pair of jeans. I need to see her again, even if it's just to say good morning. To make sure last night wasn't some weird dream.

When I unzip my tent, the cool air hits me like a splash of cold water. The campsite is already buzzing with activity. Jason and Eric are hunched over the camp stove. A few others are sitting around the smoldering remains of last night's fire, wrapped in blankets and looking hungover.

And there she is.

Daisy sits on a log near the fire pit, her hair pulled back in a braid, cradling a steaming mug between her hands. She's wearing an oversized flannel shirt tied at the waist over a white tee.

Something tightens in my chest at the sight of her. It's strange how quickly she's gotten under my skin.

I make my way over, hyper-aware of each step. She hasn't noticed me yet, and I take a moment to watch her blow gently on her coffee. There's something different about her this morning—a quiet confidence that wasn't there yesterday. I can't help but wonder if I had something to do with that.

I clear my throat as I approach. "Morning."

She looks up, and the smile that spreads across her face sends warmth flooding through me.

"Hey," she says softly.

I drop onto the log beside her, closer than necessary, our thighs almost touching. "Sleep okay?"

"Better than I expected," she admits, tucking a loose strand of hair behind her ear. The gesture draws my attention to the curve of her neck, and I have to force myself not to lean in and press my lips there.

Before I can say anything else, Olivia appears from nowhere, standing directly in front of us with her arms crossed.

"Well, good morning, Chase," she says, her voice oddly high-pitched and stretched thin. Her eyes dart between Daisy and me, one eyebrow arched so high it's practically touching her hairline. The look she gives Daisy is loaded with silent questions.

I shift on the log. "Morning, Olivia."

She keeps staring at us; her gaze lingering on how close I'm sitting to Daisy. Then, she suddenly jerks her head toward the camp stove. "Oh! I think Jason's calling me." She points dramatically, though Jason is nowhere in sight now. "I'd better go see what he wants."

As she hurries off, Daisy laughs softly beside me. "Subtle, isn't she?"

"About as subtle as a brick through a window," I agree, smiling despite myself.

She turns to me, her eyes warm in the morning light. "Did you sleep okay last night?"

I rub the back of my neck, considering how many times I woke up thinking of her. "Off and on."

"Chase!" Jason's voice cuts through our conversation. He's standing by the treeline, waving impatiently. "Need your help with the firewood, man!"

Part of me wants to pretend I didn't hear him, to stay here with Daisy in our little bubble.

"I should probably..." I gesture vaguely toward Jason, reluctance clear in my voice.

"Go," she says with a small smile. "I'll be here."

I stand, letting my fingers brush against hers as I do. "I'll catch up with you later."

Hours later, I'm shirtless and sweaty, sprawled on the grass with the rest of the guys. We just finished a brutal game of touch football that quickly turned into tackle once Jason plowed through Eric on the third play. My muscles ache pleasantly, the physical exertion a welcome distraction from the tangle of thoughts in my head.

The girls disappeared to the lake about an hour ago, taking towels and coolers with them. I caught Daisy's eye as she left, and the shy smile she gave me has been playing on repeat in my mind ever since.

"Damn, Sullivan," Trevor pants beside me, cracking open a beer from the cooler before extending one to me. "That last touchdown was sick."

I take the beer he offers, pressing the cold can against my forehead before popping it open. "Thanks, man."

We're sitting in a loose circle, six guys nursing beers and bruised egos after the game. Jason's team won, but only because he practically cheated on that last play. Not that I'm bitter or anything.

"Hey, Chase," Robbie says, leaning forward. He's a friend of Jason's I've met a few times before. "Isn't your brother Wes Sullivan? The one who plays for Vegas?" he asks, squinting at me like he's just made the connection.

I take a long pull from my beer, buying time before I have to answer. "Yeah, that's him."

"Dude!" Robbie's eyes go wide. "That's fucking awesome! I saw him play last weekend against Kansas City. He was a beast out there."

The other guys' attention shifts to me, and I feel that familiar tightness in my chest. The same one I've felt since I was ten years old, standing on the sidelines watching Wes break high school records.

"Your brother's in the NFL? That's sick," Trevor chimes in. "You must get free tickets and shit."

I force a smile. "Sometimes."

"Man, that's so cool," Robbie continues, oblivious to my discomfort.

I'm halfway through my beer when I spot them. The girls are making their way up the trail from the lake, laughing and talking, with towels slung over their shoulders and hair still damp. My eyes automatically search for Daisy among the group.

And there she is, holy shit.

She's wearing a pink bikini with gold butterflies scattered across the fabric. Her skin is glistening with water droplets, catching the sunlight. Her blonde hair is darker when wet, hanging in loose waves around her shoulders.

I sit up straighter, unable to look away. She's not flaunting herself like some of the other girls who strut around knowing exactly how attractive they appear. There's something almost shy about the way she walks, like she has no idea how the pink fabric hugs her body in all the right places.

Trevor nudges Jason. "Who's that?" he asks, keeping his voice low. "The one in the pink bikini with your girlfriend."

There's only one girl in a pink bikini...

Jason glances over his shoulder at the girls, then back at him. "That's Daisy. Olivia's cousin. She goes to Dalton too."

I try to keep my face neutral even as something possessive flares inside me. Trevor's eyes are still locked on her like he's cataloging every curve she has.

"She's shy," he continues, "until you get to know her. Very sweet girl."

And don't I know it. Sweet doesn't begin to cover it. The memory of her mouth against mine, her soft sighs in the darkness, flashes through my mind.

How her fingers had tentatively explored my shoulders, my chest. Nothing about those moments had felt shy.

"Is she single?" he asks, still staring.

My jaw clenches involuntarily. I wait for Jason's answer, trying to appear casual while my heart hammers against my ribs.

"Yeah, man," Jason says with a shrug. "Pretty sure she is."

Fuck.

Trevor grins, running a hand through his hair. "I might have to talk to her."

A surge of possessiveness hits me so suddenly it takes me by surprise. I have no claim on Daisy—not yet.

Chapter Ten

DAISY

THE SHOWER BEATS down on my shoulders, hot and steady, washing away the sand and lake water. I close my eyes and tilt my face into the spray, letting myself smile. Actually smile. Not the nervous, trying-too-hard smile I usually wear, but a real one that comes from somewhere deep inside.

I scrub shampoo through my hair, my swimsuit clinging to me like a second skin. I've never been the type to shower in a bathing suit before, but the campground's communal facilities don't exactly scream "privacy."

"Pass the conditioner?" calls Liv from the stall next to mine.

I reach for the bottle balanced precariously on the small metal shelf, careful not to drop it on the concrete floor. "Heads up," I warn before tossing it over the divider.

The sound of her catching it is followed by a triumphant, "Thanks!"

I rinse my hair, letting my mind drift back to Chase. *Chase Sullivan*. The name still sends butterflies—actual, literal butterflies—swarming through my stomach. I can't believe I spent last night kissing him under the stars, his hands gentle on my face, his eyelashes fluttering against my cheek.

And then this morning, the way he looked at me... It's impossible for me to stop the dreamy sigh that escapes me.

I rinse the last of the conditioner from my hair, marveling at how different I feel from the girl who arrived at this campsite yesterday. It's like I've shed a layer of myself—the nervous, overthinking Daisy who blends into the background. The girl who emerged from the lake today in her pink bikini felt bold, confident even.

I turn off the shower, reach for my towel and quickly pat myself dry. The confidence I experienced earlier hasn't faded— if anything, it's grown stronger with each passing hour. I wrap the towel around myself over my damp swimsuit and gather my toiletries.

"Hey, Liv," I call over the divider. "I'm going to head back to camp."

"Sure thing!" Her voice echoes in the small space. "I'll be right behind you. Need to deep condition for five more minutes. My hair is dying from all this sun."

I laugh, recognizing my cousin's familiar dramatics. "Take your time."

Slipping my feet into my flip-flops, I push open the heavy door of the shower building. The late afternoon sunlight hits my face, warm and golden. The air smells like pine and campfire smoke—a combination I've grown to love.

As I step onto the gravel path, I notice someone leaning

against a nearby tree. My eyes take a moment to adjust to the brightness, but when they do, I recognize him as Trevor—Jason's friend.

When he sees me, he straightens from his casual lean, his stare meeting mine with unmistakable interest.

I turn my head slightly, assuming he must be waiting for someone else—probably one of the other girls. But then—

"Daisy, right?" he calls out, pushing himself away from the tree and taking a few steps toward me.

I stop, clutching my shower caddy closer to my chest. "Um, yeah?"

"I'm Trevor. We met briefly yesterday at the campfire." He gestures vaguely toward our campsite. "I figured I'd walk with you."

"Oh, okay," I say, surprised. I've had little interaction with him beyond a quick introduction, and I'm amazed he remembered my name. "Thanks."

We fall into step on the narrow path, pine needles crunching under our feet.

"So, we're both at Dalton U, huh?" he says, breaking the awkward silence. "I don't think I've seen you around campus before."

"It's a big school, I guess," I reply, adjusting the towel more securely around me.

"What's your major?" he asks, stepping over a fallen branch in our path.

"Entomology," I answer.

His brow furrows before he lets out a small laugh. "Ento-what? What's that?"

"Bugs," I say simply, watching his face for the reaction I've seen a hundred times before. Right on cue, his nose scrunches up, his upper lip curling slightly in disgust.

"Bugs? Like, on purpose?" He shakes his head. "Why would anyone want to study that?"

I sigh inwardly. "They're actually fascinating. Insects make up the most diverse group of organisms on the planet. There are over a million described species."

"But they're so..." He waves his hands vaguely. "Gross. And tiny."

I don't bother defending the bugs. It's lost on this guy.

"Well, I think that's pretty cool," Trevor says, though his tone suggests otherwise. "You must be really smart. I like smart girls."

I don't bother responding, just offering a noncommittal smile as we continue down the path. He fills the silence by launching into a detailed explanation of his business major and his plans to work for his father's company after graduation. I nod occasionally, my mind drifting to Chase and wondering where he might be right now.

Does he know that Jason's friend is talking to me? Possibly hitting on me? Would he care?

"So I'm on the rowing team," he continues, his voice growing louder as if sensing my attention wandering. "We placed third in regionals last year, but this season I've been working with a private coach, so I'm guaranteed to lead us to nationals."

"That's nice," I murmur, my eyes scanning the campsite as we approach my tent. There's no sign of Chase anywhere— not by the fire pit where a few people are gathering to start dinner preparations, not among the group playing cards at the picnic table.

"Yeah, the coach says I have the best form he's seen in years," he boasts, completely missing my distraction. "I've put on fifteen pounds of pure muscle since last season. Feel this." He flexes his arm, biceps bulging as he holds it out toward me. "Go ahead, I don't mind."

"Actually," I state quickly, taking a step back, "I'm feeling pretty wiped out from swimming. I think I need to take a nap before dinner."

His confident smile doesn't falter. "Oh, yeah, sure. Get some rest. I'll see you later at dinner then?"

"Definitely."

"Save me a seat?" he asks, his grin widening as he backs away.

"We'll see," I say noncommittally, already turning toward my tent.

"Looking forward to it," he calls after me, his tone suggesting he's already mentally claiming victory.

I roll my eyes once my back is fully to him. *But isn't that what you wanted Daisy? Guys to notice you?* Yeah, but I don't want a guy who thinks he's God's gift to women explaining his workout routine to me. I unzip my tent quickly, eager to change into dry clothes and maybe take that nap I mentioned.

As I duck inside, I freeze mid-step. Chase is sitting cross-legged on my air mattress. His blue eyes meet mine, a mischievous glint dancing in them as he takes in my towel-wrapped form. "Hey, Butterfly," he says casually, like finding him in my tent is the most natural thing in the world.

"What are you—"

"So... Trevor wants you to feel his muscles, huh?"

Heat rushes to my cheeks. "You heard that?"

"Hard not to. The guy's not exactly subtle." Chase flexes

his own arm in an exaggerated imitation. "'Feel this—I don't mind.'"

I laugh despite my embarrassment and reach out to swat his shoulder. "Stop it!"

In one fluid motion, he catches my wrist and pulls me forward. I tumble onto the air mattress with a surprised squeak, landing half on top of him. Before I can catch my breath, he rolls, pinning me beneath him, his body warm against mine through the damp towel.

His eyes flicker to the open tent flap, and he reaches over to zip it closed with one hand, his other arm still braced beside my head. The zipper slides smoothly, sealing us inside our own private world.

"I missed you today," he murmurs, his voice low and intimate in the enclosed space. His eyes trace over my face like he's memorizing every detail. "Couldn't stop thinking about you."

My heart hammers against my ribs. "I missed you too," I admit, the words barely above a whisper.

He lowers his head slowly, giving me time to pull away if I wanted to. But I don't want to—not even a little bit. His lips meet mine, soft and tentative at first, then with growing confidence as I respond. I reach up to thread my fingers through his hair, pulling him closer.

The kiss deepens, his tongue sliding against mine as his weight settles more fully on top of me. The damp towel between us feels suddenly restrictive, an unwelcome barrier. Chase must feel the same way because his mouth leaves mine to trail open-mouthed kisses down the column of my throat, then over my shoulder, before his fingers find the edge of my towel where it's tucked above my chest. With deliberate slowness, he tugs at the fabric, his eyes meeting mine in silent question.

I nod, breathless with anticipation. He loosens the knot and the towel falls open, revealing my bikini underneath, still damp from the shower.

He lifts his head, eyes darkening as they sweep over me. He makes a sound—a low groan.

"God, Daisy," he murmurs, voice husky. "You're beautiful."

I feel exposed yet powerful under his gaze. The way he's looking at me—like I'm something precious, something desirable—makes me brave in ways I've never been before.

His lips return to my skin, this time moving lower. He presses kisses along the trim of my bathing suit top, his breath hot against the swell of my breasts. My back arches involuntarily, seeking more contact.

"I've been thinking about this," he confesses between kisses. "Ever since I saw you in this."

He smiles against my skin before continuing his exploration, his mouth moving to the flat plane of my stomach.

His lips trail higher, pressing a warm, lingering kiss along the fabric of my bikini top, back to the swell of my breast. The sensation sends heat pooling between my legs, making me gasp. When he lifts his head, his eyes have darkened to midnight blue, pupils blown wide with desire. He captures my mouth again in a kiss that's deeper, hungrier than before.

My hands slide down his back, feeling the muscles shift beneath his t-shirt. I want more—need more of him. Without thinking, I reach for his hand where it rests on my hip. Our eyes lock as I guide his hand lower, across my stomach, just past the waistband of my bikini bottoms.

"Are you sure?" he whispers against my lips, his fingers hovering at the edge of the fabric.

"Yes," I breathe, pressing his hand more firmly against me.

Chapter Eleven

CHASE

I GROAN as my fingers slip beneath the material, feeling her silky skin beneath my fingers. She's completely bare down there, not a hint of hair, just perfect smoothness.

"Chase," she whispers, her voice trembling slightly as my fingers explore further.

I'm surprised to find her already slick with arousal. Not just shower dampness—this is different, warmer, more revealing than undressing. The knowledge that she wants this —wants me—as much as I want her sends a rush of heat through my entire body.

"You're so wet," I murmur against her neck, my voice rough with desire.

She blushes, turning her face away. "Sorry."

I gently turn her face back toward mine. "No, don't apologize. It's incredibly sexy. Knowing that your body wants me."

Her eyes meet mine, vulnerable yet trusting. I capture her lips in another kiss as my fingers continue their exploration, circling her clit. The small gasp she makes against my mouth drives me wild. Her hips rise to meet my touch, seeking more pressure.

"Is this okay?" I ask, watching her face for any sign of hesitation.

"Yes," she breathes, her eyes fluttering closed. "Please don't stop."

I kiss her as I slide my middle finger inside her.

"Fuck, Daisy," I murmur, my voice strained. "You feel amazing."

Her body tightens around my finger as I explore her, feeling how perfectly snug she is. With each gentle stroke, she gets wetter. I've been with plenty of girls before, but something about Daisy feels different—better.

I ease a second finger inside her, watching her face carefully for any sign of discomfort. But there's only pleasure there—her lips parted, cheeks flushed pink. She's so tight around my fingers that I have to go slow, working them in gently.

Her body tightens, her hips lift slightly, offering herself, spreading her legs wider for me without realizing it.

"God, Chase," she breathes, her hand moves to grip my biceps. Her fingers dig into my muscle, holding on like she needs an anchor.

I curl my fingers, searching for that spot that will drive her wild, and when I find it, her reaction is immediate. Her back arches off the air mattress, a soft moan escaping her lips.

"Shhh," I remind her, glancing toward the tent flap. "Someone might hear."

Her eyes flutter closed, her breathing becoming more ragged with each stroke of my fingers. I can feel her tightening around me, her inner walls beginning to pulse. She's close—so close.

"Chase," she whimpers, her voice rising slightly. "I'm going to—"

I capture her mouth with mine, swallowing her words as her body trembles. My lips press firmly against hers, partly to keep her quiet but also because I need to feel connected to her as she comes apart. Her hips buck against my hand as the first wave hits her, and I feel a rush of wetness coat my fingers.

Fuck, she feels good. I want the same gush around my cock.

I continue kissing her deeply, my tongue sliding against hers as she moans into my mouth. The sound vibrates between us, and I swear I could get addicted to the feeling of her coming on my fingers. She's gripping my arm so tightly I'll probably have marks, but I don't care. All I care about is how beautiful she looks right now, completely lost in pleasure.

As her orgasm fades, I slow my movements, keeping my fingers inside her but stroking more gently, helping her to ride out the waves. Her body pulses around me, little aftershocks that make her gasp into my mouth.

When her breathing finally slows, she opens her eyes to look at me. The vulnerability in her expression makes my chest tighten—she looks both blissfully happy and adorably shy, like she can't quite believe what happened.

"That was..." she whispers, trailing off as words fail her.

"Yeah," I agree, unable to stop the smile spreading across my face. "It was."

I slowly withdraw my fingers, and she shivers at the loss of contact. I press a gentle kiss to her forehead, then the tip of her nose, then her lips. She sighs into my mouth, her body still trembling.

I watch her face as she comes back to herself, her eyes growing clearer. Then I see it—the moment she gathers her courage. Her gaze drops to the obvious bulge in my jeans, and she reaches out a hand tentatively toward my waistband.

I catch her wrist gently, stopping her. "This was for you."

Her eyebrows furrow slightly. "But don't you want—"

"Don't worry about me," I say, bringing her hand to my lips and kissing her palm. "When we have our first time together, it'll be somewhere better than this. Somewhere with actual walls."

The laugh that bubbles out of her is soft, a perfect sound that makes me smile. I trace my fingers across her hip, drawing lazy patterns on her bare skin. The touch seems to calm her, and I watch the gentle rise and fall of her chest as her breathing steadies.

But then something shifts in her expression. Her smile fades, and her eyes dart away from mine, focusing on some point over my shoulder. I can practically see the thoughts churning behind those blue eyes.

"Chase," she whispers, her voice suddenly serious. "There's something you should know."

I prop myself on one elbow, giving her my full attention. "What is it?"

"I've never done something like this before with a guy." She takes a deep breath, her cheeks flushing pink. "I'm... I'm a virgin."

The moment the words leave her mouth, she covers her

face with both hands, groaning with embarrassment. "God, that sounds so stupid when I say it out loud."

I feel something shift in my chest—not disappointment, but a strange mix of tenderness and responsibility.

I gently pull her hands away from her face. Her eyes are squeezed shut, like she can't bear to see my reaction.

"Hey," I say softly. "Look at me."

She slowly opens her eyes, vulnerability swimming in them.

Something primal stirs inside me at her confession. Untouched. She's completely untouched. A possessive heat spreads through my chest as the reality sinks in—I'll be her first.

"Hey," I whisper, brushing a strand of damp hair from her forehead. "Don't be embarrassed. Not with me."

She searches my face, looking for any sign of disappointment. "You're not... turned off?"

I almost laugh at how wrong she is. "God, no, Daisy. The opposite."

The truth is, knowing she's never been with any man makes me want her even more. Something about being the only one to touch her this way, to show her what pleasure feels like—it awakens something fiercely protective and possessive in me. She'll be mine in a way she could never be anyone else's.

"I like that I'm the first to touch you like this," I admit, my voice dropping lower. "That no one else has seen you the way I just did."

Her lips part in surprise. "Really?"

"Really." I trace my thumb across her bottom lip. "It means I get to be the one to show you everything. The one who gets to watch you discover what you like."

LULU HART

A small smile tugs at her mouth. "I definitely liked what you did."

I can't help laughing, the sound low and husky in my throat. "Oh, Butterfly," I whisper, leaning in to press my lips against her ear. "If you liked that, just wait until you see what else I can do."

Her breath catches audibly, a beautiful blush spreads across her cheeks while a small shiver runs through her body beneath me. How she reacts to my words—to my touch— makes me want to show her everything right now.

But something stops me. A voice in my head reminds me that this isn't just another hookup. This is Daisy—sweet, genuine Daisy with her butterfly pajamas and encyclopedic knowledge of insects. Daisy, who trusted me enough to tell me she's a virgin.

I pull back slightly, meeting her eyes. The desire I see there is unmistakable, but I need her to know this isn't just about sex for me.

"But there's no rush," I say, my voice gentler now. "There is no pressure for you to do anything you're not ready for."

Her eyes search mine, surprise flickering across her features. "You don't mind waiting?"

"Of course not. I want you to be sure. Completely sure."

She bites her lower lip, considering my words. "What if I'm already certain?"

The question sends heat racing through my veins, but I force myself to stay focused. "Then we'll wait until we're somewhere more comfortable than a tent in the middle of the woods," I finish, pressing a soft kiss to her forehead. "Your first time should be special, Daisy. Not rushed on an air mattress where anyone could walk by."

Her eyes shine with something I can't quite name—gratitude, maybe, or relief mixed with disappointment. She reaches to touch me, her fingers gently tracing the edge of my bruise.

"You're not what I expected, Chase Sullivan," she whispers.

I turn my face to kiss her palm. "Is that a good thing?"

"A very good thing." Her smile is soft, a little shy despite what we just shared. "Everyone talks about Chase Sullivan like he's this player who hooks up with a different girl every weekend."

"That's definitely not true." I can't help but laugh, though there's not much humor in it. "And what do you think now?"

"I think people don't know you at all," she says.

Her words hit me harder than I expect. She's right—no one at Dalton really knows me. But somehow, in the space of a day, Daisy does.

We lie here together, her body curled against mine, as the sounds of the campsite filter through the thin walls of the tent —laughter, the clatter of cooking utensils, music playing from someone's portable speaker. It feels like we're in our own little world, separate from everything else.

"I should probably go," I say reluctantly, knowing that if I stay much longer, people will notice we're both missing. "I promised Jason I'd help with dinner."

She sighs, nodding against my chest.

I press one last kiss to her lips before sitting up, running a hand through my disheveled hair. She looks so beautiful lying here, her blonde hair spread across the pillow, her skin still flushed from my touch. The sight of her makes it nearly impossible to leave.

She smiles then, a genuine smile that reaches her eyes, and it hits me how much I want to be worthy of that smile. Of her trust.

Chapter Twelve

DAISY

I'M up to my elbows in soapy water, scrubbing at a pot that's determined to keep its layer of burned chili, when I feel someone's presence behind me. The campfire crackles a few feet away, casting long shadows across our makeshift kitchen area.

"Need some help with that?"

I recognize Trevor's voice immediately and fight the urge to cringe. He's been finding excuses to talk to me all evening—passing me the salt during dinner, laughing too loudly at my offhand comment about mosquitoes, and now this.

"I'm good, thanks," I say, not turning around. "Almost done."

He steps closer anyway, reaching for a clean dish towel. "I'll dry. My mom always says I'm the best dryer in the family." He flashes what I'm sure he thinks is a charming smile.

"Really? Dish drying? That's the talent you're leading with?" I say before I can stop myself.

He laughs, apparently taking my sarcasm as flirtation. "Among other talents. I could show you sometime."

I scrub harder at the pot, wishing it would magically become clean so I could escape. The rest of the group is scattered around the campsite—some playing cards at the picnic table, others lounging by the fire. Olivia catches my eye from across the clearing and mouths, "Sorry!" with an exaggerated grimace. She's been watching Trevor's attempts with a mix of amusement and pity.

"Hey, Daisy!" Chase's voice cuts through the awkward moment like a lifeline. "I need your help with something."

I whip my head around to see him standing a couple of yards away.

"Oh!" I say, perhaps too enthusiastically. "Yes, of course." I quickly rinse the soap from my hands and grab a towel. "Sorry, Trevor. Duty calls."

His face falls. "But we were—"

"She'll be back later," Chase says. He gestures toward the trail leading away from the main campsite. "It's this way."

I follow Chase without hesitation, feeling Trevor's gaze burning into my back as we go. Once we're safely out of earshot, I let out a relieved sigh.

"Perfect timing," I whisper. "What do you need help with?"

He glances over his shoulder, then takes my hand. "Absolutely nothing," he says with a grin that makes my heart skip. "I just couldn't watch that guy hit on you for another second."

He leads me down the path, past the shower building, and around to its far side where a small clearing sits for another campsite that's empty. The moment we're out of sight, he gently pushes me against the stone wall, his body pressing close. His blue eyes lock with mine, dark with desire, and then his lips are on me, hot and insistent. I melt into him, my arms looping around his neck as he kisses me. His hands slide to my waist, fingers digging into my hips as he pulls me closer.

When we finally break apart, we're both breathing hard. He rests his forehead against mine, his breath warm on my face.

"I've been wanting to do that," he murmurs, pressing another soft kiss to my cheek.

I can't help smiling, my heart racing beneath my ribs. "Me too."

He kisses me again, slower this time, like he's savoring the taste of me. I sigh against his lips, letting myself get lost in the sensation. It's incredible how quickly this has become my favorite feeling in the world—being held in Chase's arms, hidden away from everyone else.

"I like this," I whisper when we come up for air. "Sneaking around, having our own little secret."

He smiles, tucking a strand of hair behind my ear. "Yeah?"

"Yeah. It's fun," I admit, tracing patterns on his chest with my fingertip. "Though I keep wondering what happens when we go back to campus."

The thought has been nagging at me all day—this strange, beautiful bubble we've created here in the woods feels so separate from real life. From Dalton U, where Chase Sullivan is practically a campus celebrity, while I'm just the weird bug girl.

His expression grows serious, his eyes searching mine. "That's actually what I wanted to talk to you about." He takes a deep breath, his hands still resting on my waist. "When we get back to campus, I'd like to take you on a proper date."

My heart stutters. "A date? Like, in public? Where people can see us?"

He laughs softly, brushing his thumb across my cheek. "That's generally how dates work, yes."

"But you're... you. And I'm... me." I gesture vaguely at myself.

His brow furrows. "What's that supposed to mean?"

"It means you could date literally anyone at Dalton. Girls who don't spend their weekends cataloging butterfly migration patterns."

"Maybe I don't want to date just anyone anymore." His voice drops lower, more intense. "Maybe I want to date the girl who knows more about butterflies than anyone I've ever met. Who makes me laugh and doesn't expect me to be someone I'm not."

I can feel myself blushing, warmth spreading from my cheeks down my neck.

His hand comes up, brushing my cheek. "So, Daisy... would you like to go on a date with me when we get back to campus?"

Heat floods my cheeks, but I can't stop the smile spreading. "I'd like that," I whisper, hardly believing this is happening.

Chase's smile widens, making the corners of his eyes crinkle in a way that sends butterflies swarming through my stomach. He leans in to kiss me again, his lips soft against mine.

My phone buzzes in my back pocket. I groan, pulling back reluctantly.

"Sorry," I murmur, fishing it out.

The screen lights up with a text from Olivia:

S'MORES TIME!!! Where are you?? Don't
miss this!!

I laugh, showing him the message. "Apparently, we're about to start s'mores."

"Can't miss s'mores," he agrees with a grin, lacing his fingers through mine. "Though I'm tempted to keep you all to myself a little longer."

I squeeze his hand, reluctant to let go of this moment. "We should probably head back before she sends out a search party."

He nods, pressing one last quick kiss to my lips before we walk back toward camp. As we near the glow of the campfire, my steps slow.

"Hey, I just remembered I need to grab something from my tent," I say, remembering we're having s'mores. "You go ahead, and I'll meet you at the fire in a few minutes."

He looks momentarily disappointed but nods. "Don't take too long."

I watch him walk toward the campfire, admiring the way his shoulders look in his navy blue t-shirt before I duck into my tent. Inside, I rummage through my duffel bag until my fingers find what I'm looking for—the familiar orange packaging. I grab the pack of Reese's Peanut Butter Cups and tuck them into my pocket.

When I emerge from my tent, the campfire is blazing, casting a warm glow over everyone's faces. I notice Olivia waving at me from her spot on one of the logs. The guys are standing in a loose circle nearby, passing around a bag of marshmallows and chocolate bars. I make my way over to her.

"There you are!" she exclaims as I approach. Then her eyes go wide as I pull out the orange wrapping. "Oh my God, you're an actual angel!" She snatches the Reese's from my hand. "I completely forgot to bring these. S'mores would have been a disaster without them."

Chase appears beside me, his arm brushing against mine as he sits. "What are the peanut butter cups for?" he asks, eyeing the packaging in Olivia's hands.

"For the s'mores," I explain, accepting a marshmallow and a stick from Jason. "It's the only way I s'more. You replace the plain chocolate with a Reese's cup. The peanut butter melts with the marshmallow, and it's basically heaven."

"I've never tried that," he says, sounding genuinely intrigued.

"Then you haven't lived," I reply, nudging his shoulder playfully. "Prepare to have your life changed forever."

I slide my marshmallow onto the stick and extend it toward the fire, careful to keep it above the flames. Around me, the guys are deliberately shoving their marshmallows directly into the fire, pulling out flaming sugar bombs before blowing them out.

I watch the marshmallow carefully, rotating the stick to ensure it toasts evenly to a perfect golden brown. When it's just right—puffed and golden with no black spots—I pull it back from the flames.

"Perfect roast," I announce proudly, sliding the graham cracker beneath it. I quickly place the peanut butter cup on top and sandwich it with another graham cracker, pressing down gently. The marshmallow's heat immediately starts melting the chocolate and peanut butter.

I bring the s'more to my mouth and take a bite. The moment the flavors hit my tongue—warm chocolate, creamy peanut butter, and gooey marshmallow—I can't help the sound that escapes me. A low, appreciative moan that's probably a bit too enthusiastic for a campfire setting.

"Oh my God," I mumble through my mouthful, eyes closing involuntarily. "So good."

When I open my eyes, Chase is watching me with an expression I can't quite place—part amusement, part something deeper that makes my cheeks flush. His eyes haven't left my face, and there's a softness in his smile.

"Want to try?" I ask, extending the s'more toward him. Without hesitation, he leans forward, his eyes still locked on mine as he takes a bite.

His eyes go wide as he chews, and my stomach drops for a second. Oh no, maybe he hates it. I've been so enthusiastic about this weird combination, and now he's going to think I have terrible taste and—

But then his expression transforms. His lips curve into a smile that reaches all the way to his eyes.

"Daisy," he says, swallowing the bite, "how have I gone my entire life without trying this?"

Relief and pleasure wash over me. "I know, right?"

He's still looking at me with that warm intensity that makes my insides flutter. Then he reaches out, his thumb brushing against the corner of my mouth in a gentle sweep. The touch sends electricity shooting through me.

"You had a little..." he murmurs, his voice dropping low enough that only I can hear.

Instead of wiping his thumb on a napkin, he brings it to his own mouth and licks the sticky mixture off. My breath catches in my throat as I watch him, the firelight dancing across his features, turning his eyes to midnight blue. The gesture is so casually intimate it makes my heart race.

"Wouldn't want to waste any," he says with a small smirk that sends heat flooding through my body.

I'm vaguely aware that we're surrounded by people, but in this moment, it feels like we're the only two people in the world.

Chapter Thirteen

CHASE

I'VE NEVER SEEN a marshmallow burst into flames so fast. Eric's stick is a torch within seconds, his drunken reflexes way too slow to save it. The look of complete devastation on his face makes me laugh harder than I should.

"Dude, that's the third one you've cremated," Jason says, tossing him another marshmallow from across the fire pit.

I lean back on the log, my stomach pleasantly full of s'mores—not the regular kind—Daisy's peanut butter cup version. The fire crackles, sending sparks dancing into the night sky. Beside me, Daisy licks a smudge of melted chocolate from her thumb, completely unaware of how the simple gesture makes my heart rate spike.

"Alright, people," Jason announces, clapping his hands together. "It's time for the best part of any camping trip."

"S'more s'mores?" Trevor calls out, and a few people chuckle.

Jason shakes his head, his expression turning serious. "Scary stories."

A collective murmur ripples through the group. Some groan, others lean forward eagerly. I glance at Daisy beside me, catching the way the firelight dances across her face, highlighting the curve of her cheek, the soft line of her jaw. Her eyes meet mine, and she smiles—that small, private smile.

"Everyone gather around," Jason commands, gesturing for us to move closer to the fire. "This is tradition."

I watch as people shift, finding spots on logs and camping chairs. I stay exactly where I am, my thigh pressed against Daisy's, unwilling to break that point of contact even for a moment. Trevor makes a beeline for the empty spot on Daisy's other side, but Olivia swoops in at the last second, dropping onto the log with a triumphant smile. I catch Olivia's eye, and she winks at me.

"Here," Olivia says, thrusting a thick wool blanket toward me with a knowing smile. "It's getting cold."

"Thanks," I say, accepting it.

I unfold the blanket, draping it over Daisy and my laps. Under the cover of wool, I let my hand find hers, our fingers intertwining. She gives my palm a gentle squeeze, and a ridiculous grin spreads across my face.

"Okay," Jason says. "Who wants to go first?"

"I'll go," Matt volunteers, standing from his spot. He's already pulling out his phone and turning on its flashlight.

"Oh God," someone mutters as Matt positions the light under his chin, illuminating his face in that classic horror-movie way that stopped being scary around third grade.

"On a night like this one," he begins, his voice dropping to what he clearly thinks is a spooky tone, "a group of college students went camping in these very woods."

"Really, Matt? The 'it happened right here' setup? Could you be more cliché?" Olivia rolls her eyes.

"Shh!" he hisses, waving his free hand dramatically. "You're ruining it!"

Beside me, Daisy stifles a giggle.

"As I was saying," he continues, "these students were sitting around a campfire just like we are now when they heard a strange scratching sound coming from the woods."

"Let me guess," Trevor interrupts, "it was a hook-handed killer?" He laughs at his own joke.

Matt glares at him. "No, it wasn't a hook-handed killer. If you'd let me finish—"

"Was it Bigfoot?" Eric calls out, making exaggerated stomping motions with his feet.

"No, it wasn't—"

"Oh! I know!" Olivia chimes in. "It was the ghost of a camper who died in these woods twenty years ago to the day!"

Matt's face is getting redder by the second. I can't help but smirk as his "scary" story falls apart before it even gets going.

"Guys, seriously," Matt protests, the flashlight under his chin flickering as he gestures. "This is good if you'd just—"

"Was it a chupacabra?" Daisy asks innocently beside me. I squeeze her hand under the blanket, trying not to laugh.

"No! It wasn't a chupacabra, or Bigfoot, or a ghost!" Matt snaps. "It was—"

"A bear?" Jason suggests with a grin, and Daisy's entire body tenses beside me. I know she's remembering her "yo bear" impression.

Matt's face is now practically glowing red in the firelight. He switches off his flashlight with an angry click.

"Fine! You want to know what it was?" he shouts over the laughter. "It was the SILENCE! The silence that comes before death! Because they were all already dead from the beginning! They just didn't know it yet! They were in purgatory the whole time!"

The giggling dies down as everyone stares at Matt. Crickets chirp in the awkward quiet that follows.

"That's it?" Eric finally asks. "That's the big twist? They were dead the whole time?"

"It's like every bad horror movie ending rolled into one," Olivia mutters.

Matt throws his hands up. "You guys don't get it! It's metaphorical. The silence represents the void of existence that awaits us all!"

"Wow," Jen says flatly. "Mind. Blown."

Matt stands there for a moment, looking around at our unimpressed faces, then drops back onto his log with a huff. "Whatever. You people have no appreciation for nuance."

Jason clears his throat. "Right. Well, thanks for that... enlightening tale, Matt." He stands, rubbing his hands together. "I'll go next."

Olivia bounces in her seat, clapping her hands with excitement. "Oh yes! You guys are in for a treat. My boyfriend tells the best scary stories. Remember the one about the hitchhiker last year? I couldn't sleep for days."

Jason grins, looking pleased with himself. The firelight casts dramatic shadows across his face as he takes a deep breath and squares his shoulders. Unlike Matt, he doesn't need a flashlight prop or cheap effects. There's something in his stance alone that commands attention.

"This is a true story," he starts, his voice lowering to a steady tone that immediately silences the group. "A group of friends—about six or seven—stayed in an old, abandoned cabin deep in the woods for the weekend. The cabin had been there for decades; it was cheap to rent, and after a few too many drinks, they figured, why not? The first night was fine. They laughed, told stories. But something felt... off. The cabin was too quiet. The kind of quiet where you start hearing things that aren't there—like a faint tapping in the walls, or maybe the sound of footsteps when you're sure no one else was awake."

Daisy shifts closer to me under the blanket.

"By the second night, it got worse. Someone swore they heard whispers," he continues. "At first, they thought it was the wind. But the whispers weren't coming from outside—they were coming from inside the walls. At first, it was subtle. A soft "ssssss" sound, barely noticeable, like someone had their ear pressed against the wall. But it got louder."

The campfire crackles, sending a shower of sparks up above. Around us, everyone has gone completely still, their faces illuminated by the dancing flames. Even Matt looks interested, leaning forward with his elbows on his knees.

"One girl who had been dismissive of the weirdness tried to find the source. "It's just an old house. It creaks and moans," she said. But as soon as she walked to the wall, she froze." Jason pauses and then drops his voice. "There was something there. A strange pattern in the wood—almost like a seam, where the boards had been cut and re-nailed together.

"Guys, check this out," she said, tapping the wall with her fingers."

As he continues his story, Daisy leans into my side, her head finding the perfect spot on my shoulder. Our fingers are still intertwined beneath the blanket, but now her grip tightens.

I turn slightly, breathing in the scent of her shampoo—something floral and sweet that I'm already associating with her. Without thinking, I put my lips to the top of her head, a gesture that feels so natural I almost can't believe we've only known each other like this for two days.

She sighs contentedly against me. The weight of her, warm and trusting against me, makes something in my chest expand. It's such a simple thing—her head on my shoulder, our hands clasped together—but it feels significant. Important.

"Suddenly, a gust of wind slammed against the windows, and a loud crash came from behind the wall. The group scrambled, their panic rising. One guy who had been joking about ghosts all weekend grabbed a flashlight and started banging on the wall, shouting, "Come out, whatever you are!" There was no answer, only the sound of something crawling behind the wall. "Get out!" someone screamed."

Daisy's breath hitches against me as Jason gets to an intense part of his story. When she lifts her head from my shoulder, her eyes meet mine in the firelight. There's something captivating about the way she's fully immersed in the story—excited rather than scared.

She smiles at me, a private little curve of her lips that makes my heart skip. I move in, drawn by something I cannot name, and press my lips gently against hers. It's brief, chaste—a soft connection that feels right at this moment. When I pull back, her eyes are wide with surprise, but there's a pleased flush on her cheeks that wasn't there before.

She settles back against my shoulder, fitting perfectly into the crook of my arm. I become aware of eyes on us. Glancing around the circle, I catch Olivia watching us with barely contained glee. Trevor's staring too, his expression considerably less pleased. Even Matt has paused his sulking to observe us with raised eyebrows. I wasn't subtle; I don't care. Let them see. The message is clear: she's with me.

"Suddenly, the wall in front of them split open. It wasn't a normal crack—it was like the wood itself was stretching and twisting. And from inside the gap, a pale, thin hand reached out. One girl screamed and ran for the back door. But just as she reached it, she froze. The door… was gone. The entire wall had closed in on them, trapping them in. The last thing they heard before everything went black was a voice, soft and sickly sweet, whispering their names from the walls: "You should've never come…" The next morning, the group was found scattered around the cabin. Shaken, disoriented, but alive. The cabin? Completely silent again. To this day, no one's rented that cabin again."

As he finishes his story, a chorus of "ooohs" rises around the campfire. Olivia dramatically clutches her chest while Carrie and Madison both visibly shiver, rubbing their arms.

"I have goosebumps," Madison says, extending her arm for everyone to see.

"Me too," Carrie agrees. "That was seriously creepy, Jason."

A brilliant flash of lightning illuminates the entire campsite, turning night to day for a split second. Daisy jumps against me. One-one-thousand, two-one-thousand—

CRACK! Thunder booms directly overhead, so loud I feel it in my chest.

"Holy shit," someone whispers.

For a moment, nobody moves. Then the first fat raindrop hits my cheek, followed immediately by another, and another. Within seconds, it's a downpour.

"Scatter!" Jason yells over the sudden roar of rain. "Early night, people! See you in the morning!"

Chapter Fourteen

CHASE

Everyone leaps up at once, logs and chairs abandoned as they sprint toward their tents. Daisy and I are on our feet instantly.

"Come with me," I say, my voice urgent against the thunder.

She doesn't hesitate, dashing for my tent. The rain pounds against our backs, soaking through our clothes in seconds. I fumble with the zipper, hands slippery and cold, finally yanking it open. We tumble inside together, and I quickly zip it closed behind us, sealing out the downpour.

She collapses onto my air mattress, her chest heaving as she catches her breath. Then suddenly, she bursts into laughter—bright and musical—as water drips from her hair on my sleeping bag. The sound fills the small space, more beautiful than any music I've ever heard. In the dim light filtering through the tent fabric, her eyes sparkle with joy.

"We're soaked!" she gasps between laughs.

I can't help myself. She's irresistible like this—rain-drenched and radiant. I move toward her, my hands finding her waist as I lower her back against the air mattress. Her laughter fades into a soft gasp as our eyes lock, and then my lips are on hers, hungry and insistent. She responds immediately, her arms wrapping around my neck, pulling me closer as the kiss deepens.

Water from my hair drips onto her face, but she doesn't seem to mind. Her hands slide under my wet shirt, fingers tracing cold patterns against my skin.

"We should get out of these soaked clothes," I murmur against her lips, already feeling the chill settling into my bones.

The rain drums against the tent, creating a rhythm that matches my heartbeat. Thunder crashes overhead, but it feels distant compared to the electricity between us.

Daisy nods, her teeth chattering slightly. "Good idea."

"I have dry clothes you can borrow."

She bites her lower lip, looking suddenly shy. "Actually, I think..." She pauses. "Maybe we could just..." I raise an eyebrow, waiting. "You know, get under the blankets? Use body heat... to warm up?"

My heart hammers against my ribs. "Yeah," I manage, my voice rougher than I intend. "That would work."

We move awkwardly in the confined space, peeling off our soaked clothes. I try not to stare as she pulls her wet t-shirt over her head, revealing a simple white bra. She shimmies out of her jeans, the wet denim clinging stubbornly to her legs until she's left in a matching white thong. Fuck me, her ass is perfect.

I strip to my boxers, suddenly self-conscious despite my years of hookups. She's watching me, her eyes traveling over my chest, my shoulders, my arms. There's something reverent in her gaze that makes me feel both powerful and vulnerable at once.

I grab my sleeping bag and unzip it fully, spreading it out like a comforter. "Come here," I say softly, holding it open for her.

When she slides under the makeshift blanket next to me, I wrap it around us both, cocooning us in warmth. Our bodies press together, skin against skin, and I inhale sharply at the contact. She's cold from the rain, but already warming against me.

"Better?" I ask, my voice barely audible over the storm raging outside.

"Much," she whispers, her breath warm against my collarbone.

Our legs tangle together naturally, her smooth calves brushing against mine. She playfully runs her toes over my ankle, and I return the gesture, sliding my foot along her calf. We play this silent game of footsie under the covers, each touch sending small currents of electricity through my body.

The storm outside intensifies, rain hammering against the tent like thousands of tiny fingers.

She shifts closer, the curve of her body fitting perfectly against mine. I pull her tighter against my chest, one arm wrapped around her waist, her back pressed to my front. Her damp hair tickles my chin.

I'm trying my hardest not to get turned on right now.

The rain creates a soothing rhythm on the tent canvas, nature's own lullaby surrounding us.

"This is nice," she whispers, her voice sleepy and content.

"Yeah," I murmur into her hair.

Her breathing slows, becoming deeper, more rhythmic. My hand finds hers under the sleeping bag, our fingers intertwining naturally.

"Chase?" Her voice is almost inaudible over the patter of rain.

"Yeah?"

"I'm glad I came on this trip."

I smile. "Me too, Butterfly."

The warmth between us grows, banishing the last of the chill from the rain. Outside, the storm continues, occasional flashes of lightning illuminating the tent in brief, white bursts.

I feel her breathing slow, her body growing heavier against mine as sleep begins to claim her. My hand moves of its own accord, stroking her damp hair in long, gentle motions. There's something profoundly intimate about this moment— more intimate than any hookup I've ever had. Just holding her, feeling the rise and fall of her chest against mine, listening to the soft sounds she makes as she drifts toward sleep.

I listen as her breathing changes, becoming slow and even. She's falling asleep in my arms, trusting and vulnerable. The realization stirs something protective in my chest—something I haven't felt in a long time. Maybe ever.

The next morning comes too soon. I wake to the sounds of everyone packing up camp, and reality crashes back. We're headed home today. Back to Dalton. Back to real life.

Sunlight filters through the tent, casting everything in a soft golden glow. I blink slowly, awareness creeping in. The rain has stopped completely, replaced by the cheerful sounds of birds.

Sometime during the night, Daisy turned toward me, her face now nestled against my chest, an arm draped over my torso. Her blonde hair spills across my arm, tickling my skin. She's still asleep, her breathing deep and even, lips slightly parted.

I watch her for a moment, memorizing every detail—the sweep of her cheek, the fan of her eyelashes against her skin, the small freckle near her temple I hadn't noticed before. My body responds to her closeness, hardening against her thigh, but I ignore it. This moment feels too perfect to disturb.

Gently, I brush a strand of hair from her face and kiss her forehead. Her skin is warm and soft against my mouth.

She stirs, eyelids fluttering before opening fully. For a moment, confusion clouds her features before recognition dawns, followed immediately by a shy smile.

"Morning," I whisper.

Her eyes widen suddenly, and she clamps a hand over her mouth. "Oh God," she mumbles through her fingers, "dragon breath. Morning breath. Whatever you want to call it. It's horrible."

I laugh softly, reaching for her wrist. "Dragon breath? That's why you're hiding from me?"

I gently pull her hand away from her mouth, my fingers wrapping around her wrist. "Come here," I murmur, tugging her closer.

"Chase, seriously—" she protests, but I silence her with my lips.

I kiss her softly at first, testing, then deeper as she melts against me. Her mouth is warm and tastes faintly of sleep, but

111

there's nothing unpleasant about it. Nothing that would make me pull away. If anything, I want more of her—this sleepy, unguarded version of Daisy.

When we finally break apart, her cheeks are flushed pink, eyes wide with surprise.

"See?" I whisper against her lips. "No dragon breath."

She laughs, the sound vibrating through her chest and into mine where we're pressed together. "You're either lying or your sense of smell is broken."

"Neither," I assure her, stealing another quick kiss. "Just the perfect morning."

We stay tangled together for another moment, savoring the quiet before the inevitable chaos of packing. Outside, I can hear Jason shouting instructions, the metallic clang of tent poles being disassembled, car doors slamming.

"We should probably..." she says reluctantly, gesturing vaguely toward the sounds of the campsite.

"Yeah," I sigh, equally hesitant to go. "Real life awaits."

The two-hour drive back to Ambrose passes quicker than I expected.

I'm reluctant to leave when Daisy's still heading back to the campus dorms with Jason and Olivia. The thought of saying goodbye, even just until tomorrow, feels strangely difficult.

"I'll help Chase with his bag," Olivia announces suddenly, practically leaping from the passenger seat. She shoots a meaningful glance at Jason. "You should get out, stretch your legs."

He catches on immediately. "Right. I'll just... check the oil or something."

Their lack of subtlety would be funny if I weren't so desperate for a moment alone with Daisy. I'm grateful when they both give us a semblance of privacy.

"So," I say, turning to Daisy next to me in the backseat. Her blonde hair is pulled into a messy bun. She's wearing denim shorts and a pale yellow t-shirt that makes her look like actual sunshine. She's looking at me with those blue eyes that somehow are both innocent and knowing at the same time.

"So," she echoes, with a small smile playing on her lips.

I reach out and tuck a piece of hair behind her ear, letting my fingers linger against her cheek. "I had a good time this weekend."

"Me too," she says softly, leaning into my touch.

"I want to see you again," I tell her. "Tomorrow? After your morning class?"

She nods, her smile widening. "I'd like that."

I lean in, breathing her in. My heart is pounding as I press my lips to hers—a gentle kiss that carries the promise of all the things I want to say. It's brief but perfect, our connection sweet and lingering despite the knowledge that Jason and Olivia are probably watching.

When I pull away, her eyes stay closed for just a moment longer, and I commit that image to memory—Daisy with her face tilted up toward mine, lips parted, a flush of pink on her cheeks.

"I'll text you tonight," I promise.

She nods, finally opening her eyes.

I reluctantly reach for the door handle, knowing I can't delay the inevitable any longer. As I step out of the car, the cool afternoon air hits my face, a stark contrast to the warmth of being next to her.

"Thanks for the ride," I call to Jason, who's pretending to check something under the hood.

"No problem, man," he replies, closing the hood with a decisive thud. "See you tomorrow?"

"Yeah, tomorrow."

As I walk up the path to my house, I can't resist looking back one last time. Daisy waves from the backseat. I wave back, feeling something unfamiliar and warm spreading through my chest.

I watch until Jason's SUV disappears around the corner. I've never felt this way about a girl before—like I want to be better for her. And I will. I will find my passion again.

The weekend changed something between us, creating something I never expected to find on a random camping trip.

With a sigh, I hoist my duffel bag over my shoulder and head toward my house. The weekend's glow still surrounds me as I dig for my keys, thinking about texting Daisy as soon as I get to my room.

The lock clicks open, and I push through the front door, dropping my bag with a heavy thud in the entryway. The house is quiet, but I can sense immediately that I'm not alone.

That's when I notice them. Luke is sitting ramrod straight on the living room couch, his face a mask of tension. And beside him—our father.

They both turn to look at me, and the identical expressions of barely contained anger on their faces make me freeze in place.

My father speaks first. "Where the hell have you been?"

Chapter Fifteen

CHASE

"Suspension?" The word sticks in my throat as I stare at the official university letterhead. My father's words fade to white noise as my eyes scan the document, catching phrases that punch like fists: "academic probation," "multiple failing grades," "violation of attendance policy."

"Chase, are you even listening to me?" Dad's voice cuts through the fog. His face is flushed with a specific shade of crimson that appears when his disappointment transforms into rage. "Your brothers and I have been calling you for days."

I run a hand through my unwashed hair, still gritty with lake water and campfire smoke. "I went camping with Jason," I mumble. "There was no cell service out there."

"Convenient," Luke says from the couch, his arms crossed tightly over his chest. The bruises on his knuckles are still visible—a matching set to the ones on my face.

Dad waves the paper in front of me again. "The dean gave me this personally. Do you understand what that means?"

"I didn't know," I say, my voice sounding hollow even to my own ears. "I swear I didn't know it had gotten this bad."

"You didn't know?" Dad's voice rises, incredulity sharpening his words. "How do you not know you're failing three classes? How do you not notice you haven't submitted assignments in weeks?"

"I was busy," I mutter, unable to meet his eyes.

"Busy?" His voice rises another octave. "I had to track you down like a fugitive! When you weren't answering, I called Luke, only to find out he and Bebe are staying at Amelia's house."

My father steps closer, his eyes narrowing as he examines my face. The bruising around my eye has faded to a sickly yellow-green, but it's still visible.

"And I'm guessing that black eye and Luke's busted knuckles aren't a coincidence?" He looks between us, his mind connecting dots I'd hoped would stay disconnected. "What the hell is going on with you two?"

Luke says nothing, just stares at me with cold eyes.

Dad's continuing lecture becomes a distant drone, like a lawnmower several houses away. I catch fragments—"family reputation," "legacy," "disappointed"—but they wash over me without sticking.

I came back from camping feeling almost hopeful. Daisy had awakened something in me—a desire to get my shit together, to be someone better. Someone worthy.

But it's too late. The suspension letter in my father's hand confirms what I've been avoiding for months: I've already crashed and burned.

"I was going to fix it," I say.

Dad's laugh is bitter. "Fix it? Chase, this isn't a C- that you can bump up with extra credit. You've failed three classes. You've missed so many sessions of constitutional law that Professor Hargrove personally called me."

"I was planning to talk to my advisor tomorrow," I insist. "I was going to work something out."

"It's done." Dad folds the letter. "The decision is final. You're suspended for the rest of the semester."

I slump against the wall, the weight of it all suddenly too heavy.

Luke shifts on the couch, his expression unreadable. There's no satisfaction there, which surprises me. If our roles were reversed, I might enjoy seeing him crash and burn after what happened with Bebe.

"Pack your bags," Dad says.

The words jolt me back to attention. "What?"

"You heard me." His tone is final, brooking no argument. "Pack your things. You're coming home with me today."

"Home? I'm not going home," I say, the shock of his demand hitting me like a bucket of ice water. "I live here."

Dad's eyes narrow, the lines around his mouth deepening as his jaw tightens. "Not anymore, you don't."

"What the hell does that mean?" I push away from the wall, anger cutting through my numbness.

"It means exactly what I said. I bought this house for my sons to live in while attending college. You are no longer attending college; therefore, you no longer live here."

"You're kicking me out?"

"I'm not kicking you out, Chase. I'm taking you home." He gestures vaguely around the living room. "Luke and Bebe deserve to have their home back. Without... complications."

119

Luke looks away, his jaw tight. We both know what "complication" means. *Me.* I'm the complication.

"I can find an apartment," I say desperately. "I don't have to live here. I can get a job, pay my way—"

"With what money?" Dad asks sharply. "Your trust fund is contingent on your education."

"So that's it?" I ask, my voice cracking slightly.

He doesn't answer. His silence is confirmation enough.

I grab armfuls of clothes from my dresser and throw them into my duffel bag, not bothering to fold anything. What's the point? My life is already a wrinkled mess. A sock falls to the floor, and I kick it across the room with unnecessary force.

Behind me, I can sense Luke's presence before I turn to see him standing in the doorway, watching me. His arms are crossed, his face unreadable except for a tightness around his eyes that could be anger or something else entirely.

"It didn't have to be this way," he mumbles.

I shove a handful of t-shirts into the bag, compressing them with my fist to make room for more. "You're right," I reply, my voice raw. "Instead of pushing me while I'm down, you could help me."

His jaw tightens. "How exactly am I supposed to help you? You kissed my wife. You're failing out of school. You've been on drugs."

"I don't know," I admit, pausing to look at him. "But this isn't it."

I grab my two duffel bags and my backpack, hefting them over my shoulders. Dad looks up expectantly as I descend the stairs, relief crossing his face that I'm complying without further argument.

"I'm not going with you," I announce, walking straight past him toward the front door.

I don't wait for his response. The door slams behind me with a finality that should feel satisfying, but instead leaves me hollow. The late afternoon sun hits my face as I stand on the sidewalk, suddenly directionless. I have nowhere to go. No home. No school. No brother who gives a damn.

But I do have somewhere I need to be.

Twenty minutes later, I'm trudging across Dalton University's manicured lawn toward the dorms. My bags feel heavier with each step, reality settling in that I've just burned my last bridge.

Daisy's dorm is ahead—Byrd Hall, a five-story brick building with a pretentious white portico.

I stand outside the entrance, waiting. The electronic keycard lock means I can't just walk in. Students stream in and out, most giving me curious glances as they pass. I must look like hell—bruised face, rumpled clothes, bags slung over my shoulders like I'm some homeless drifter.

After a few minutes, a group of girls approaches, laughing among themselves. Someone swipes her card and holds the door. I dart forward, catching it before it closes.

"Thanks," I mutter, slipping inside.

One girl stops mid-sentence, her eyes widening as she looks at me.

"Oh my God," she says, her voice rising. "You're Chase Sullivan!"

I freeze, not expecting to be recognized. She's petite with curly brown hair, wearing a Dalton U sweatshirt.

She giggles, twirling a strand of hair around her finger. "I thought so! You're like, a legend. My sister was in your brother's class, and she told me all about the Sullivans." Her gaze fixes on my bruised face but politely avoids commenting. "I'm Megan, by the—"

"Megan, by any chance do you know Daisy? I'm supposed to meet her, but I don't know her room number."

Her eyes light up with recognition. "Oh! Daisy's on the fourth floor. Room 417." She leans in conspiratorially. "Are you two like, together? Because that would be so—"

"Thanks," I cut her off, already moving toward the stairwell, not wanting to discuss my relationship status with a stranger.

The space smells like a mixture of cheap air freshener and stale pizza. By the time I reach the fourth floor, I'm breathing hard—more from anxiety than exertion.

The hallway stretches out in both directions, identical doors with whiteboards bearing residents' names. I follow the numbers until I find 417. "Daisy" is written in neat handwriting on the small whiteboard, surrounded by little doodles of butterflies.

I stand here for a moment, suddenly hesitant. What if this is a mistake? What if she doesn't want me here? But the alternative is facing my father, returning to the house in disgrace. Taking a deep breath, I knock on her door.

For several long seconds, there's no response. My heart sinks. Maybe this entire impulsive plan was—

The door swings open, and there she is. A smile spreads across her face, bright and effortless when she sees me, a smile like sunshine breaking through storm clouds. Then her eyes drop to the bags at my feet, and the smile falters, confusion creeping in.

"Chase? What's—"

I don't explain. I can't explain. Words feel impossible right now. She seems to understand something's wrong because she steps back, holding the door wider, inviting me in without question.

I drag my bags inside her small dorm room, letting them fall to the floor with a heavy thud. Then I'm moving toward her, drawn by some magnetic pull I can't resist. My arms wrap around her, pulling her close, burying my face in her hair.

She doesn't speak, just hugs me back, her arms tight around my waist. Her hands are splayed across my back, holding me steady as I breathe her in. I say nothing. I can't. If I open my mouth right now, I might break completely. So I hold her, letting her warmth seep into me, counteracting the cold emptiness that's been spreading through my chest since I read that suspension letter. She doesn't push me away or demand explanations. My face remains buried in her hair, my eyes squeezed shut against the burning sensation behind them.

Minutes pass. I don't know how many. Time feels meaningless with her in my arms. Eventually, I loosen my grip enough to look at her, finding her eyes full of concern but no judgment.

"I got suspended for failing three classes," I whisper, my voice hoarse. "My dad kicked me out of my house, and my brother hates me."

Chapter Sixteen

DAISY

I'VE NEVER SEEN anyone look so completely broken before. Chase's arms feel like a fortress around me, strong yet somehow fragile. I feel tremors running through his body as he holds me, like he's barely keeping himself together.

I reach up to touch his face, my fingers gentle against the fading bruise. There's something devastating about seeing someone so confident brought this low. The Chase Sullivan I know would never have shown this kind of vulnerability— would have let no one see him break. But here he is, standing in my tiny dorm room, looking utterly lost.

"I'm so sorry," I whisper, because what else can I say? No platitudes will fix this.

He pulls away, his eyes red-rimmed though no tears have fallen. He runs a hand through his hair, making it stand up in messy spikes. "I thought I'd already hit rock bottom, you know?" His laugh is hollow. "But apparently there's always further to fall."

I guide him to my bed, pushing aside a pile of textbooks to make room. He sits heavily, like his legs can no longer support him. I sit beside him, close enough that our shoulders touch and take his hand in mine, threading our fingers together.

We stay in silence for a while. The afternoon light filters through my thin curtains, casting everything in a soft glow that feels at odds with the heaviness in the room.

"I'm not planning on staying," he finally says, his voice rough around the edges. "I just... I really wanted to see you."

His eyes drift over to his pile of bags by the door and then catch on something else. My suitcase, propped against the wall next to my desk.

"Were you going somewhere?" he asks, nodding toward it. "That's not the one you brought on the camping trip."

I shake my head. "No, I'm not going anywhere."

He nods, dropping the subject—thankfully. The suitcase is more than just luggage to me. It's a relic from my own time of despair—my own grief that I had to overcome and accept.

I trace my finger along the back of his hand, feeling the slight ridge of a vein beneath his skin. It reminds me of the countless times I've had my own veins prodded and poked. Iron overload. Such a simple phrase for something that's slowly killing me.

"Chase," I start, then stop. The words feel trapped in my throat.

He looks at me, his eyes focusing despite his own pain. "What is it?"

I almost tell him everything—about the hemochromatosis, the iron that's been steadily accumulating in my organs since birth, the liver damage that's finally caught up with me. About how I'm on a transplant list, waiting for the call that could save my life. Or the call that might never come.

But as I open my mouth, I see the desperation in his eyes, the way his shoulders slump under the weight of everything that's already gone wrong in his life. He's been suspended, kicked out of his home, rejected by his family. And now here I am, about to tell him that the girl he wants to take out on a date might not have much time left.

"You can stay here," I say instead, squeezing his hand. "For tonight."

His eyes search mine. "Are you sure? I don't want to impose."

"Yeah, I'm sure."

Relief washes over his face, softening the hard lines of worry. He leans toward me, his palm coming up to cup my cheek. The kiss he gives me is gentle, almost reverent, nothing like the heated exchanges we shared at the lake. This is something different—a thank you, a promise, a moment of connection amid chaos.

When he pulls back, his eyes drift to my lap where my hands rest. For the first time, a hint of a smile touches his lips.

"I like your pajamas," he says, a small smile finally breaking through the sadness on his face. His finger traces one of the silky blue butterflies printed on my sleep shorts. "These are cute."

I feel a blush warming my cheeks. I'd completely forgotten I was wearing them when I answered the door.

"Thanks."

"I want to see your butterfly collection," he says, nodding toward my shelf where several framed specimens hang.

"I'd love to show you," I say, grateful for the chance to

think about something other than the problems weighing on both of us. I stand and walk over to my collection, feeling a small surge of pride as Chase follows me.

I point to a frame containing a brilliant blue morpho butterfly, its wings iridescent. "This one's my favorite. Morpho didius. The blue isn't actually pigment—it's structural. Microscopic scales on the wings reflect light in a way that creates the color."

He leans closer to examine it, his breath fogging the glass. "How does that work?"

"The scales are like tiny prisms," I explain, surprised by his genuine interest. "They refract light at certain wavelengths. If you looked at it under a microscope, the scales themselves wouldn't be blue."

I move to another frame, this one containing a delicate white butterfly with black-tipped wings. "This is a cabbage white. They're super common, but I love them because they're survivors. They can adapt to almost any environment."

"What about this orange one?" he asks.

"The monarch butterfly," I say, touching the frame gently. "They migrate thousands of miles each year between Canada and Mexico. It takes multiple generations to complete the journey—the butterflies that start the trip aren't the ones that finish it."

"That's incredible," he says. "So it's like a relay race across generations?"

"Exactly. The great-grandchildren somehow know the exact route their ancestors took, even though they've never made the journey before. Scientists still don't fully understand how they navigate."

Chase's finger traces the outline of the monarch's orange

wings through the glass. "Nature's GPS," he murmurs, then looks at me with a small smile.

"I've been collecting since I was ten," I add. "My dad thought it was just a phase, but..." I shrug, gesturing to my shelf of specimens.

"I did a study on monarch butterflies in my environmental law seminar last year," he says.

I turn to him in surprise. "You studied butterflies in law school?"

He nods. "Yeah, we had to choose an endangered species affected by environmental policy. Most people picked wolves or polar bears—obvious choices. I went with the monarch butterfly."

"That's... unexpected," I say, genuinely surprised. I try to picture Chase—with his confident swagger—passionately defending butterflies in a classroom full of future corporate lawyers.

"The monarchs' migration routes are being destroyed by development and pesticides," he continues, his fingers still tracing the frame. "Their population has declined by about 90% in the last two decades. I argued that current environmental protections do not preserve their habitats."

I stare at him, seeing a side I never expected. "I didn't know you were interested in environmental law."

"Yeah, well," he shrugs, looking almost embarrassed by his enthusiasm. "I've always been drawn to it, actually. Conservation issues, protecting natural resources. It feels like work that matters, you know?"

"Chase Sullivan, secret environmentalist."

"It doesn't exactly fit with the reputation, does it?" He attempts to return my smile. "My dad always pushed me toward business law—mergers, acquisitions, corporate litigation. That's where the money is."

"What would you want to do instead?" I ask, studying his face carefully. "If your dad weren't pushing you to corporate law?"

He looks away, his profile etched against the afternoon light filtering through my dorm window. "Environmental advocacy, maybe. Or public interest law. Something that doesn't just make rich people richer."

The vulnerability of his admission makes my heart ache.

"So what happens now?" I ask quietly. "What's your plan?"

"I'll go back to my dad's," he says. "Take responsibility for the mess I've made. Figure out how to fix it." His fingers find mine, intertwining them together. "I can't go back to school for the rest of the semester—that's non-negotiable at this point. But I can work, maybe at my dad's office, or... I don't know. Find something to do."

"Will he help you?" I ask.

"I'm sure he will," Chase admits. "On his terms."

I hear the effort it takes for him to say these words, to accept his new reality.

Chapter Seventeen

DAISY

THE SCENT of formaldehyde clings to my lab coat as I carefully position the last butterfly specimen under my microscope. There's something peaceful about being alone in the laboratory after hours, just me and my insects, categorizing beauty that most people never stop to notice.

"So this is where the magic happens," a familiar voice says, cutting through the silence.

I nearly drop my forceps, my heart leaping into my throat as I spin around to find Chase leaning against the doorframe, arms crossed over his chest. His hair is slightly mussed, like he's been running his fingers through it.

"Chase!" I exclaim, suddenly hyperaware of how I must look—hair pulled back in a messy bun, safety goggles making my eyes look huge and buggy, blue latex gloves covering my hands, bulky white lab coat swallowing my frame. Not exactly cute. "What are you doing here?"

He pushes off from the doorframe and strolls into the lab, looking around with genuine curiosity. "Thought I'd surprise you." His eyes land on the specimen I've been working on. "Is that a butterfly?"

I resist the urge to cover my face or try to fix my appearance. "How did you know where to find me?" I ask, setting down my forceps beside the microscope.

"Olivia," he says with a small shrug, coming closer. "I texted her when you didn't answer your phone."

Of course.

He moves toward me with purpose, each step bringing him deeper into my little sanctuary of science and solitude. When he reaches me, he positions himself directly in front of me, stepping between my legs as I'm perched on the high stool.

My breath catches at his closeness. Even in this sterile lab with its harsh fluorescent lighting, he looks unfairly handsome.

"These are cute," he says as he extends his arm and gently lifts my safety goggles. His fingers brush against my temples as he slides them up to rest on top of my head. "There you are."

"You're in a good mood," I observe, noticing the lightness in his expression.

"I am," he says, his voice low and intimate. He closes the distance between us, and kisses me softly. His lips are warm against mine, and I melt into him despite the clinical surroundings of the lab.

When he pulls back, his eyes are bright with something I haven't seen in them before—hope.

"I've officially moved back in with my parents and talked

to my dad," he tells me, his hands coming to rest on my waist. "Things got pretty heated at first. There was a lot of yelling, mostly from him."

"And?" I ask, my heart clenching with worry. I want so badly for things to work out for him.

I think about last night when he explained he couldn't stay over at my dorm after all. He'd gone back to his parents' house instead, saying that defying his father further would probably make it worse for him.

Chase is walking such a delicate line with him right now. One misstep and he could lose everything—his chance to return to school, his financial support, maybe even his relationship with his family.

"We came to an agreement." The corner of his mouth lifts in a small smile. "I'll be able to re-enroll next semester if I work at his office until then, proving I can handle responsibility."

"That's wonderful!" I exclaim, unable to contain my excitement. I wrap my arms around his neck, careful not to touch him with my gloved hands.

He presses his forehead against mine. "Of course, my dad threw in some non-negotiable terms as well." He shrugs, not elaborating further, but the shadow that passes over his face tells me there's more to the story. His smile returns quickly though, brightening his eyes. "But in the end, it'll be worth it. I'm getting my life back on track."

"I'm thrilled for you," I say, meaning it with every fiber of my being.

His eyes drop to my lips, his hands tightening at my waist. "I'm happy too," he murmurs. "Happier than I've been in a long time."

Then he's leaning in again, capturing my mouth in a kiss that's different from the first—deeper, more insistent. His tongue traces the seam of my mouth, and I part my lips, welcoming him in. The taste of him is intoxicating, and I forget about the sterile lab, the specimens, the latex gloves still on my hands.

I lose myself in the kiss, forgetting everything around me. His thumb traces my bottom lip, and I shiver at his touch.

"I want to take you out tonight," he says suddenly, his voice husky. "An actual date. No camping trips, no dorm rooms, no hiding in labs. Just you and me."

My heart skips. "Tonight?"

"Yes, tonight. In about three hours." His smile is confident now, the Chase Sullivan I first met shining through. "So finish up here and get that cute butt of yours home to get ready."

I laugh, surprised by his spontaneity. "Okay, yes. I'd love that."

"Good. I'll pick you up at eight."

As he walks toward the door, a thought occurs to me. "Wait! What should I wear?"

He pauses in the doorway, turning back with that devastating half-smile that makes my knees weak. "Something comfortable." His eyes sparkle as he adds, "With butterflies, if you've got it." He winks.

I'm still smiling as he disappears into the hallway, his confident stride echoing against the linoleum floor. For a moment, I sit here, my heart hammering in my chest, feeling like I'm floating. *Did that really just happen? Did Chase Sullivan ask me on a date?*

The walk back to my dorm feels quicker than usual, my steps light with anticipation. By the time I reach my room, I have just under two hours to get ready.

After a quick shower to wash away the lab chemicals, I stand wrapped in a towel before my closet, scanning my options. Most of my clothes are practical—jeans, t-shirts, sweaters for the cold lecture halls. Not exactly date material.

Then I spot it—the pale blue halter top I bought on a whim last summer. Tiny embroidered butterflies flutter across the fabric in varying shades of blue and silver. I've never worn it, always telling myself it was too fancy for everyday classes but too casual for formal events. But tonight feels like the perfect occasion.

I slip it on, adjusting the tie at the back of my neck. The soft material drapes nicely, showing just enough skin to feel special without being overdone. I pair it with a simple navy skirt that hits above my knees and grab my cream-colored cardigan in case it gets chilly later.

Standing before the mirror, I barely recognize myself.

I tilt my head, examining my reflection. It's cute and casual but still feels like me—not trying too hard but special enough for a date. I pick up my phone from the desk and snap a quick mirror selfie, turning slightly to capture the butterfly details on my top.

I send the picture to Liv with a simple message:

What do you think?

Her response comes almost instantly, making my phone buzz in my hand.

> OMG you look amazing! Why are you all dressed up?

I bite my lip, smiling as I type:

> I have a date with Chase tonight.

Three dots appear immediately, followed by:

> WHAT?! Details, please!!

> He surprised me at the lab and asked me out. Picking me up at 8. Don't know where we're going yet.

My phone rings instantly. Of course she's calling—a text conversation won't satisfy her curiosity. I answer with a laugh.

"So it's official now?" she asks without preamble, her voice practically vibrating with excitement.

"I don't know if it's 'official' official. He's got something he's working through, and I don't want to pressure him. I want to keep this light and fun."

"Daisy, he's obviously crazy about you," she says. "You deserve this."

I smile, feeling a flutter in my chest at her words. "Thanks, Liv."

"Have you told him about your condition yet?"

The warmth fades instantly, replaced by a familiar heaviness. "No," I admit. "I will when the time is right."

"Daisy—"

"I know what you're going to say," I interrupt, sitting on my bed. "But I don't want to burden him with my health issues right now."

She sighs. "Okay, but please tell me you're planning to do something with your hair." Her voice shifts into what I call her 'makeover mode.' "You can't just leave it down and plain like that. You should try that braided crown thing I showed you last month. It would look amazing with that top, and it'll show off your neck with the halter style. Then some light eyeshadow to bring out your—"

"Liv," I cut in gently but firmly. "Thank you for caring so much, but I'm going to do this my way."

There's a brief pause before she sighs. "You're right. I'm being too pushy again, aren't I?"

"A little," I laugh. "But I love you for it."

"I just want everything to be perfect for you," she says, her voice softening.

"I know. But perfect for me might look different from perfect for you." I glance at my reflection again. "I'm thinking of curling the ends a bit and leaving it down," I say, glancing at the clock. "I've got to get moving if I want to be ready by eight."

After ending the call with Olivia, I set my phone down and feel a rush of butterflies in my stomach. This is actually happening.

I plug in my curling iron and turn to my small jewelry box as I select my grandmother's delicate silver earrings. They catch the light as I fasten them, tiny butterfly wings that match my top perfectly.

The mirror reflects a version of myself I rarely see—cheeks

flushed with anticipation, eyes bright with hope. I carefully apply mascara, then a touch of shimmery eyeshadow that makes my blue eyes look deeper. The lip gloss goes on last—a soft pink that causes my lips to look fuller.

"This is your night," I whisper to my reflection, surprising myself with the certainty in my voice.

Chapter Eighteen

CHASE

I CHECK my watch for the third time, my heart racing with anticipation as I walk through campus toward Daisy's dorm. I've changed shirts twice, settled on my best jeans, and even picked up flowers—real ones, not the gas station variety I might have grabbed in the past. Yellow daisies mixed with some wildflowers because I'm not exactly subtle.

My phone buzzes in my pocket just as Byrd Hall comes into view. Probably Daisy wondering where I am, although I'm five minutes early. I pull it out, smile already forming, then feel it die on my lips when I see the name on the screen.

Celeste.

"Fuck," I mutter, stopping in the middle of the sidewalk.

For a moment, I consider letting it go to voicemail. But my father's conditions echo in my head: therapy twice a week and take Richard Astor's daughter on a few dates. The first requirement is annoying but manageable. The second makes my skin crawl.

I answer with a sigh. "Yeah."

"Chase!" Her voice is high and breathy, like she's surprised I answered. "I was hoping to catch you. I was wondering if we could get together soon," she continues, not waiting for my response. "Daddy mentioned your father called him, and I thought—"

"Yeah, about that," I cut her off, glancing at my watch again. Four minutes until I'm supposed to meet Daisy. "Listen, Celeste, I can't talk right now."

She makes a small huffing sound—like a pout. "Oh. Well, when would be better? I'm free this weekend and reservations should be made in advance."

I close my eyes, pinching the bridge of my nose. Dad was crystal clear about his expectations: take Richard's daughter out. Make it look sincere. Keep the Astors happy. He understands I don't actually like Celeste, but appearances matter to our families. To my father. To The Keepers.

"I don't know yet," I say vaguely, watching a couple exit the dorm building. "I'll call you tomorrow, okay?"

"Perfect!" she practically squeals. "I was thinking of Wesello's for dinner? They have a private back room that Daddy always reserves—"

"I'll call you tomorrow," I repeat firmly, cutting her off.

I end the call and shove my phone back in my pocket, cursing under my breath. The Keepers. Always lurking in the background of my life, like some Victorian-era secret society with its outdated traditions and expectations. Two families coming together, preserving wealth and influence—it's like something out of a Jane Austen novel, except with trust funds and political connections instead of dowries and estates.

But Celeste is exactly what I can't stand about Keeper

women—perfectly groomed, perfectly obedient, with all the personality of a department store mannequin. Trained from birth to be the perfect society wife, who organizes charitable events and looks pretty at political fundraisers. The kind of woman who has opinions but only the right ones, who'd never dream of challenging the status quo.

I stare at the bouquet in my hands, feeling like a fraud suddenly. Here I am, about to take out a girl I genuinely care about, while simultaneously agreeing to fake-date someone else to keep my father's connections happy. The guilt settles in my stomach like a lead weight.

I shove those thoughts aside and hurry the steps to Daisy's dorm. No point in dwelling on problems I can't solve right now. Tonight is about Daisy. Only Daisy. I'll deal with Celeste later.

Standing outside her door, I take a deep breath and knock, shifting the bouquet from one hand to the other. When the door swings open, everything else fades away.

Daisy stands there in a pale blue top covered in tiny embroidered butterflies, which has my brain short-circuiting for a solid five seconds. Her blonde hair falls in soft waves around her shoulders.

The delicate fabric ties behind her neck in a neat little bow, leaving her shoulders completely bare. My eyes trace the gentle curve where her neck meets her shoulder, and I swallow hard. It's somehow both adorably cute and devastatingly sexy at the same time.

I can't help but imagine what it would be like to stand behind her, fingers grazing those shoulders before gently tugging at that single bow that holds everything together.

"Hi," she says, with a shy smile playing on her lips.

"Hi," I manage, suddenly feeling like a nervous teenager. "These are for you." I thrust the flowers toward her, watching her eyelashes flutter as she takes in the yellow daisies nestled among wildflowers. "Daisies," I add unnecessarily, feeling heat creep up my neck. "Pretty unoriginal, I know. But I saw them and thought of you."

She holds the bouquet carefully, bringing it to her face and inhaling with a smile. "These are beautiful. You know, no one has ever brought me daisies before."

"Really?" I ask, surprised. "I would've thought with your name..."

She laughs, shaking her head. "I'm not named after the flower. My mom was obsessed with The Great Gatsby in college. I'm named after Daisy Buchanan."

"Literature, not botany," I say with a smile. "That's unexpected."

"Ironic, right? Named after a fictional socialite, ended up a science nerd consumed by insects." She looks at the flowers again, her expression softening. "These are lovely, Chase. Thank you."

I can't help myself—I step forward, cupping her face in my hands, and kiss her. When I pull back, her cheeks are flushed pink, her eyes bright.

"You look beautiful," I tell her, my voice low.

Her blush deepens. "You don't look so bad yourself."

She steps back, opening the door wider. "Come in for a minute while I put these in water," she says, gesturing toward a small kitchenette in the corner of her dorm room.

I follow her inside, taking in the details of her space that I had seen briefly yesterday. Her room is neat but lived-in, with framed butterfly specimens arranged on the wall above her desk. Books are stacked on every available surface, most with scientific titles I can barely pronounce. And that suitcase... the same one that I saw yesterday is still sitting in the same spot. Strange...

She fills a glass with water from the tiny sink in the kitchenette area, carefully arranging the flowers I brought her.

"So where are we going tonight?" she asks, glancing over her shoulder at me.

"I thought we'd try this little place off campus," I say, leaning against the wall. "It's called Mariposa. Spanish for butterfly." I watch her face light up at the connection. "It's nothing fancy—just good food, a pleasant atmosphere. Casual."

"That sounds perfect," she says, placing the makeshift vase on her desk. "I've never heard of it."

"It's a hidden gem. Small, family-owned. They make these incredible empanadas," I finish, offering my hand to her. "Ready?"

She takes it without hesitation, her fingers intertwining with mine in a way that feels both casual and significant. As we step out of her dorm and into the cool evening air, I'm struck by how natural it feels to be holding her hand, like we've been doing this for months.

We walk across campus. A few students pass us, some doing double-takes when they recognize me. I'm used to being noticed—being a Sullivan comes with that territory—but tonight feels different. There's no need to posture or perform. I'm just a guy walking with a girl he likes.

"Chase! My man!"

I look to see Richie from my constitutional law class waving as he approaches with a few guys I vaguely recognize.

His eyes immediately drop to our linked hands, a grin spreading across his face.

"Hey, Richie," I say, giving Daisy's hand a reassuring squeeze. "This is Daisy."

"Nice to meet you," he says, his smile genuine as he nods to Daisy. "You two headed somewhere?"

"Dinner," I reply. "Later, man."

I guide her away before he can ask more questions. His eyes follow us, and I know the gossip will be all over campus by morning. Chase Sullivan, off the market—*again*.

Twenty minutes later, we're stepping into Mariposa. The restaurant is small but warm, with string lights crisscrossing the ceiling and colorful murals covering the walls. The hostess —a middle-aged woman with a kind smile—greets us in Spanish before switching to English.

"Table for two?" she asks, grabbing menus.

"Yes, please," I say.

She nods knowingly, a hint of amusement in her eyes as she observes our linked hands. "Follow me."

She leads us through the cozy space to a corner table by a window.

The hostess gestures to the small table illuminated by flickering candles. I slide into the chair across from her, suddenly aware of how intimate this feels—the two of us in this quiet alcove, sheltered from the rest of the world.

"This is lovely," Daisy says. "I can't believe I've never been here before."

"One of Ambrose's best-kept secrets," I tell her, watching as she unfolds her napkin and places it in her lap. "I found it last summer."

The waiter approaches with water and a basket of warm

tortilla chips. "Can I get you two something to drink?" he asks with a friendly smile.

"I'll have a lemonade," Daisy says.

"Make that two," I add, not wanting alcohol to complicate tonight.

As he leaves, Daisy opens her menu, and I find myself watching her face instead of looking at my own.

"The carne asada sounds amazing," she says, then reads further and makes an appreciative hum. "Oh, but so does the chile relleno."

I can't help but smile at her little noises of approval. There's something so genuine about the way she reacts to things—no pretense, just honest responses. When she reaches the seafood section, her nose scrunches up, and she quickly flips to the next page.

"Not a fan of fish?" I ask, nodding toward the menu.

She looks up, slightly embarrassed. "Is it that obvious?"

"You made a face," I tell her, reaching across the table to touch her hand. "It's cute. Have you decided what you want?" I ask, still not having looked at my menu.

"I think the butternut squash enchiladas," she says, making another little hum of approval.

"Alright," I say, leaning forward. "Let's skip the boring small talk. We're playing a game."

She quirks an eyebrow. "A game?"

Chapter Nineteen

DAISY

CHASE NODS toward the couple across the room. "See them? The guy in the ugly blue tie?"

I follow his gaze. "Yeah."

"They're not on a date," he says. "She's a jewel thief, he's her getaway driver. And they're plotting their next heist over crème brûlée."

I laugh, immediately catching on to his game. I scan the restaurant and point to an elderly couple by the window. "Those two? They're former CIA operatives who faked their deaths in the 80s. They meet once a year in random restaurants to exchange intel on their grandchildren, who have no idea their sweet grandparents used to assassinate foreign dignitaries."

His eyes sparkle with delight. "That's good! I like the grandchildren twist."

"The husband still keeps a garrote wire in his orthopedic shoe," I add, and he bursts out laughing.

Our waiter appears, notepad in hand. "Have you decided what you'd like to order?"

"I'll have the butternut squash enchiladas," I say, closing my menu.

He doesn't even glance at his menu. "The carne asada for me. And can we get some queso fundido?"

"Excellent choices," the waiter says, collecting our menus. "I'll put that right in for you."

As he walks away, Chase leans forward, his eyes twinkling with mischief. "Let's try a new game. Two Truths and a Lie."

"I haven't played that since freshman orientation week. You tell three facts about yourself, and I have to guess which one is the lie?"

"Exactly," he says, his fingers drumming lightly on the table.

"You should go first," I say, taking a sip of my lemonade. "Since it was your idea."

He sits back in his chair as he considers what to say.

"Alright," he says finally. "Number one: I once got arrested for climbing the water tower during freshman year." He holds up a second finger, his eyes holding mine. "Two: I think about kissing you pretty much every time you speak." I'm pretty sure I'm blushing now. "And number three: I've never been skiing, despite my family owning a cabin in Aspen."

I consider each statement carefully, weighing them against what I know about him.

"I think..." I tap my finger against my chin, "the lie is number one. You never got arrested for climbing the water tower."

His brows shoot up in surprise. "How did you know?"

"Because if Chase Sullivan was put in jail, it would be

legendary gossip. Everyone would know," I say, feeling oddly proud of my deduction. "Plus, you have that look people get when they're trying too hard to sell a lie."

"What look?" he asks, feigning offense.

"That one right there," I laugh, pointing at his face. "Too innocent to be believable."

I do a little victory wiggle in my seat, shoulders shimmying side to side in what Olivia calls my 'happy dance.' Chase watches me with amusement, his smile growing wider.

"Alright, Detective Daisy," he says, leaning forward. "Your turn. Two truths and a lie."

I take a deep breath, suddenly feeling nervous. I think for a moment, deciding what to share. I need to include something flirty like he did, but not be too obvious to which statement is the lie.

"Okay," I say, meeting his eyes across the table. "Number one: I spent an entire summer cataloging butterfly specimens at the Smithsonian as an intern." I pause, gathering my courage for the flirty statement. "Number two: I can't stop thinking about how it feels to wake up next to you." My cheeks burn as I say it, but I push forward. "And number three: I've never broken a bone in my body."

I watch as he considers each option, his eyes never leaving mine.

"Well," he announces, "the lie has to be number one. The Smithsonian thing. That's too specific to be true."

I shake my head, feeling a small thrill of victory. "Wrong! I really did intern at the Smithsonian the summer after high school. I helped organize their lepidoptera collection."

"No way," he says, looking genuinely surprised. "So which is the lie then?" he asks, his eyes gleaming.

I feel heat rush to my cheeks, unable to meet his gaze. The answer is obvious now—I've never broken a bone. But admitting that means confirming I've thought about waking up next to him... multiple times.

His hand reaches across the table, palm up in invitation. I place my palm in his, and he links our fingers together, the warmth of his skin against mine sending tingles up my arm.

"You don't have to say it," he says softly. "I think I know."

Our waiter arrives with perfect timing, setting steaming plates before us. The aroma of spices and roasted vegetables fills the air between us, momentarily distracting from the intimacy of the moment.

"Can I get you anything else?" the waiter asks.

"We're good, thanks," Chase answers without looking away from me.

The food is incredible—my enchiladas are rich and flavorful, the butternut squash toasted perfectly with just the right balance of spices. Chase cuts into his carne asada, offering me some of his.

The conversation flows easily as we eat. He tells me stories about his childhood—adventures with his brothers all the way to paintball competitions.

I gave him more useless but interesting facts about all things bugs, and he engaged and asked questions.

When the check comes, Chase insists on paying despite my protests.

"Next time can be your treat," he says with a wink that makes my heart skip.

Next time. The promise of it lingers between us as we step outside. He reaches for my hand automatically, his fingers sliding between mine like they belong there.

The walk back to campus is peaceful, with streetlights casting a golden glow over the sidewalk. The campus feels quieter. We walk in comfortable silence.

"I had a good time tonight," I tell him as we approach campus.

"Me too," he says, squeezing my hand. "Best date I've had... ever."

We reach my dorm building, and I feel a flutter of nervousness as we stand outside the entrance. The air has shifted—charged—and I don't want the night to end yet.

"Do you want to come up?" I ask, the words tumbling out before I can overthink them.

I see the realization hit him for what I'm asking, and for a moment I worry I've been too forward. But then his expression softens.

"I'd love to," he says.

My heart hammers against my ribs as I swipe my keycard and lead him inside. The elevator ride to the fourth floor feels charged with electricity, his presence behind me making me hyperaware of every breath, every movement.

When we reach my room, I fumble with the key, suddenly nervous. Once in, I drop my purse and cardigan on my desk chair and move toward my bed, turning on the small lamp on my nightstand. The soft glow bathes the room in a warm light —not too bright, but enough to see each other. I want to create a mood, something intimate but not too obvious.

Now what? I stand awkwardly in the middle of the space, unsure what to do with my hands or where to look. *Should I sit on the bed? Offer him water?* My confidence in asking him up has evaporated, leaving me frozen in place.

Chase seems to sense my uncertainty. He steps closer,

taking my hands in his. "Come here," he says softly, leading me toward my bed. The mattress dips as we sit side by side, our thighs touching.

His eyes find mine, deep blue and impossibly tender. When he leans in to kiss me, I meet him halfway. This kiss is different from our others—deliberate, unhurried. His lips move against mine with purpose, and when his tongue traces the seam of my mouth, I open to him eagerly.

I sink into the sensation, the taste of him mingling with the sweetness of the lemonade we shared at dinner. His hand comes up to my face, thumb stroking my cheek as our kiss deepens. I melt against him, all my earlier nervousness dissolving into a warm, liquid heat that pools low in my belly.

He pulls back slightly, his breath hot against my lips, and then I feel the flutter of his eyelashes against my cheek—those butterfly kisses that make my heart race. He trails them along my jawline and down to the sensitive skin of my neck, each delicate touch sending shivers through my body.

"Chase," I sigh, my fingers threading through his hair.

His mouth finds mine again, hungrier this time. My confidence grows with each passing moment. I reach behind my neck, my fingers finding the knot that holds my halter top in place. I untie it, letting the fabric loosen around me. I drag the top off me, exposing my simple white strapless bra underneath.

His eyes darken as he watches me, his gaze intense but reverent. He swallows hard, then gestures toward my bra, his voice dropping to a husky whisper.

"May I?"

I nod, unable to form words as anticipation races through me. He shifts closer, his hand sliding around to my back. With surprising dexterity, he unclasps my bra with one hand, then gently pulls it away from my body. The cool air of my dorm room kisses my skin, and I resist the urge to cover myself.

His Adam's apple bobs noticeably as he swallows, and the raw appreciation in his eyes makes me feel beautiful in a way I never have before.

"You're perfect," he whispers, his voice thick with emotion. "So perfect, Daisy."

Chapter Twenty

DAISY

His touch ignites my skin like a match to paper, burning away every coherent thought.

He gently pushes me back onto the mattress, my head sinking into the pillow as he climbs over me. The weight of his body against mine feels both thrilling and safe, like I've been waiting for this pressure my entire life. His eyes meet mine, seeking silent permission before his mouth drops to my breast.

His tongue against my nipple sends electricity shooting through my entire body. I gasp, arching involuntarily as he begins licking and sucking with a tenderness that makes my toes curl. His lips are warm and insistent, drawing out sensations I've never experienced before.

"Chase," I breathe, my fingers finding their way into his hair, threading through the soft strands. I hold him to me, not wanting him to stop, not wanting this moment to end.

His tongue swirls around my nipple before he moves to the other breast, giving it the same attention. The sensation makes me dizzy with pleasure. Heat pools between my legs, and I shift beneath him, seeking some relief. I feel his hand slide down my side, his fingers tracing the curve of my waist before finding the zipper of my skirt. He drags it down.

"Is this okay?" he whispers against my collarbone, his breath hot on my skin.

"Yes," I breathe, lifting my hips to help as he slides the fabric off my legs.

The cool air hits my exposed skin, and I'm suddenly aware that I'm lying beneath Chase Sullivan in nothing but my white thong. His eyes travel my body with such reverence that I forget to be self-conscious.

He hooks his fingers into the thin fabric at my hips, pausing for a moment before gently tugging it. I lift my hips again, helping him remove the last barrier between me. He tosses my underwear aside, adding it to the small pile of discarded clothes on the floor.

I should feel vulnerable, lying completely naked while he's still fully dressed, but the way he's looking at me—like I'm something precious—makes me feel powerful, like a goddess worthy of worship. I watch as his eyes drink in every inch of me, making my skin tingle wherever his gaze lands.

He moves down my body, pressing soft kisses along my stomach, each one sending shivers across my skin. When he reaches my hip bone, he pauses, looking up at me with those impossibly blue eyes.

"You're so sexy," he whispers against my inner thigh.

His hand slides up my leg, and his thumb brushes against the most sensitive part of me. I gasp at the contact, my hips instinctively lifting toward his touch. He traces gentle circles, exploring me with a reverence that makes my heart pound.

"You're wet," he murmurs, his voice thick with desire.

My cheeks flush with heat, but there's no embarrassment —only a primal satisfaction at how my body responds to him. When his finger slowly slides inside me, I can't help the moan that escapes my lips.

"Chase," I exhale, my fingers clutching at the sheets beneath me.

He withdraws his fingers, and I whimper at the loss of contact. He settles back on his heels, his fingers reaching for the buttons of his shirt. He undoes them one by one, revealing more skin with each movement.

His chest is smooth and lean, not bulky with muscle like a gym rat, but defined in all the right places. His skin is golden in the soft lamplight, and I have a sudden urge to trace the subtle contours of his abs with my fingertips. He has the kind of body that comes from good genes rather than obsessive workouts—natural and unforced.

"Your turn to stare," he says with a small smile, and I realize I've been doing exactly that.

He stands beside the bed, his hands moving to his belt. The metallic sound of the buckle sends a thrill through me as he unfastens it. My eyes follow his movements as he unbuttons his jeans and slowly slides down the zipper. With a slight push, the denim falls to his ankles, pooling around his feet.

I swallow hard as his thumbs hook into the waistband of his boxer briefs. I hold my breath as he takes them off, revealing himself to me completely. His erection springs free, stiff and ready, and my eyelids lift at the sight of him. His cock is magnificent—long and thick, with a smooth, flushed head. There's something about the way it stands proud from his body that makes my mouth go dry. I've never seen anything so purely masculine, so undeniably sexual.

My eyes trail from his erection up the subtle V of his hips, admiring how the muscles there create perfect lines pointing to his center. There's a light dusting of hair on his chest that narrows to a thin trail leading down.

He bends to retrieve his jeans, fishing his wallet from the back pocket. I watch as his fingers extract a small foil packet—a condom. The reality of what we're about to do hits me with full force, sending butterflies swarming through my stomach.

He returns to the bed; the mattress dipping under his weight as he positions himself between my legs. The feeling of his naked skin against mine is electric, every point of contact emitting sparks through my body. He leans down, capturing my lips in a kiss that's tender yet urgent, his tongue sliding over mine in a preview of what's coming.

When he pulls back, our eyes lock. "Are you sure about this?" he asks, his voice husky with desire but tinged with concern. "We can stop."

I reach up to touch his face, my palm against his cheek. "Yes," I whisper, my voice trembling with certainty. "I want this. I want you."

His eyes darken, pupils expanding until there's just a thin ring of blue around the edges. "God, Daisy," he breathes, "I want you so fucking bad."

Before I can respond, he's moving across my skin, pressing hot, open-mouthed kisses along my stomach, over my hip bones, down to my inner thighs. My breath catches as I realize what he's about to do. I've never experienced this before, and nervous anticipation makes my heart race.

"Chase, you don't have to—" I start, but my words

dissolve into a gasp as he settles between my legs, his breath warm against my most intimate place.

The first touch of his tongue sends a jolt of pleasure so intense that my back arches off the bed. I can't control the whimper that escapes my lips as he explores me with his mouth, finding places that make stars explode behind my eyelids.

"You taste so good," he groans against me, the vibration of his voice adding another layer to the overwhelming sensations. I feel myself spiraling higher with each stroke of his tongue, each gentle suck. My hands tangle in his hair, not pushing or pulling, just needing something to anchor me as pleasure builds.

I've felt nothing like this before—his mouth working magic between my legs, creating sensations that make coherent thought impossible. The wet heat of his tongue circles and flicks in a rhythm that's driving me wild. I'm breathing in short, desperate gasps now, my hips moving of their own accord, seeking more of the exquisite pressure.

"Chase," I moan, my voice barely recognizable to my own ears. "Oh God, that feels so good."

He hums in response, the vibration sending another jolt of pleasure through me. His hands grip my thighs, holding me open for his mouth as he continues his delicious torture. I can feel myself climbing toward something monumental, every nerve ending in my body alive and tingling.

Suddenly, he pulls away. My eyes fly open to find him sitting back on his heels, chest heaving, lips glistening. The sight of him like this, eyes dark with desire, mouth wet from pleasuring me, makes my heart race even faster.

"I can't wait anymore," he says, voice rough with need. "I need to be inside you now."

I nod wordlessly, my body aching for him as he wipes his mouth with the back of his hand. He reaches for the condom packet beside us on the bed, tearing it open with his teeth. I've never found condoms particularly sexy before, but I watch, transfixed, as he takes himself in hand, forearms flexed, and rolls the latex over his length with practiced ease. There's something incredibly erotic about seeing him prepare like this —the raw masculinity of it sending another wave of heat through me.

He moves closer, his hands finding the undersides of my knees. With gentle pressure, he spreads my legs wider, positioning himself between them. I feel completely exposed, completely vulnerable, and yet completely safe with him.

"Are you ready?" he asks.

"Yes," I whisper, reaching for him.

I feel the blunt pressure of him against my entrance, the tip of him pressing in, and my breath catches in anticipation. He pushes forward slowly. The sensation is intense—a stretching fullness unlike anything I've experienced before. I gasp, my body tensing instinctively.

"Tell me if you need to stop, okay?" he says, his eyes searching mine, looking for any sign of discomfort. "We can go as slow as you need."

I nod, unable to form words as I adjust to the unfamiliar sensation. Chase shifts his weight, reaching for my hands. His fingers interlace with mine as he pins them gently on either side of my face, the gesture somehow both dominant and tender. I feel strangely secure like this—anchored by his touch as he hovers above me.

He rolls his hips forward with exquisite gentleness. I close my eyes, focusing on the feeling of him filling me. It's intimate in a way I never imagined, this connection between us.

"Are you okay?" he asks, his voice threaded with concern despite the obvious restraint it's taking.

I nod.

"You feel amazing," he murmurs against my ear. "So perfect around me."

The initial discomfort is fading, replaced by a growing warmth that spreads through my belly. I notice how his eyes keep searching mine, checking for signs of pain or unease. It's so sweet how attentive he's being, how he's holding back despite the strain evident in the tense muscles of his shoulders and the controlled rhythm of his breathing.

"You can go deeper," I whisper, my voice barely audible even in the quiet room.

When he pushes a little more, I feel a sudden sharp pinch followed by a release of pressure. I gasp, my fingers digging into his shoulders as I realize what just happened—my hymen breaking, the final physical barrier between us gone.

"Did I hurt you?" he asks immediately, freezing in place.

"Just for a second," I reassure him, surprised by how quickly the discomfort fades into something warmer, more pleasurable. "It's better now. Keep going."

He covers my mouth with his, kissing me deeply as he moves with more confidence. Each thrust sends waves of pleasure radiating through me, building on the sensations his mouth created earlier. His strokes grow a little faster, a little deeper, and he slides in and out of me with more ease now.

"God, Daisy," he groans, his voice strained. "You feel incredible. I'm so close already—you feel too good." His eyes lock with mine, intense and vulnerable all at once. "I want you to come with me," he whispers. The raw honesty coming from him makes my heart stutter.

He shifts slightly, changing the angle, and suddenly he's hitting a spot that makes me cry out. My nails dig into his back as the pleasure intensifies, building to something I can barely comprehend.

He slips his hand between our bodies, his fingers finding the sensitive bundle of nerves at my center. He touches me there, creating slow, deliberate circles with his thumb that perfectly match the rhythm of his thrusts. The dual sensation is overwhelming—him inside me while his fingers work their magic.

I wrap my legs around him, pulling him deeper, urging him on. "Oh God," I gasp, my head pressing back into the pillow as pleasure spirals through me.

The way he's touching me is so intimate, so intentional—like he's memorizing what makes me respond. He continues those perfect circles, applying just the right amount of pressure. There's something profoundly connecting about the way he watches my face, as if cataloging every reaction, every flutter of my eyelids, every parted-lip gasp.

"That's it," he encourages softly, his voice a reverent whisper. "Let go for me."

The tension builds with each synchronized movement—his hips rolling into mine while his fingers maintain their hypnotic pattern. I'm climbing higher than before, my body trembling beneath him. The pleasure is so intense it's almost unbearable, gathering like electricity before a storm.

"Chase," I whimper, clinging to him as the sensation threatens to overwhelm me. "I think I'm—"

"I know," he breathes against my ear, his voice strained but tender. "I can feel you. Come for me."

And I do. The tension snaps like a rubber band stretched too far. My inner muscles clamp around him, squeezing rhythmically as wave after wave of pleasure crashes through me. My vision blurs at the edges as I arch against him, a rush of wetness flowing between us.

"Fuck," he groans, his rhythm faltering. "Oh God, Daisy —I can't—" His words cut off as his body tenses above me. His fingers dig into my hips as he gives me short, quick thrusts, his face contorting in pleasure. I feel the pulsing inside me as he comes, each twitch sending aftershocks through mine.

I wrap my legs tighter around him, suddenly wishing there wasn't a barrier between us. I want to feel him entirely, to have him finish inside me without the latex separating us. The thought surprises me—I've never felt that way before, never wanted someone so completely.

Chase stays still for a moment, his forehead pressed against mine as we both catch our breath. Then he drags out, the empty feeling making me sigh with disappointment. He sits back on his heels between my legs, and notice his cock is still semi-hard, the condom cloudy with his release. There are small pinkish streaks—evidence of my virginity.

"You're bleeding a little," he says softly, concern replacing the bliss on his face. "Are you okay?"

"I'm fine," I assure him, propping myself up on my elbows.

"Just a minute," he says, his voice gentle. "Don't move."

He slides off the bed with surprising grace, and I watch as he makes his way to my small bathroom. I hear water running briefly, then the sound of the toilet flushing.

163

When he returns, he's no longer wearing the condom and is holding a damp washcloth in his hand. Our nakedness should feel awkward or embarrassing, but there's something so natural about the way he moves, completely comfortable in his skin. The soft light from my bedside lamp casts golden shadows across his lean muscles.

"Let me take care of you," he says, sitting beside me on the bed.

The warmth of the cloth is soothing as he gently cleans between my legs. I can feel my face getting hot—not from embarrassment, but from the tenderness of his actions. He's so careful, so attentive, his eyes occasionally meeting mine to check that I'm comfortable.

"Thank you," I whisper, not knowing what else to say. The words feel inadequate for the moment.

Chapter Twenty-One

CHASE

I CHECK my watch for the third time in five minutes, as if staring at it will somehow make the nurse call my name faster. The plastic chair beneath me is uncomfortable in that uniquely medical way—designed to keep you from getting too comfortable, like they're worried you might decide to move in.

"Sullivan, Chase?"

Finally. I stand, ignoring the knowing glance from the girl across from me. *Yeah, I'm here for an STD test. So are half the people in this waiting room. Welcome to college.*

The nurse leads me down a hallway decorated with posters about protected sex and the importance of regular testing. I've seen them all before, but this time they hit differently. This isn't my usual post-breakup checkup—this is about Daisy.

After finding out Ava was cheating, I figured it was better safe than sorry. The irony isn't lost on me—the guy who used to hook up without a second thought, now anxiously waiting for a clean bill of health before things with Daisy get more serious.

"Room three," the nurse says, handing me a clipboard. "Fill this out while you wait."

I sit on the paper-covered exam table; the material crinkling beneath me as I scan the questionnaire. Sexual history. Types of protection used. Date of last sexual encounter.

Last night.

Daisy. Just thinking about her makes something warm unfurl in my chest. Last night was... different. I've had plenty of sex before—good sex, even great sex sometimes—but it's always been about the physical release, about getting off. With her, every touch felt like it meant something. The way she looked at me, trusted me, gave herself to me completely—it cracked something open inside me I didn't know was there.

I fill out the form quickly, checking boxes and scribbling answers. Last question done, I click the pen and set the clipboard aside. The doctor should be here any minute, but "any minute" in a clinic can mean anything from five minutes to half an hour.

I drum my fingers against my thigh, already bored out of my mind. There's a small rack of magazines on the wall— might as well kill time. There're no Sports Illustrated or People here—just medical journals and wellness pamphlets. I grab the one on top, a health magazine with a smiling woman holding an apple on the cover. Not exactly my usual reading material, but it's better than staring at the anatomical poster of STDs.

I flip through the glossy pages, barely registering the articles about superfoods and workout routines. It's all words and pictures blurring together until something catches my eye

—a photo of a teenage girl sitting on a hospital bed with a packed suitcase beside her. She's smiling, but there's something in her eyes that appears forced, like she's trying to be brave.

The headline reads "Always Ready: What Every Transplant Patient Should Know." I scan the article; my attention suddenly focused. It talks about how potential transplant patients often keep a packed suitcase ready for when "The Call" comes—the news that a donor organ is available—they need to be ready to leave at a moment's notice.

Where have I seen that? My aunt had a kidney transplant a few years ago and had a bag ready. But that's not what I'm thinking of...

My heart stops.

That suitcase. *Daisy's suitcase. The one by her door.*

No way—it has to be a coincidence, right? But the two times I've been to her place—it hasn't moved. Not an inch.

"Shit," I mutter, the realization hitting me.

Could Daisy be waiting for a transplant? Is she sick? She doesn't look sick, but then again, not all illnesses are visible. The questions pile up, each one more terrifying than the last.

I have an overwhelming urge to text her to demand answers. *But what would I even say? Hey, I saw your suitcase and read a random magazine article. Are you dying?* Yeah, that would go over well.

I toss the magazine back and pick the clipboard—mind racing and feeling like a jerk for missing that—if the suitcase is what I think it's for. I hit my head with the clipboard, *hard*, just as the nurse and doctor walk in.

Great. Just perfect. They probably think I'm having some kind of breakdown.

The science building looms ahead, all glass and steel, gleaming in the afternoon light. I pace near the entrance, checking my watch every thirty seconds. Students filter out in small groups, laughing and comparing notes.

Then I see her.

Daisy's whole face glows when she spots me, her entire expression transforming like I've just made her day by simply existing. She breaks into a jog, blonde hair bouncing with each step. I catch her in my arms, lifting her off the ground as I pull her into a tight hug. She feels so small against me, so fragile yet somehow strong.

"Hi," she says breathlessly when I set her down.

I cup her face in my hands and kiss her, right there in front of the science building where anyone can see. Let them look. I don't care anymore who knows about us or judges because of how quickly I moved on from my last relationship.

"Hi yourself," I say against her lips. "How was class?"

"Fascinating actually. We were looking at genetic mutations in fruit flies and how they—" She stops herself, blushing slightly. "Sorry, I'm nerding out again."

"I like when you nerd out," I tell her, taking her hand in mine. "Come on, let's grab a coffee. I'm dying for caffeine."

She falls into step beside me, our fingers intertwined.

"So," she says, swinging our hands between us, "how was your morning?"

"I... went to the student health center," I admit, rubbing the back of my neck. "Not because I have any symptoms or anything—just taking precautions, you know? After everything with…" I trail off carefully, not wanting to kill the mood by bringing up my ex.

But there's no judgement there, just understanding.

She squeezes my hand reassuringly. "That's responsible of you."

"I should have the results in a few days," I continue. "I just wanted to be sure before we…"

"I appreciate that," she says, a slight blush coloring her cheeks. "I've been on birth control for a couple of years now." She tucks a strand of hair behind her ear. "It helps regulate my period."

We reach the campus coffee shop, joining the short line of students waiting to order. Daisy shifts her weight from one foot to the other, looking suddenly shy.

"And, you know," she continues, her voice dropping to almost a whisper, "in case we decide… *not* to use protection." Her eyes meet mine briefly before darting away.

My heart rate kicks up a notch. The thought of being with Daisy without a barrier between us sends a rush of heat through my body. *Christ, if sex with her was that incredible with a condom, what would it feel like to be completely bare inside her?* To feel her warmth directly, to finish inside her… The idea alone makes me half-hard in the middle of this coffee shop.

"That would be…" I clear my throat, lowering my voice. "I'd like that. Once we get the all-clear, of course."

Her eyes lock with mine, and the shy smile that curves her lips makes my heart race. There's an innocence to her expression, but something knowing in her look that drives me crazy.

The barista calls for the next customer, snapping me back to reality. We step up to the counter and order—a black coffee for me and a caramel latte for her. While we wait, I slip my arm around her waist, pulling her against my side. She fits perfectly there, like she was designed to tuck into the space beside me.

"Let's sit outside," I suggest once we have our drinks. "It's too nice to be cooped up in here."

I guide her through the bustling coffee shop and out into the courtyard. The late afternoon sun filters through the trees, casting golden dappled shadows across the open space. We find a wood and iron bench tucked under a large oak tree, away from the main foot traffic. I sit close to her, our knees touching as we face each other.

She takes a sip of her latte, a tiny bit of caramel foam clinging to her upper lip. I want to kiss it away but find myself staring at her instead. Her skin is clear and bright; her eyes are alert and full of life. If she's sick—truly sick enough to need an organ transplant—I can't see any sign of it. She looks the picture of health, vibrant and beautiful.

She notices me staring and tilts her head. "What? Do I have something on my face?"

I swallow hard, setting my coffee on the bench between us. "No, it's not that. I just..." I take a deep breath. "I'm sorry."

"For what?" Her brow furrows.

"For being a jerk. For you listening to all my problems— my suspension, my dad—when you've got something serious going on." The words tumble out. "I saw your suitcase," I blurt out, watching confusion flicker across her face. "The one in your dorm. It's always there, in the same spot? Ready to go?"

She blinks at me several times, her expression shifting from puzzlement to something else—something guarded. Her eyes dart away from mine, focusing on a point over my shoulder.

"What about it?" she asks quietly, her fingers tightening around her coffee cup.

"At the health center this morning, I saw an article about transplant patients. How they keep packed suitcases ready for when they get 'The Call.' My aunt had a kidney transplant and did the same thing." I reach for her hand, but she pulls it back. "Daisy, are you sick? Are you waiting for a transplant?"

She's silent for so long I think she might not answer. The surrounding courtyard continues buzzing with activity, but it feels like we're in our own bubble, separated from everyone else by the weight of what hangs between us.

"Daisy," I say softly. "You don't have to tell me if you're not comfortable. I just want you to know that I'm here, willing to listen if you need me. You've been there for me through all my stuff, and I want to be there for you too, whatever it is."

Chapter Twenty-Two

DAISY

MY HEART HAMMERS against my ribcage like a butterfly desperate to escape. The truth hovers between us, delicate and dangerous. Chase's eyes—those impossible blue eyes that see too much—are fixed on me with an intensity that makes my skin prickle.

I watch a few leaves rustle in the breeze, buying myself precious seconds. The courtyard suddenly feels too open, too exposed for this conversation.

"Would you believe me," I say, forcing a lightness into my voice, "if I told you I have a side hustle as a magician for kids' parties?" I attempt a smile. "I keep the suitcase by the door for anyone who needs emergency cheering up. You know, pull a rabbit out of a hat, make some balloon animals—instant happiness."

His expression doesn't change. The joke falls flat between us, landing with all the grace of a stone.

"Daisy," he says quietly. "You don't have to do that with me."

"Do what?" I ask, though I know exactly what he means.

"Deflect. Make jokes when things get serious." His hand finds mine again, warm and solid.

I sigh, meeting his gaze. I know he's right. He deserves the truth—especially after everything he's shared with me.

I look at our intertwined hands, focusing on the contrast between his tanned skin and my paler complexion.

"It's called hemochromatosis," I finally say, my voice barely audible above the ambient noise of the courtyard. "It's a genetic disorder where my body absorbs too much iron from food."

"Iron?"

I nod, finding it easier to continue now that I've started. "My body can't get rid of the excess iron, so it builds up in my organs. Mainly my liver." I swallow hard. "It's failing because of it."

"That's why you have the suitcase," he says softly, the realization dawning in his eyes.

"I've been on the transplant list for three years," I confirm, observing his face for signs of pity or, worse, disgust. "Just waiting for a match. The suitcase stays packed because when the call comes, I'll only have a few hours to get to the hospital, no matter where I am."

Chase's hand tightens around mine. His thumb traces small circles against my skin.

"You look so healthy," he says, searching my face with amazement.

I offer a slight smile. "I have good days and bad days. The treatments help—phlebotomies to remove excess iron, medication to bind it." I shrug. "Today's a good day. You wouldn't know anything was wrong just by looking at me. On other days, I can barely get out of bed."

His expression shifts, a mixture of concern. "How long have you known?"

I take a deep breath, feeling the familiar tightness in my chest whenever I talk about this. "I was diagnosed when I was twelve, but it wasn't severe then. Just regular monitoring, some dietary changes." I pause, looking down at our hands. "Then, about three years ago, my liver enzymes started climbing. The doctors did a biopsy and found significant damage."

"That's when you went on the transplant list?"

I nod, swallowing hard. "That's when everything changed."

His eyes are intense, focused entirely on me. He's listening in a way that makes me feel both exposed and understood.

"At that time," I continue, "I had this moment where it all just... hit me. I was sitting in my bedroom studying for finals when I suddenly realized my liver could fail at any moment. Just like that—game over." I snap my fingers for emphasis. "And I completely lost it."

I feel a tightness in my throat as I remember those dark months. "I snapped. Stopped going to classes, stopped answering calls. What was the point, you know? Why bother with an education? Why make plans for a future that might not happen?" The memory of that hopelessness washes over me. "My high school boyfriend, Brandon—we'd been together almost two years when I got on the transplant list. At first, he was supportive. Came with me to appointments, held my hand during blood draws. Then one day, he just... couldn't anymore." I pause, feeling the familiar ache of that rejection. "He texted me. Can you believe that? After everything, he sent a text saying he couldn't handle the pressure of dating someone who might die. Like my illness was some inconvenience he hadn't signed up for."

Chase's jaw tightens, a flash of anger crossing his face. "What an asshole."

"Yeah," I agree, surprised by the emotion in his voice. "My parents weren't much better, though in a different way. They were so terrified of losing me they basically tried to wrap me in bubble wrap. Wanted me to stay home, not go to college after high school, focus on my health." I shake my head, remembering the fights. "They were drowning in their own grief about potentially losing their only child—they couldn't see they were suffocating me." I take a sip of my latte, now lukewarm. "It was Liv who pulled me back from the edge," I continue, feeling a small smile form despite the heaviness of the conversation. "When everyone else was walking away or smothering me, she... showed up. Every day. Even when I wouldn't answer the door, she'd slide notes under it. Sometimes stupid memes or gossip, other times longer letters reminding me why life was worth fighting for."

His eyes haven't left my face, his attention unwavering.

"She'd bring her homework and sit outside my door, talking to me through it. One day she announced she was going butterfly hunting and needed my expertise." I laugh softly at the memory. "It was such an obvious ploy to get me outside, but it worked. That was the first day I felt like myself again in months."

"She sounds like an amazing cousin," he says, his voice gentle.

"She is. After that, she helped me see that living in fear of dying wasn't really living at all. That I could choose either to wait for death or embrace whatever life I had left." I glance up at the dappled sunlight filtering through the leaves above us. "I've been living by that philosophy ever since," I say, watching a butterfly flit between flowers nearby. "Making the most of each day, not letting fear dictate my choices." I turn back to Chase, suddenly feeling guilty. His face shows no judgment, only concern and attentiveness. It makes what I need to say next both easier and harder. "I'm sorry I didn't tell you sooner. Not that I didn't trust you or didn't want you to know. You have so much going on already with your suspension and your family situation. I didn't want to add my medical drama to your pile."

He shakes his head, squeezing my hand. "Don't apologize. I understand."

"Do you?" I search his face. "Because I need you to know it wasn't about keeping secrets. I just... I've seen what happens when people find out. They either run away like Brandon, or they treat me like I'm made of glass like my parents. I didn't want either of those things to happen with us. But I understand too if you need to walk away."

He reaches out to brush a strand of hair from my face, his touch gentle. "I'm not going anywhere," he says firmly, his eyes never leaving mine. "And I will not treat you like you're fragile either. You're the strongest person I know, Daisy."

His confidence makes my heart flutter. I want to believe him, but experience has taught me otherwise.

"You say that now," I whisper, "but you haven't seen the bad days. The days when I struggle to get out of bed, when my skin turns yellow from jaundice, when I'm too exhausted to even hold a conversation."

He shifts closer, both hands now holding mine. "Then I'll be there on those days too. I'll bring you butterflies to catalog on the days you can't go looking for them yourself."

Something in his expression changes, a determined light entering his eyes.

"Daisy, you're going to get that transplant," he says with such certainty that I almost believe him. "I know it."

Chapter Twenty-Three

CHASE

IF THERE'S a special circle of hell for the terminally bored, it probably looks a lot like my father's accounting office.

Invoices look the same after the first hundred. Same boxes, same numbers, same mind-numbing tedium. I've been staring at the software for so long my vision's starting to blur, and I swear to God if I have to enter one more plumbing repair bill, I might actually go crazy.

This is my punishment—sorry, my "opportunity to demonstrate responsibility"—as part of our deal: I work for him during my suspension, proving I can handle mundane tasks without screwing up, and in return, I get to re-enroll next semester. The path to redemption is paved with paperwork.

Eight hours a day, three days a week, sitting in this windowless back office of Sullivan Property Management, entering data like some kind of trained monkey.

I check my watch. 2:17 PM. Still two hours and forty-three minutes of this hell to go.

My phone buzzes on the desk, and I grab it like a drowning man reaching for a life preserver. A text from Daisy.

This lecture is sooooo boring. Save me.

A smile spreads across my face instantly. I glance over my shoulder to make sure my father isn't lurking in the doorway before typing back.

I'm dying here too. Drowning in invoices. Save ME.

I text back, grinning at my phone.
Three dots appear immediately.

What are you wearing? Does my hero wear a suit?

I snort, glancing at my wrinkled button-down that I barely bothered to iron this morning.

Not exactly a suit. More like a business-casual prison uniform.

Send pic.

I hold the phone up, angling for a quick selfie that captures my bored expression and the stack of invoices beside me. I send it with the caption:

Exhibit A: Dying of boredom.

Her response comes quickly.

> Hmm. Actually, not bad. The whole "office slave" look works for you.

I smirk at my phone, about to type back something flirtatious when another text from her pops up.

> I went to the mall last night. Got something I think you'll like...

My eyebrows shoot up. *Is she implying what I think she is? Is she talking about lingerie? Some kind of sexy outfit?* The thought of Daisy in something she bought specifically for me sends heat rushing through my body.

> Oh really?

I type back, trying to sound casual.

> What did you get?

Her flirting is the only bright spot on this monotonous day.

Three dots appear, disappear, then reappear. She's thinking about her answer.

> Something blue. That's all I'm saying. Want to see it tonight?

My pulse quickens. Blue is my favorite color, and she knows it. I'm already imagining what this mysterious blue something might be when reality crashes down on me like a bucket of ice water.

"Shit," I mutter, remembering the deal with my dad to take Celeste out on a date—*fake* date.

Damn, I forgot...

I type back quickly.

Can we do tomorrow instead? Dad's making me do something for him tonight.

I hate even referring to the fake date as "something for him" like I'm a puppet on my father's strings, but it's technically true. While I wait for her response, I run a hand through my hair, frustrated that I have to postpone seeing her.

I tap my fingers against the desk while waiting for her reply, suddenly anxious. The last thing I want is for Daisy to think I'm blowing her off, especially when things between us have been so good.

Three dots appear, and I hold my breath.

Sure, tomorrow works.

It's not entirely a lie. This whole arranged date thing is definitely "family stuff," even if the details would probably make her question my sanity for agreeing to it.

Looking forward to tomorrow then.

I'll keep the blue thing a surprise.

I smile at my phone.

> My imagination is going to be running wild until then.

> Especially during this mind-numbing invoice hell.

ᴏ W

Before I can respond, my phone rings in my hand. My brother Wes's name flashes on the screen, and I have a twinge of guilt. I've been avoiding his calls since the Bebe incident, which I'm a hundred percent certain Luke has told him everything about.

For a moment, I consider letting it go to voicemail like I have for the past two weeks, but something makes me swipe to answer. Maybe it's guilt, or I'm just desperate for a distraction from invoice hell. I can't avoid my family forever.

"Hello?"

"Well, he lives," Wes's voice comes through immediately, sounding both relieved and irritated.

"Ha, ha," I reply dryly. "What's going on?"

"What's going on?" Wes repeats, his tone sharpening. "What's going on is that I've heard my little brother is spiraling. Dad called me; Luke called me. Hell, even Bebe reached out to check if I'd heard from you."

I pinch the bridge of my nose. "I was spiraling," I admit. "But it's getting better. I'm working on it."

"Really? Because from what I hear, you got suspended, got into a fistfight with Luke, and are now working as dads glorified secretary as punishment."

"Data entry specialist, thank you very much," I correct

him, trying to keep my tone light despite the shame burning in my chest. "And it's not a punishment; it's me proving myself."

"Chase, what's going on with you?"

The question hits me harder than I expected. Not because it's difficult to answer, but because for the first time in months, someone's asking me directly instead of yelling accusations. I stare at the pile of invoices in front of me, suddenly finding it hard to swallow.

"I don't know, man," I admit, my voice dropping to barely above a whisper. "I just... I got lost somewhere along the way. And I did such a good job of hiding it I didn't even realize how bad things were until it all blew up in my face."

There's silence on the other end for a moment. I can almost picture Wes's face—that thoughtful expression he gets when he's analyzing a problem.

"You know what this sounds like?" he finally says. "Remember those depression commercials we used to make fun of? The ones with people walking around holding smiley face signs in front of their actual sad faces?"

I let out a short laugh. "Yeah, I guess it sounds like that. Actually, I have an appointment with a therapist tomorrow. Dad set it up. So I guess we'll find out if I'm clinically depressed or just being a dumb kid who can't handle the pressure."

"That doesn't sound like you at all," Wes says, his voice softening with concern. "You've always been the one who had everything figured out. Most likely to succeed, remember?"

"Yeah, well," I sigh, staring at the ceiling tiles above my desk. "Even the guy voted most likely to succeed can have his internal battles. You don't see it all, Wes. Nobody does. That's kind of the problem."

There's a long pause on the line. I can hear the faint sounds of a locker room in the background—voices echoing, lockers slamming shut.

"I'm sorry I haven't been there," Wes finally says, his voice heavy with regret. "I should have checked in more."

"Don't be ridiculous," I tell him, straightening in my chair. "It's not like you can just drop the NFL and come running home because your brother is having a quarter-life crisis."

"Still," he says, "family should be there for each other."

"Hopefully, once all this blows over and the season ends, we can get together for paintball," I say, my voice lightening at the thought. "You, me, and Luke. Like old times."

"I'd like that," Wes says. "The three Sullivan brothers, causing chaos on the paintball field again. Though I'll probably be rusty as hell."

"You? Rusty? Mr. NFL superstar with all those fancy training drills?" I laugh, feeling more like myself than I have in weeks. "I'm the one who should be worried. My cardio these days consists of walking from my desk to the coffee machine."

Wes chuckles, and the familiar sound warms something in my chest. For a moment, it feels like nothing has changed between us, like we're still the same brothers who used to spend hours strategizing the perfect ambush in the woods behind our house.

"So, anything else new with you? Besides the academic meltdown and family drama?"

I hesitate, my thoughts immediately turning to Daisy. Just thinking about her brings a smile to my face.

"Actually, yeah. I met someone."

"You have?" There's genuine surprise in Wes's voice. "That's great. Tell me about her."

A smile spreads across my face as I think about how to describe her. "Her name's Daisy. She's a sophomore majoring in entomology. Smart as hell, beautiful but shy, really into butterflies—she collects them. And she's..." I trail off, searching for the right words. "She's different, Wes. Makes me want to be a better man," I continue, surprised by how easily the words flow. "She doesn't judge me for my mistakes, just encourages me to fix them. And she's got a quiet strength about her that's... I don't know... inspiring."

I catch myself before mentioning her health issues. The fact that she's dealing with hemochromatosis, that her body is slowly poisoning itself with too much iron. That she's waiting for a liver transplant that might not come in time. It feels like a betrayal to share something so personal, even with Wes. Daisy hasn't told many people about her condition. It's her story to tell, not mine.

"Wow," Wes says after a moment of silence. "I've never heard you talk about anyone like this before. It sounds like you love her."

Love. Do I love Daisy? The feeling in my chest whenever I think about her, the way my day gets instantly better when she texts, how I can't wait to see her again—maybe that is love.

I smile into the phone, though Wes can't see me. "Yeah, maybe," I admit softly. "But don't jinx it, okay?"

The truth is, I'm terrified of saying it out loud. Like naming this feeling might make it more fragile, more likely to shatter. I've never had something this good, this real before. And with everything else in my life falling apart, she is the one bright spot I can't afford to lose.

"I get it," Wes says, and I hear a rustling in the background. "Listen, I've got to get to practice. Coach will have my ass if I'm late. But Chase?"

"Yeah?"

"Don't be a stranger, okay? No more ignoring my calls."

"Yeah, I promise." I reply, feeling a weight lift that I didn't even know was there. "Go be a superstar. I'll answer next time."

"Good. Take care of yourself, little brother."

We hang up, and I lean back in my chair. *Love.* Such a small word for something that feels so massive. I've never said those three words to anyone before—not romantically, anyway. Never felt anything close to what I feel when I'm with Daisy.

Chapter Twenty-Four

CHASE

I'M STARING at the ceiling of my bedroom, counting the tiny cracks in the plaster—thirty-seven so far—when there's a knock at my door. The sound is sharp, authoritative. It's dad.

"Chase." His voice confirms it. "Celeste is here."

My stomach drops like I'm on a roller coaster. I check my watch—6:15 PM. Right on time, because of course she is. Celeste Astor has probably never been late for anything in her life.

"Okay," I call back. "I'll be down in a minute."

I hear his footsteps retreating, and I close my eyes, willing myself to get up. My phone sits on the nightstand, the screen dark. Daisy hasn't texted since this morning—a simple "good morning" with a butterfly emoji that made me smile despite everything. I haven't told her about what I'm doing tonight. I haven't figured out how.

What would I even say? Hey, by the way, I'm taking another girl to dinner because my father is controlling and won't let me go back to college if I don't. But don't worry, I don't actually like her.

I drag myself off the bed, not bothering to change out of my faded jeans and plain navy t-shirt. What's the point? This isn't an actual date. No need to pretend I put any effort into this. Running a hand through my hair, I take a deep breath and head downstairs, each step feeling heavier than the last.

The sound of laughter carries from the foyer—my father's practiced chuckle and Richard Astor's booming guffaw, punctuated by Celeste's delicate, tinkling laugh.

I pause at the bottom of the stairs, taking in the scene. Richard Astor stands next to my father, both men in expensive suits despite the casual nature of the evening. They aren't coming with Celeste and me to dinner, my mom is making them meatloaf at home. Typical Keeper behavior though—even a simple dinner requires looking the part.

And then there's Celeste.

She's wearing a pale pink dress that probably cost more than my entire wardrobe, her dark hair swept up in some complicated twist that exposes the diamond studs in her ears. Her makeup is flawless, her smile perfect and practiced as she notices me and turns it up a notch.

"Chase," she says, her voice warm with an enthusiasm I know isn't genuine.

I stare right past her, focusing on a point somewhere over her shoulder. My father clears his throat, the sound carrying a warning I know all too well.

"Here," Dad says, fishing his car keys from his pocket and holding them out to me. "Take the Audi."

I take the keys without enthusiasm. My father's idea of generosity—letting me borrow his overpriced status symbol for a date I don't want to be on. Our eyes meet for a brief moment, and I see the silent command there: *Behave yourself. Be nice.*

"Have fun tonight," he adds with forced cheerfulness, clapping me on the shoulder.

Richard Astor claps me on the back too, his massive hand landing with enough force to make me wince. "You two kids enjoy yourselves now. The reservation at Marcello's is under my name. Just tell them when you arrive."

I turn toward the door without acknowledging Celeste, who's still standing there with that perfect smile frozen on her face. I can feel my father's eyes burning into my back as I walk away, silently demanding I show better manners.

Too bad.

The front door closes behind me with a soft click, and I hear the quick tap of heels as she hurries to catch up. I keep walking, my strides purposefully long as I head toward my father's sleek black Audi parked in the circular driveway.

"Chase, wait," she calls, her voice breathless.

I don't slow down, letting her trail behind me like a lost puppy. I click the key fob, the Audi's lights flashing in response. Behind me, I slide into the driver's seat and shut the door.

Through the windshield, I watch as she finally reaches the passenger side, slightly out of breath, her perfect hair now less perfect. She stands there, one manicured hand on the door handle, the other smoothing her dress. Her eyes meet mine through the glass, expectant, waiting.

Is she serious?

I stare at her for a beat, then turn the key in the ignition. The engine purrs to life, and still she waits, like we're in some

1950s movie and I'm supposed to hop out and play the gentleman.

Not happening.

After what feels like an eternity, understanding finally dawns in her eyes. Her smile falters for a split second before she recovers, pulling open her own door and carefully lowering herself into the passenger seat.

"Your father's car is beautiful," she says as she buckles her seatbelt before adjusting her dress, tugging it down over her knees. "The restaurant should be lovely. Daddy says their osso buco is divine."

Without responding, I reach for the stereo controls and crank up whatever's playing—some alternative rock station my father would hate. The bass thrums through the car, hopefully drowning out any chance of conversation. I pull out of the driveway, accelerating harder than necessary, taking petty satisfaction in the way Celeste grabs the door handle to steady herself.

The drive to Los Angeles takes nearly an hour, filled with the most painful small talk imaginable. Every time I turn the music up, she somehow finds a way to talk over it, asking questions about school, about my family, about my "plans for the future" like we're at a job interview instead of a forced date.

"My father says you're considering law school," she says, her voice pitched just loud enough to be heard over the music. "Me too. Harvard has an excellent program. The Astors have been going there for generations."

I grunt in response, eyes fixed on the road ahead. Traffic thickens as we approach the city, brake lights glowing red in the gathering darkness. Part of me hopes we'll be late, that the restaurant will give away our reservation, but I know better. Nothing ever goes wrong for the Astors.

The valet, a young guy in a crisp red uniform, rushes around to Celeste's side of the car. He opens her door with a flourish and offers his hand. She takes it, emerging from the car with practiced grace. She gives him a dazzling smile, then turns to me with a pointed look—eyebrows slightly raised, lips pursed in subtle disapproval.

I know exactly what that look means: *That's how a gentleman behaves, Chase.*

I roll my eyes and hand the keys to the second valet, not bothering to wait for a tip receipt. I follow Celeste into the restaurant, hanging back as she approaches the maître d'.

"Astor, party of two," she announces, her voice carrying that distinct upper-class lilt that all Keeper women seem to perfect by puberty.

The maître d' consults his list, then nods with deference. "Of course, Ms. Astor. Your table is ready. Please follow me."

Inside, Marcello's is exactly what I expected—all dark wood, white tablecloths, and crystal chandeliers. The kind of place where they don't put prices on the menu because if you have to ask, you can't afford it.

He leads us through the dimly lit restaurant, past tables of well-dressed couples and business associates. The place reeks of old money—plush carpet that muffles our footsteps, waiters in crisp white shirts and black bow ties. I hate it immediately.

We're escorted to a secluded table in the corner, partially hidden behind a decorative screen covered in some sort of gold leaf pattern. Privacy for the elite. The maître d' pulls out Celeste's chair while I drop into mine.

A waiter materializes beside our table almost instantly,

setting down heavy linen napkins in our laps and ornate menus bound in leather. He produces a bottle of water—some imported Italian brand with a fancy cursive name—and fills our glasses.

"May I get you something to drink this evening?" he asks, his accent faintly Italian, possibly genuine.

"Water is fine," I say, avoiding looking up from the menu I'm pretending to read.

"I'll have a glass of the Pinot Grigio," Celeste says with a polite smile. "The Veneto, if you have it."

The waiter nods appreciatively. "Excellent choice, Miss."

After he leaves, Celeste folds her hands on the table, leaning forward. "This place is known for its amazing risotto. My father brings clients here all the time." She pauses, waiting for me to respond.

I don't.

I flip a page of the menu, ignoring her.

"I'm considering business law myself," she continues. "Though Daddy thinks international relations might be more practical for—"

"Sounds great," I cut her off, still not looking up from the menu.

Her silverware clatters against the table. I finally glance up to see her perfect composure finally crack. Her shoulders drop, and her practiced smile vanishes.

"For God's sake, Chase," she hisses, eyes flashing with genuine emotion for the first time tonight. "You clearly don't want to be here with me, so why did you even agree to this? I'm not an idiot. I know when I'm being treated like garbage."

The raw hurt in her voice catches me off guard. I set the menu down, finally looking at her—really looking at her. Her cheeks are flushed, her perfectly manicured hands clenched into fists on the table. Behind the makeup and designer dress, I see something I wasn't expecting: a real person.

"I..." The excuse dies in my throat. What can I say? That my father forced me? That I need to do this so he'll pay for school next semester?

She shakes her head, a bitter laugh escaping her lips. "Don't bother. I get it. Your dad convinced you just like mine did."

"Do *you* even want to be here?" I ask.

"Not really," she admits. "It was pretty obvious we didn't hit it off when we met last year."

I remember that night—her in a blue silk dress, me in a suit I hated, both of us making awkward conversation by the pool while our fathers watched approvingly from across the patio.

"But Daddy was so insistent," she continues, a flash of vulnerability crossing her face. "He kept saying what a good match we'd be, how the Sullivans and Astors have always been aligned in the society. How you just needed to mature a bit. I'm... trying to make him happy, I guess."

"I'm doing the same thing," I admit, feeling a weight lift as I say it aloud, suddenly feeling like the world's biggest jerk. Here I've been behaving as though she's the villain in my story, when she's just as trapped as I am. "I'm sorry for being such an ass tonight. I've been taking out my frustration on you, and that's not fair."

Her expression softens. "It's okay."

We sit in silence for a moment as the waiter returns with Celeste's wine. After he leaves, I straighten, lowering my voice.

"Look, maybe we can work together on this. What if we

go on a few dates—fake ones—but actually pleasant ones—and make our fathers happy? We'll be friends, nothing more. Then after a few weeks, we tell them we tried it, but there just wasn't any chemistry."

A genuine smile replaces her practiced one. "That's... brilliant. No drama, no disappointment—two adults who tried and realized they're better as friends."

"Friends," I say, extending my hand across the table.

She takes it, her grip surprisingly firm. "Friends it is."

As we shake on our new arrangement, relief washes over me. For the first time tonight, I smile—a real one, not the forced grimace I've been wearing since I walked downstairs to find her in the foyer.

"So," I say, picking up my menu with renewed interest, "what's good here besides the risotto?"

The rest of dinner passes in a completely different atmosphere. Without the pressure of forced romance hanging over us, conversation flows naturally. Turns out, Celeste is actually pretty funny when she's not trying to be the perfect Keeper daughter. She does a spot-on impression of her etiquette coach that has me nearly choking on my pasta.

By the time we're sharing a tiramisu (her suggestion, and a good one), I realize I'm enjoying myself. Not in the way I enjoy being with Daisy—that's something entirely different—but in the way you enjoy hanging out with someone who gets what it's like to be trapped in the same bizarre world you are.

Chapter Twenty-Five

DAISY

THE PAINTBRUSH TREMBLES in my hand as Chase presses against my back, his fingers deftly tying my apron strings. His breath is warm against my neck, and my pulse flutters like butterfly wings.

"You know," he murmurs, his lips brushing my ear. "it seems counterintuitive that I'm helping you add a layer when all I can think about is removing one."

Heat rushes to my cheeks as his hands linger at my waist. All around us, other couples chat and laugh, completely oblivious to the electricity crackling between us. The paint and sip studio is dimly lit, with soft music playing in the background and the scent of wine mingling with acrylic paint.

"Behave yourself," I whisper, turning my head slightly so he could see my smile. "We're in public."

His answering grin is wicked as he steps around to face me, his eyes dropping briefly to the neckline of my wrap dress. "I'm being very well-behaved, considering what's been on my mind since you mentioned that mysterious blue thing you bought."

I bite my lip, suddenly hyperaware of what I'm wearing beneath this innocent-looking dress. The lingerie I'd bought—the "blue thing" I'd been teasing him about—was already making me feel daring in a way I wasn't used to. The delicate blue lace felt like a secret weapon beneath my dress.

I take my seat in front of the blank canvas, feeling Chase's eyes on me as I settle onto the stool. My fingers reach for the champagne flute filled with pale yellow lemonade.

"To artistic genius," he says, extending his paintbrush toward my canvas in a mock toast. His eyes crinkle at the corners when he smiles, making my heart flutter. "May our masterpieces be worthy of the Louvre."

I laugh and clink my brush against his. "Or at least worthy of my dorm room wall."

The instructor, a woman with paint-splattered overalls and wild curly hair, claps her hands at the front of the room. "Alright, everyone! This afternoon we'll be painting 'Starry Night.' I want you to relax, have fun."

When the instructor demonstrates the first strokes, I actually try to follow along, drawing careful lines with a steady hand. Beside me, Chase's canvas looked like chaos within two minutes. A crime scene of color.

"Wow," I whisper, biting my lip to hold back a laugh. "Is that supposed to be the sky?"

"Obviously," he says, utterly serious. "A post-modern interpretation. Very advanced."

I laugh, shaking my head, until something cool flicks against my hand and look down. Yellow. He has the audacity to grin like he hadn't just assaulted me with acrylic.

"You did not just—"

Before he could defend himself, I dip my brush in black and swipe a line across his forearm. He gasps dramatically, hand to his chest. "You wound me."

The room buzzes with chatter and laughter, but between us, it felt like a bubble. His shoulder brushes mine when he leans in to see my painting, his voice low.

"Yours looks good."

"Because I'm not goofing off."

"Goofing off?" His eyes glint. "I'm creating."

By the time the class ends, my cheeks hurt from smiling. The instructor has everyone hold up their canvases. His is so bad—so completely, unapologetically bad—and he still bows dramatically as if he'd won an award.

"I'm a natural," he declares, his voice full of mock seriousness as he gestures to his chaotic canvas. "Clearly Van Gogh reincarnated."

I can't help but giggle, glancing between his messy canvas and mine. While my painting actually resembles "Starry Night" with its swirling blues and yellows, Chase's looked like a toddler had been given free rein with finger paints.

The idea strikes me suddenly. "Hey, we should trade paintings."

His eyebrows shoot up in surprise. "Are you serious? You want to trade this masterpiece of modern art for your actually decent painting?" He picks up his canvas, tilting it this way and that as if trying to find an angle where it might look better.

"Absolutely," I say, reaching for his canvas. "I want to keep it so I'll always remember your incredible, unique, one-of-a-kind talent."

His expression softens as he hands over his painting, our fingers brushing in the exchange. Something flickers in his eyes —warmth, tenderness, and something deeper that makes my heart race.

"Well, in that case," he says, taking my painting with exaggerated care, "I'll treasure this forever," he finishes, carefully holding my canvas with both hands like it's a priceless artifact.

My heart swells as he studies my painting with genuine appreciation. Then he sets it gently on the table and steps closer to me, his eyes never leaving mine. Before I can say anything, he leans in and presses his lips to mine in a tender kiss that makes my knees weak.

When he pulls back, his eyes are soft, but there's a hint of vulnerability. "Hey, if anyone asks who painted this masterpiece," he says, gesturing to his artwork, "would you tell them I did it?"

"You want me to claim your artistic genius?" I tease.

His smile turns shy. "I was thinking you could say your boyfriend painted it."

My breath catches. *Boyfriend.* The word hangs between us, loaded with meaning. We've been seeing each other for a couple of weeks now, but we haven't labeled what we are. A smile spreads across my face, warmth blooming in my chest.

"Yes," I say softly. "I would definitely say my boyfriend painted it."

Something shifts between us in that moment, something profound and real. We've moved from casual dating into something official, something that suddenly feels solid and true.

"Boyfriend," I whisper, testing the word on my tongue. It feels right.

Chase's eyes brighten, crinkling at the corners as his smile widens. "Girlfriend," he replies, his voice low and intimate despite the bustling activity around us.

And just like that, I realize what's happened between us. This isn't just a label—it's a promise, a commitment. We've built something real together, something that matters.

He leans down and kisses me again, this time with more certainty, more intention. His lips move against mine with a new confidence, like he's staking a claim. My hands find their way to his chest, feeling his heartbeat racing beneath my fingers.

When we break apart, I'm breathless, my cheeks flushed with heat. I walk out of the paint class hugging his awful painting to my chest, grinning like an idiot—as Chase's *girlfriend*.

The night air is cool against my flushed skin as we walk back to my dorm, our hands intertwined. Chase's thumb traces circles on my palm, each slight movement sending tingles up my arm. We're both quiet, but it's a charged silence, filled with anticipation.

"What are you thinking about?" he asks.

I glance at him, heat rising to my cheeks. "You know exactly what I'm thinking about."

His answering smile is wolfish. "Tell me anyway."

Instead of answering, I pull him into the shadow between

two buildings and kiss him, my hands sliding up his chest underneath his shirt. His warm skin feels like satin over steel beneath my fingertips, the firm planes of his chest rising and falling with quickening breath. The contrast of soft and hard makes me dizzy with want.

"God, Daisy," he groans against my mouth, suddenly moving forward until my back meets the cool brick wall. The rough texture catches at my dress as Chase presses his body flush against mine, one hand braced beside my head while the other traces along my collarbone.

His fingers dip beneath the neckline of my dress, eyes darkening as he discovers the delicate blue lace underneath. "Is this it?" he whispers, voice husky. "The blue thing?"

I nod, unable to form words as his fingertips trace the edge of the lace.

"Beautiful," he murmurs, his gaze hungry as he studies what little he can see. "I want to see all of it."

I slide my hand between us, palm pressing against the front of his jeans, feeling him harden under my touch. His sharp intake of breath sends a wave of power through me.

"Not here," I whisper, even as my body contradicts my words.

Chase's answer is to hook his hand beneath my thigh, lifting my leg to wrap around his waist. The new position allows him to press against my center, the friction of denim against the thin fabric of my underwear making me gasp. He rocks his hips forward deliberately.

"We should keep walking," I whisper, though I make no move to push him away.

"Yeah," he agrees, but kisses me again anyway.

By the time we finally reach my dorm, the twenty-minute

walk has felt like hours of sweet torture. Every brush of his hand, every knowing glance between us has built a tension that's nearly unbearable.

The key card beeps and the door swings open. We barely make it inside before Chase's hands are cupping my face, his mouth finding mine in the darkness. I fumble for the light switch but abandon the effort when his lips trail down my neck, igniting sparks beneath my skin.

My fingers slide beneath his shirt, tracing the firm planes of his stomach, feeling the muscles tense under my touch. I tug at the fabric, suddenly desperate to feel more of him. He breaks our kiss just long enough to pull his shirt over his head, tossing it carelessly to the floor.

My breath catches at the sight of him. The dim light filtering through the blinds casts shadows across his chest, highlighting every curve and contour.

I reach for his belt, my fingers trembling slightly as I work the metal clasp. I manage to undo it, sliding the leather through the loops with a satisfying hiss. He watches me, his eyes dark with desire, his breathing shallow.

I place my hands on his chest and gently push him backward until his legs hit the mattress. He sits on the edge of my bed, his eyes fixed on mine, his chest rising and falling with quickened breaths. I step back, suddenly wanting to slow this moment down, to make it last. I reach over and switch on the small lamp on my nightstand, bathing the room in a soft golden glow.

Chase watches me intently as I reach up and pull the elastic from my ponytail, letting my hair cascade around my shoulders. I shake my head, feeling the weight of my hair against my back. His eyes darken, and I see him swallow hard.

"You're so beautiful," he murmurs, his voice rough with desire.

My fingers find the knot at my waist, the one that holds my wrap dress together. I tug at it gently, feeling the fabric loosen around me. He continues watching as I drag the tie free. The dress parts slightly, revealing a sliver of the blue lace beneath.

His breath catches audibly.

My voice is barely above a whisper as I ask, "Is this what you've been thinking about all day?"

Chapter Twenty-Six

CHASE

My brain short-circuits the moment her dress slips from her shoulders.

"Christ," I whisper, unable to form a more coherent thought as the fabric pools around her feet, revealing what she's been hiding beneath it all evening.

Blue lace lingerie hugs her curves—delicate lace against creamy skin, the color making her eyes appear even more impossibly blue. The exact shade of cobalt I once told her was my favorite color. The bra cups her breasts perfectly, straps crossing over her collarbone. The matching panties sit low on her hips, connected to lacy garters that hold up sheer thigh-highs.

I can't breathe. Can't think. Can barely remember my own name.

"You like it?" Daisy asks, and there's something in her voice —a mixture of shyness and newfound confidence that makes my heart hammer against my ribs. She does a small, tentative turn, giving me a view of the back where the panties reveal the perfect curve of her ass, the rounded cheeks peeking out from beneath the lace. She bends at the waist slightly, looking over her shoulder at me with those blue eyes—clearly teasing me— before straightening again with a smile that's equal parts shy and seductive.

"Jesus, Daisy," I manage to say, my voice rough. I'm still sitting on the edge of her bed, hands gripping the mattress to keep from reaching for her too quickly. "You're trying to kill me."

She laughs softly. "Is that a yes?"

"That's a hell yes," I manage, my voice rough even to my own ears.

She takes a step toward me, closing the distance between us. My breath catches as her hands find my knees, gently pushing them further apart as she lowers herself down, knees to the carpet. The sight of her kneeling between my legs in that blue lace sends a jolt of electricity through my entire body.

"I want to touch you," she whispers, her eyes locked with mine, that mesmerizing blue holding me captive.

I can only nod, words failing me completely. Her fingers find my jeans, working the button. The zipper slides slowly, the sound unnaturally loud in the hushed room. I lift my hips, helping her as she tugs my jeans down my thighs. My boxer briefs follow, my cock jutting free, already hard as steel and aching for her.

Her delicate fingers wrap around my shaft. The gentle pressure of her touch sends electricity racing up my spine. I grip the edge of the mattress, knuckles turning white as she begins to move her hand in slow, experimental strokes, watching my face for reactions. I can't help the low groan that escapes me as her hand moves with more confidence.

When her hand reaches the head, she pauses, noticing the bead of moisture that's formed there. With a curious expression, she runs her thumb through it, using the slickness to glide back over the sensitive tip in a circular motion that makes my hips jerk involuntarily.

"Holy shit, Daisy," I groan, watching as she smears the wetness around.

She leans forward, and as she does, I guide her mouth to the tip of my cock, my hand grasped around her chin, and time seems to suspend as her lips part. My thumb drags over her plump, full lower lip the moment before she wraps her mouth around me.

"Oh, fuck," I gasp, my head falling back as her warm, wet mouth slides further, taking me deeper. The sensation is incredible—soft, slick and hot, her tongue flattening against the underside of my shaft as she moves.

I thread my fingers through her hair, gathering the golden strands away in a makeshift ponytail, holding her in place as I thrust in shallow dips so only the crown of my cock pumps in and out of her mouth. The sight of her lips stretched around me, her cheeks hollowing as she sucks, is almost too much to bear.

"God, you're beautiful," I whisper, my voice raw with desire.

Her eyes flick up to meet mine, and the connection nearly stops my heart. Those blue eyes, the same incredible shade as the lace barely covering her body, watching me intently as she pleasures me. There's something innocent yet decidedly wicked in her gaze, and the combination is driving me wild.

My body grows hotter with every stroke of her tongue against my cock. I feel the familiar tightening low in my belly, the mounting pressure that signals I'm close.

"Daisy," I gasp, tugging gently on her hair. "You need to stop, or I'm going to—I can't hold back much longer."

She looks at me through her lashes, her eyes filled with a mixture of pride and desire. With one final, torturous suck, she releases me, the pop of her lips echoing in the quiet room.

I'm on my feet in an instant, pulling her up into my arms and crushing my mouth against hers. I can taste myself on her lips. Without breaking our kiss, I slide my hands down to the backs of her thighs and lift her. She responds immediately, wrapping her legs around my waist, her arms encircling my neck.

I turn us around, carrying her a few steps to her desk. I sweep aside her textbooks with one arm, sending papers fluttering to the floor as I seat her on the wooden surface. The height is perfect for me to stand between her legs. My hands slide up her thighs, fingers caressing the thigh-highs before moving higher. I trail my fingertips over the lace of her panties, my breath catching when I realize there's an opening right where the fabric should cover her pussy.

"Fuck," I groan as my fingers slide through her, finding her impossibly wet. The discovery makes my cock throb with need. "Crotchless? You've been wearing these all day?"

Her eyes are dark with desire as she nods, biting her lower lip.

"I got my test results back," I tell her, my voice rough with need. "I'm clean."

"Good," she breathes, her eyes never leaving mine. "I want to feel you without anything."

My heart skips a beat. I step closer between her parted thighs, my hands gripping her hips. I gently tug her forward until she's perched right at the edge of the desk.

I take my cock in hand, guiding it to her pussy. Her slick heat against my tip nearly buckles my knees. I press forward slowly, observing her face as I ease inside. Her mouth falls open in a silent gasp, her fingers digging into my shoulders.

"You okay?" I murmur, holding still to let her adjust.

"Yes," she whispers, her inner muscles fluttering around me. "Just... give me a second."

I stay perfectly still, though it takes every ounce of willpower I possess. The sensation of being inside her—hot, tight, perfect—is overwhelming. I press my forehead against hers, our breath mingling as we both adjust to the incredible sensation of being joined like this.

"I've never..." I begin, then swallow hard. "I've never felt anything like this."

The truth is, I've had unprotected sex before, but this—this is different. *This is Daisy. This is us.* This is something that matters.

When her hips shift, I take it as my cue. I begin to move inside her, drawing back slowly before pushing forward again. The friction is exquisite, every nerve ending in my body singing with pleasure.

Her eyes flutter closed, her lips parting as soft sounds escape her throat. Each thrust draws a new expression from her—a gasp, a flutter of eyelashes, the tightening of her fingers against my skin.

I capture her mouth with mine, swallowing her moans as I drive deeper. The kiss is messy, desperate, all tongue and teeth and shared breath. Being inside Daisy without a condom is mind-blowing—the heat, the wetness, the way I can feel every subtle contraction of her body around me. I've experienced nothing so intense, so all-consuming.

"Chase," she gasps against my mouth, her voice breaking on my name. "Oh God, Chase."

I increase my pace, driven by the sound of my name on her lips. Her legs tighten around my waist, drawing me deeper with each thrust. I slide one hand between us, my thumb finding her clit, circling the sensitive bud in time with my movements.

"Is this good?" I whisper in her ear, already knowing the answer from the way her body trembles against mine.

"Yes," she breathes, her head falling back, exposing the delicate line of her throat. "Don't stop. Please don't stop."

I press my lips to her neck, tasting the salt of her skin. The desk creaks beneath us, the sound mingling with our ragged breathing and the slick sounds of our bodies where we're joined. I'm lost in her—in the feel of her, the scent of her, the sound of her pleasure. The pressure builds at the base of my spine.

Her body suddenly goes rigid beneath me, her inner walls clenching around me with unexpected force. Her eyes fly open, locking with mine in a moment of pure connection as her lips form that perfect 'O' shape. Looking at her—completely undone, *completely mine*—pushes me over the edge. I thrust deep one final time, burying myself to the hilt, our pelvis' grinding together, as my release crashes through me, pulsing jets of my cum inside her in hot waves.

"Daisy," I gasp, as we fall apart together, her body milking every drop from me, my hips still moving in shallow thrusts as we ride out the aftershocks.

For several heartbeats, we remain frozen in this perfect moment, bodies joined, foreheads pressed together, breathing each other's air. I've never felt so connected to another person —physically, emotionally, completely.

When I finally begin to withdraw and pull completely free, I'm caught by the sight below. Her pussy is still pulsing, the pink flesh quivering with tiny contractions. I watch in fascination as a pearly mixture of our cum begins to seep from her. Something primal stirs in me at the sight—a visceral, possessive feeling I've never experienced before.

Without thinking, I guide my still-firm cock back to her pussy, using the head to gently push our combined wetness back inside her. The movement draws a surprised gasp from her.

"What are you doing?" she asks, her voice breathy and curious rather than objecting.

"I don't know," I admit, continuing the gentle motion, watching as I push our mingled essence back into her body. "I just... I want to stay inside you. I want to keep us together."

A soft smile curves her lips as she reaches out to touch my face. "That might be the most romantic thing anyone's ever said to me."

I kiss her, slow and deeply as I continue the gentle rocking motion. To my surprise, I feel myself growing fully hard again inside her; the oversensitivity giving way to a renewed desire. Daisy feels it too—I can tell from the way her breath catches, the way her hips shift subtly to meet mine.

"Again?" she whispers against my lips, a hint of wonder in her voice.

"I want you," I whisper, my voice husky with emotion. "I could probably do this all night—be with you, be connected to you like this. It's hard to explain, but there's something about being inside you that feels... right. Like I've found where I belong."

Her eyes soften, and she cups my face in her hands. "I understand. I feel it too." Her thumb traces my lower lip as she adds, "It's like finding a missing piece you didn't even know was gone."

The perfect description makes my chest tighten with emotion. I kiss her again, savoring the taste. When I pull back, I see something vulnerable in her eyes.

"I never thought it could be like this," she admits, her voice barely above a whisper. "With anyone."

"Me neither," I confess, surprised by how true it is. I've had sex before, but never like this—never with this bone-deep connection that makes every touch feel like coming home.

I shift us carefully, lifting her from the desk without breaking our connection. Her legs tighten around my waist as I carry her the few steps to her bed. We tumble onto the mattress together, laughing softly as we bounce. The movement causes me to slip deeper inside her, drawing gasps from us both.

"You feel so good," I murmur, bracing myself above her on my elbows. I start to move again, slower this time, savoring every subtle shift of her body beneath mine. This isn't just sex —I know that with absolute certainty.

I'm making love to Daisy.

The realization hits me with startling clarity as I move inside her. I haven't said those words to her yet—those three words that have been building in my chest for weeks now— but this is how I'm showing her. With every thrust, every caress, every kiss, I'm telling her what I'm not yet brave enough to say aloud.

I study her face in the soft lamplight, memorizing every detail—the flush spreading across her cheeks, the way her lips part with each breath, the flutter of her eyelashes against her skin. I want to remember everything about this moment, to carry it with me always.

Chapter Twenty-Seven

DAISY

"You're dating Chase Sullivan? *The* Chase Sullivan?" Olivia's shriek could probably be heard three floors down as she nearly drops the takeout bags on my tiny dorm room floor. "As in officially boyfriend-girlfriend, changed-your-Facebook-status dating?"

I can't help the ridiculous grin that spreads across my face. "Yes, that Chase Sullivan. And no, I haven't updated any social media yet. We just made it official yesterday."

She sets our dinner on my desk, yes—the same one I had sex on last night—although she doesn't know it and launches herself at me, wrapping me in a hug so tight I can barely breathe.

"I knew it! I absolutely knew it!" She pulls back, gripping my shoulders. "You realize I deserve at least seventy percent of the credit for this relationship, right?"

I laugh, extracting myself from her grasp to grab the food. "Seventy percent sounds high."

"Are you kidding?" She flops onto my bed, kicking off her shoes. "I gave you that ridiculous bear conversation starter. Not to mention all the crucial relationship advice I've given you. So really, I'm the fairy godmother of this whole situation."

I roll my eyes but can't help smiling. "Fine. You get some credit. And if things go well—like, really well—you can be my maid of honor. But that's a *big* if! We've only been official for a day."

Olivia squeals, clapping her hands together. "I knew it! I'm already planning my speech. It's going to make everyone cry."

"Please don't jinx this," I laugh, unpacking our Chinese food containers. "We're nowhere near that point yet."

"I'm happy for you," she says, her voice softening as she grabs her chopsticks. "Chase is a good guy. And after watching you yearn for him for months on end, it's about time."

She pauses, twirling lo mein around her chopsticks. "Speaking of Chase, you know Ava's heard about you two, right?"

My stomach tightens. "How would she know already?"

"Oh, honey, the campus is small, and Chase Sullivan is news. It was not like he was hiding you. Her roommate saw you two at that Mexican place looking all couple-y." She shoves a forkful of rice into her mouth. "I ran into her at the library yesterday, and let me tell you, she said Ava had opinions."

"What kind of opinions?" I ask, stabbing at my kung pao chicken.

"According to her—and I'm quoting here—'If Chase had taken me on proper dates instead of just expecting me to hang around his house or at parties all the time, maybe I wouldn't have cheated.'" Liv rolls her eyes dramatically. "Like that justifies hooking up with someone else."

I nearly drop my chopsticks. "That's such bull. She's seriously trying to blame him for her cheating?"

"That's what I said!" Liv points her fork at me.

"Well, she can keep her revisionist history to herself," I mutter, feeling a flash of protectiveness toward Chase. "Cheating is cheating."

She gives me a pointed look, her fork suspended mid-air. "You know, you must be pretty special to him."

"What do you mean?" I ask, though something warm unfurls in my chest at her words.

"Think about it, Daisy. Chase never took her on actual dates. They hung out at parties or at his place. But you?" She gestures with her chopsticks for emphasis. "He's taking you to restaurants, the botanical gardens, the movies, paint classes—the whole boyfriend experience. That means something."

I pause, a forkful of kung pao chicken halfway to my mouth. She's right. He has been taking me on real dates—thoughtful, planned outings where we talk and laugh and get to know each other. But then I remember what he said that night at the lake, that he was never fully invested in Ava.

Olivia leans forward, lowering her voice conspiratorially. "Did you ever find out what happened with that black eye he was sporting?"

I shake my head, pushing food around my container. "No, I haven't pushed him about it. He seemed pretty uncomfortable when I asked, so I dropped it."

"Well," she says, her eyes widening dramatically, "I heard something interesting. Jenna from my bio lab? She's friends with some upperclassmen who know the Sullivans. Apparently, Luke's been seen around town with bruised knuckles."

"Wait, you think Luke punched Chase?"

She raises an eyebrow, leaning in even closer. "Well, usually there's only one reason two men will fight like that..." I wait, knowing she's building up to something. "A woman," she finally says, her voice dropping to a theatrical whisper.

"You think Luke and Chase fought because of a woman?" I ask incredulously. The idea sounds ridiculous. "Like, what—they're fighting over the same girl? And besides, Luke is married and Chase was dating Ava..."

She shrugs, taking another bite of her lo mein. "Maybe. I'm just saying it's the most common reason brothers come to blows. Tale as old as time."

"They're brothers who lived together. I'm sure they had a lot more reasons."

"Yeah, you're probably right," she says. "You know I'm one for gossip."

That she is...

Liv takes a sip of her soda, then fixes me with a sly grin. "So... have you two sealed the deal yet?"

I'm in the middle of swallowing a bite of chicken when her question registers. The food catches in my throat, and I start coughing violently, my eyes watering as I reach for my water bottle.

"Oh my God!" she squeals, her eyes wide. "You totally did! I was just fishing, but that reaction—" She points her chopsticks at me accusingly. "You slept with Chase Sullivan!"

"Shhh!" I hiss, glancing nervously at my door. "Do you want the entire floor to know?"

"So it's true!" She leans forward eagerly. "Was it the blue lingerie? I knew that would work! The second you showed me what you bought, I was like, 'That boy doesn't stand a chance.'"

I feel my cheeks burning as I set down my water. "Actually... we... before that."

Her jaw drops. "Before the lingerie? When?!" She reaches across the space between us to smack my arm. "You sneaky little hoe! I can't believe you didn't tell me immediately!"

I laugh, rubbing my arm where she hit me. "Ow! I was going to tell you tonight—that's why I asked you over for dinner. And I've been with exactly one guy in my entire life, and suddenly I'm a hoe?" I counter, raising an eyebrow. "That seems like an unfair label."

"It's not about the number, honey. It's about keeping vital information from your best friend."

We both burst into laughter, and I'm grateful for the way she's making this conversation feel normal, not awkward.

"So," she says, leaning forward, "how was it? And I want details—but not a graphic play-by-play."

I take a sip of water, trying to hide my smile behind the bottle. "It was... really good. Like, surprisingly good for a first time together." My cheeks are burning, but there's something freeing about finally telling someone. "It happened after we went to that Mexican restaurant. He walked me back to my dorm, so..."

"So..." She leans forward, her eyes sparkling with curiosity. "What kind of lover is he?"

I burst out laughing, nearly spitting out my water. "What kind of—what does that even mean?"

"You know," she says, waving her hand impatiently. "Is he

rough and wild, or more soft and gentle? Does he take charge or let you lead? These are important details, Daisy!"

My cheeks burn hotter than the kung pao chicken on my plate. I stare down at my food, memories of Chase's hands on my skin flashing through my mind.

"He's... attentive," I finally say, my voice softer than I intended. "Like, focused on making sure I was comfortable. But also..." I bite my lip, searching for the right words. "intense, you know? There were moments when he was so gentle it made my heart hurt, and then other times..." I trail off and fan myself with my hand.

"That good, huh?" She puts down her chopsticks to slow-clap. "Well, congratulations, my dear. Welcome to the land of sexual bliss. It's about time you joined us here."

I throw a fortune cookie at her, which she catches effortlessly. "Stop it."

"What? I'm genuinely happy for you!" She unwraps the cookie and cracks it open. "Seriously though, I'm glad your first time was good. Most people don't get so lucky."

Chapter Twenty-Eight

DAISY

I NEVER REALIZED how love could sneak into the smallest corners of my life until I met Chase. It isn't always fireworks or sweeping gestures—it's the quiet moments, the everyday things, the parts of life that used to feel ordinary. With him, they're anything but.

He brings me coffee after my biology class because it works out with his lunch break.

Not just any coffee—my coffee. Caramel latte.

His face lights up in a way that still makes my stomach flip after three weeks together. He weaves through the crowd, careful not to spill the drinks, holding mine a little higher like its precious cargo.

He adds a tiny butterfly drawn on the sleeve, complete with a smiley face in the center, clearly added after purchase.

I take a sip, and it's perfect. The way he delivers my coffee shouldn't matter. It's just a cup. But if it isn't one of the sweetest things a guy has ever done for me...

And suddenly coffee wasn't coffee anymore. It was proof.

As part of his deal for redemption with his father—he has a curfew, so unfortunately we haven't been able to wake up together but... he's brought over a toothbrush and we brush our teeth together...

It's become our little nighttime ritual before he leaves. I scrub away at my molars when Chase catches my eye in the bathroom mirror. Suddenly, he puffs his cheeks out like a chipmunk, his mouth completely covered in minty foam. He crosses his eyes and wiggles his eyebrows at me.

I snort before I can help myself, toothpaste dripping down my chin as I double over laughing. I try to keep brushing, but it's impossible with him making new faces every few seconds —now he's doing some kind of rabid vampire impression, foam dripping dramatically from the corners of his mouth.

"Sthop," I mumble through my own foamy mess, but I'm giggling so hard I can barely stand. I have to grip the edge of the sink to keep from falling over.

He grins at me, toothbrush still hanging from his mouth, and something about the complete silliness of it all makes my heart swell. No one else gets to see this side of Chase.

But I do.

I hand him a towel and shake my head. "You're ridiculous."

"And you love it."

He's right.

There are afternoons when we collapse onto my bed, limbs tangled, our books balanced on our stomachs. Sometimes we read silently, sometimes out loud.

I've found my favorite reading position is with my head in his lap. I'll settle there, book held above me, while he leans against my headboard with his own book—usually about law. Without fail, within minutes, his free hand finds my hair. Sometimes I think he doesn't even realize he's doing it—like his hand is magnetically drawn to my hair, operating on its own while he loses himself in whatever he's reading. His fingers begin their gentle exploration—sometimes twirling strands around his fingertips, sometimes just barely grazing my scalp in patterns I can't see but can feel.

I pretend to focus on the page in front of me, but the truth is I don't remember a single word I read. I remember only the warmth of him beneath me, steady and safe.

He'd walk in the rain for me.

It rains one evening as we're walking back to my dorm. We're already too far from anywhere dry, so by the time it pours, we're drenched. He shrugs out of his jacket and tosses it over my head, leaving himself to soak through.

"Don't," I protest, pulling at it to give back.

"Too late." He grins, his hair plastered to his forehead.

He stands there, water dripping down his face, his white t-shirt turning transparent against his skin, and he looks so completely ridiculous with his hair slicked like a wet puppy. Yet somehow he also looks impossibly handsome—gallant in the most absurd way, like a knight who forgot his armor but remembered his heart.

I grab the lapel of his jacket that's hanging over my head and tug him toward me, pulling him down until his lips meet mine. The rain beats against us, but I don't care anymore. His surprised laugh vibrates against my mouth before he kisses me back, his hands finding my waist.

When we break apart, we're both drenched, his jacket having slipped off my head entirely. Water streams over our faces, and I can taste the rain on his lips.

"Now we're both soaked," he says, pushing wet hair from my face.

"Worth it," I reply, and I mean it.

We bicker sometimes. Of course we do.

I hate it. My chest burns, my hands shake, and I say things sharper than I mean. He pushes back, stubborn and unyielding, and the words slam between us like doors.

But then—always, *always*—he reaches for me.

"I don't want to win," he says once, voice rough. His eyes

are storm-dark, but his hands are gentle when they find my waist. "I just want you."

And that's it. The fight crumbles.

It's never just the big moments.

It's the way his thumb draws circles against my skin absentmindedly.

The way he whispers "hey" every time he sees me after even a few hours apart.

It's the butterfly kisses.

It's all these tiny flashes, ordinary moments strung together, that whisper the truth louder than any grand gesture ever could.

I am his.

And he is mine.

I—am in love.

Chapter Twenty-Nine

CHASE

THE TRUTH about mall pretzels is they're basically just vehicles for salt and butter—nutritionally worthless but emotionally essential when you're killing time in retail purgatory.

"You've got a little..." Celeste gestures vaguely at my face as we stroll past a display of mannequins..

I wipe at my mouth, salt crystals falling onto my shirt. "Better?"

"You missed it completely." She rolls her eyes. After three "dates," we've settled into something resembling actual friendship—based on our conspiring fathers. "Here." She hands me a napkin from her pretzel bag.

We've hit a comfortable rhythm that comes with lowered expectations. Our first date at Marcello's was awkward until we agreed to drop the charade, the second (coffee at some overpriced café her father recommended) was where we actually started talking like normal humans, and now this—a movie at the mall followed by aimless wandering. Our last performance before we tell our fathers the romantic spark isn't there.

"That movie was terrible," I say, tossing my empty pretzel wrapper into a nearby trash can. "I can't believe we paid actual money to see that."

"Oh my God, look!" She suddenly grabs my arm, tugging me toward a storefront with glittering displays. "Can we go in here? I love this place."

The sign reads "Fairchild's Fine Jewelry" in elegant gold lettering. Not exactly where I'd choose to spend my time, but Celeste is already pulling me through the entrance before I can object.

"Sure, why not," I mutter, following her into the brightly lit interior.

The store is all gleaming glass cases and soft recessed lighting designed to make everything sparkle. A middle-aged woman in a tailored suit immediately approaches us with a practiced smile.

"Let me know if I can help you find anything special today," she says.

"We're just browsing, thanks," I reply quickly.

Celeste is already moving from case to case, her eyes wide with excitement. I trail behind her, hands in my pockets, nodding absently as she points out different pieces.

"These are gorgeous," she says, leaning over a display of rings, her face lighting up. "Look at this one! It's exactly what I've been wanting." She points at an emerald ring with a platinum band, her finger hovering above the glass. "It's perfect. I'm definitely bringing my dad here to buy it for me.

He promised me something special for my birthday next month."

I nod absently, about to make some comment about rich girl problems, when something in the adjacent case catches my eye. A delicate silver necklace with a butterfly pendant, its wings inlaid with tiny diamonds that catch the light, creating a subtle shimmer. It's not ostentatious or flashy—it's elegant and understated.

Just like Daisy.

I move toward it almost without thinking, drawn to the piece as if it's magnetized. The butterfly's wings seem to flutter in the light as I shift position, creating the illusion of movement.

"That's beautiful," Celeste says, appearing at my side. Her voice is softer now, more genuine.

"It would look perfect with your dress," a salesperson says, suddenly appearing beside us. She's younger than the first one, with a sleek ponytail and eager eyes. "Would you like to try it on?"

"No, we're just—" I start to say.

"Yes, we'd love to see it," Celeste interrupts, her voice taking on that practiced Keeper-daughter sweetness.

The salesperson beams, completely ignoring my objection as she unlocks the case with a key. She carefully lifts the butterfly necklace from its velvet display, the silver chain dangling between her manicured fingers.

"Here you go, Sir," she says, placing it in my palm before I can protest. The pendant is surprisingly light, the silver cool against my skin. The diamonds reflect the light, producing tiny prisms that dance across my hand.

Celeste turns away from me, lifting her dark hair off her

neck with both hands. "Would you mind?" she asks, glancing back at me over her shoulder.

I hesitate, feeling suddenly awkward. This feels too intimate somehow, like we're playing into the exact charade we've been trying to avoid.

I step behind her with a tight smile at the saleswoman, who's looking at us like we're the cutest couple she's seen all day. The butterfly pendant dangles from my fingers as I bring the chain around her neck, my hands fumbling slightly with the clasp. I can feel the saleswoman watching, probably thinking this is some romantic gesture between a boyfriend and girlfriend, and all I can think about is how wrong this feels.

When I finally secure the clasp, she turns around, her fingers immediately going to the butterfly resting against her collarbone.

"How does it look?" she asks, a genuine smile on her face as she glances down at the pendant.

I stare at the necklace—the perfect necklace that was meant for Daisy, not Celeste—and feel something deflate inside me. *The magic is gone.* The moment I imagined— Daisy's face lighting up when she opened the box, her understanding immediately why I chose a butterfly—has vanished. This necklace was supposed to be special, something that showed Daisy I pay attention, that I understand what matters to her.

I can't possibly buy it for her now that Celeste has worn it. It feels tainted somehow, like I'd be giving Daisy a gift that another woman tried on first. *A woman whom I've failed to mention.*

"It looks beautiful on you," I say, the words tasting strange in my mouth. Not because they're untrue—the necklace does look nice against her skin—but because they feel like a betrayal of the person I'd imagined wearing it.

The saleswoman clasps her hands together, delighted. "It's absolutely perfect! Would you like me to ring it up for you? We can process the payment right here."

I freeze suddenly, unsure what to say. Before I can stumble through an awkward explanation, Celeste touches the butterfly pendant one last time, then looks at the saleswoman with a polite smile.

"Not today, thank you," she says smoothly. "We're still browsing."

She turns her back to me again, lifting her hair just like before. "Could you help me take it off?"

When I finally manage to unhook the clasp, I hand the necklace back to the disappointed saleswoman, who carefully returns it to its display.

We exit the store in silence, and I feel strangely hollow. The moment we're out of the store's view, Celeste turns to me with a curious look.

"So who is she?" she asks, her voice casual but her eyes sharp with interest.

"What?" I stare at her in confusion, genuinely caught off guard by the question.

She smirks, brushing a strand of hair behind her ear. "Oh, come on, Chase. There's only one reason a man looks at jewelry like that. That butterfly necklace practically hypnotized you. So who is she?"

Heat rush to my face, caught in a truth I wasn't ready to share. For a moment, I consider deflecting, but what's the point? Celeste and I agreed to be honest with each other. "Her name is Daisy," I admit. "She's... different from anyone I've ever met."

"Different how?" she asks as we walk again, passing a group of teenagers crowded around the food court entrance.

"She's smart. Studies entomology—you know, insects. Especially butterflies." I can't help the smile that spreads across my face. "She collects them and has this entire display case in her dorm room."

"Is it serious?"

I nod, surprised by how easy it is to talk about this. "Yeah," I say softly. "It is."

Her smile fades, her eyes getting a faraway look. "You're lucky, you know. To have found someone who makes you feel that way."

"I guess I am," I admit, surprised by her sudden wistfulness.

She sighs dramatically. "Meanwhile, I'll probably be single forever."

I laugh, thinking she's joking, but when I look at her face, I can see she's actually serious. "Come on, that's ridiculous. You're smart, pretty, you come from one of the most powerful Keeper families. Guys must be lining up."

"Oh, they line up all right," she says with a bitter edge I've never heard from her before. "But it doesn't matter. Did you know my grandfather was a complete control freak? Even from the grave, he's still running my life."

"What do you mean?"

She stops walking, leaning against the railing overlooking the mall's lower level. "My trust fund—which is my entire inheritance—comes with strings attached. My grandfather wrote specifically that I'd have to marry a Keeper to access the full trust. And not just any Keeper—one with council descendants."

"Council descendants?" I ask, raising an eyebrow. "Like... people descended from the original Keeper Council?"

"Exactly," she utters with a dramatic sigh. "Do you have any idea how few eligible bachelors that leaves me? Literally one." She points directly at me. "You."

I almost choke. "Me?"

"You're the last single council descendant who's of age," she says, looking genuinely distressed now. "After you, I'd have to wait for little Hugh George to grow up, and he's what— eight? So that's another ten years." She laughs, but it's hollow. "I guess I could just pray he's into cougars when he's eighteen and I'm pushing thirty-five."

"Is that why our fathers are so keen on getting us together? Because of your grandfather's will?"

"Partly," she admits. "Though I think they genuinely believe we'd make a good match. The Sullivans and Astors."

I shake my head, still trying to wrap my mind around this revelation. "So what are you going to do?"

She tosses her hair over her shoulder, but her smile fades quickly. "I've been talking with Steven Alberts."

"Steven?" I raise my eyebrows in surprise. "Isn't he—"

"Gay? Yes." She shrugs, trying to appear nonchalant, but I can see the conflict in her eyes. "But he's also from a council family and under similar pressure. We've been discussing a lavender marriage."

"A lavender marriage?" I repeat. "You'd really do that? Marry someone you don't love just for money?"

She turns to face me fully, one perfectly manicured hand still resting on the railing. She studies me for a long moment, her expression unreadable. Then she lets out a small, bitter laugh.

"What else am I supposed to do? That money is all I'll have." Her voice has lost its practiced Keeper-daughter lilt, replaced by something rawer, more genuine. "Keeper daughters aren't exactly bred and trained for the workforce. Yes, we still go to college and get degrees, but we're ornaments, trophies, political chess pieces."

I open my mouth to argue, but she cuts me off with a sharp gesture.

"What marketable skills do I have?" she continues. "I can plan a perfect dinner party. I can make small talk with diplomats. I know which fork to use for salad and how to write the perfect thank-you note. That's what I was raised for —to be the perfect Keeper wife, not have a career. That trust fund is my only chance at freedom. Without it, I depend completely on my father. Do you have any idea what that's like? To have every decision, every purchase, every life choice scrutinized and controlled?"

I look at her, really seeing Celeste Astor for the first time. Not the polished Keeper daughter, but the woman trapped inside that carefully constructed image.

"Money is power, Chase," she says, her eyes suddenly fierce with conviction. "Especially for women in our world. Without my own money, I have no control over my life. None. I'll always be at someone else's mercy—my father's, a husband's, whoever holds the purse strings."

A heaviness settles in my chest as I realize what she's saying. She genuinely believes that a loveless marriage is her best option—her only option. That the path to freedom requires sacrificing the possibility of actual love.

Chapter Thirty

DAISY

I WAKE to the gentle pressure of arms around my waist, the familiar scent of pine and something uniquely Chase filling my senses before I even open my eyes. For a moment, I think I'm dreaming—one of those sweet, hazy dreams where reality bends just enough to give you what you want most.

"Morning, Butterfly," he whispers against my hair, his breath warm against my neck.

I turn in his arms, blinking sleep from my eyes, a smile spreading across my face despite the heaviness in my limbs. "Chase? What are you doing here?" My voice comes out raspy, morning-thick. "How did you get in?"

The sunlight filtering through my half-closed blinds catches in his blond hair, highlighting strands of gold I never noticed before.

"Olivia gave me the spare key you gave her," he says, tracing lazy patterns on my shoulder with his fingertips. "She said you were still sleeping, having an off day, but I couldn't wait to see you."

I nestle closer, savoring the solid warmth of him. "Best wake-up ever."

I wince as the motion brings a dull ache through my abdomen. The pain has been building since yesterday—a familiar, unwelcome visitor.

"What's wrong?" he asks immediately, his smile fading. His eyes scan my face with concern.

"Just the usual," I admit, not wanting to lie but hating to burden him with this so early in the morning. "My body's throwing a little tantrum today."

His brow furrows as understanding dawns. "Your hemochromatosis?"

I nod, trying to push myself to a sitting position but finding my arms oddly weak. The fatigue has settled deep in my muscles, making everything feel like I'm moving through molasses.

His hand gently cups my cheek. "Is it bad?"

"Not great," I admit, hating the weakness in my voice. "But I've had worse."

He shifts to help me, his hands gentle but firm as he arranges my pillows behind me. "What can I do? Tell me how to help."

The worry in his voice makes my heart ache. We've only been together a few weeks, and already he's seeing the less glamorous side of dating someone with a chronic illness. I study his face, searching for signs of that familiar retreat I've seen in others—the slight backing away, the flicker of fear or disgust—but find nothing but genuine concern.

"Honestly? I'm really tired and achy today," I explain.

"You should just continue to be the awesome, supportive boyfriend you are," I say, reaching for his hand and giving it a squeeze.

His eyes soften as he settles back next to me with a smile. "I can do that."

Despite the dull ache radiating through my body, I lean in to kiss him. The movement sends a sharp pain through my side, but I refuse to let it show on my face. His lips are soft against mine, and for a moment, the pain recedes, replaced by a warmth that spreads through my chest.

When we break apart, he brushes a strand of hair from my face. "I have to go to work," he says, his voice apologetic. "But I can stop by on my lunch break. Bring you some soup, or chocolate, anything comforting maybe?"

"You don't have to do that."

"I want to," he says simply, with such conviction that I can't argue. His thumb traces small circles on the back of my hand. "Let me take care of you, Daisy."

The words rise in my throat, three simple syllables that feel monumental. *I love you.* They hover on the tip of my tongue, threatening to spill out.

But looking at him now, his face etched with concern, I hesitate. *What if he feels pressured to say it back just because I'm sick? What if he thinks I'm only saying it because I'm vulnerable right now?* I don't want our first "I love you" to be tangled up with my illness, something he might later question was genuine or born from a moment of weakness.

"You're too good to me," I say instead, hoping he can hear what I'm not saying. The words I'm holding back.

He leans in to kiss me again. This one lingers, sweet and tender, his hand cradling my face like I might break. When he pulls away, reluctance is written across his features. "I should probably go…"

His body says otherwise, still half-draped over mine, his fingers tracing patterns on my arm.

"You should definitely go," I say, mustering enough strength to gently push at his chest. "Your dad might be looking for reasons to be disappointed in you."

Chase brushes his lips against my forehead, lingering there. "I'll be back before you know it. Text me if you need anything."

He leans down for one more kiss, then straightens, his silhouette outlined by the morning light. I watch him gather his jacket, memorizing the way he moves, the slight hesitation before he turns to leave. At the door, he pauses, glancing back at me with a grin that makes my heart flutter despite the pain.

"Rest up, Butterfly."

The door closes behind him with a click that echoes in the sudden emptiness of my room. It sounds strangely loud, final —like a period at the end of a sentence I wasn't ready to finish.

I sink back into my pillows, feeling the ache intensify now that Chase's warmth is gone. The pain radiates from my abdomen outward, wrapping around my ribs like fingers squeezing too tight. I try shifting positions, curling onto my side, then my back, then my other side, seeking relief that doesn't come.

Eventually, the pain medication I took earlier takes effect, dulling the sharp edges of my discomfort just enough that I can feel my eyelids growing heavy. I surrender to the exhaustion, letting it pull me under like a wave I'm too tired to fight.

I drift in and out of consciousness, caught in that hazy

space between sleeping and waking where time loses all meaning. In this twilight state, I imagine butterflies with diamond wings fluttering around my room, their delicate bodies carrying away particles of my pain with each beat of their wings.

A sharp knock jolts me awake.

I blink groggily, disoriented. The knocking comes again, more insistent this time. Squinting at my bedside clock, I'm surprised to see it's only been an hour since Chase left. Did he forget something?

"Who is it?" I call out, my voice still thick with sleep.

Silence answers me.

I wait, listening for a response, but hear nothing except the distant sounds of music from someone else's dorm and the constant hum of the building's ancient heating system.

"Chase?" I try again, pushing myself up on my elbows. The movement sends pain shooting through my abdomen. I gasp, clutching my side as I slowly lower my feet to the floor. The room tilts for a moment, and I grip the edge of my mattress until the dizziness passes.

"Just a second," I call out again, though no one has answered.

I wrap my cardigan tightly around myself, each step sending little jolts of discomfort through my body. The floor feels ice-cold against my bare feet as I shuffle the short distance to the door. By the time I reach it, I'm breathing harder than I should be, sweat beading along my hairline despite the chill.

Leaning against the doorframe for support, I turn the handle and pull it open, ready to see Chase's smiling face.

But there's no one there. The hallway stretches empty in both directions.

I frown, looking down—and that's when I see it. A newspaper folded neatly on the floor outside my door. I stare at it in confusion. We don't get newspaper delivery in the dorms. Most students wouldn't even know what to do with a physical newspaper these days.

Bending over sends a sharp stab through my side, making me gasp. I grit my teeth, steeling myself against the wave of nausea that follows as I reach for the newspaper. My fingers close around the cool paper, and I clutch it to my chest, using the wall for support as I make my way back to bed.

Briefly, I just lie here, waiting for the room to stop spinning, the newspaper still pressed against my chest. When my breathing finally steadies, I unfold the paper with shaking hands.

And then I read it.

The headline jumps out on the front page of The Ambrose Chronicle:

CHASE SULLIVAN AND CELESTE ASTOR JEWELRY SHOPPING, IS IT LOVE?

I blink, certain I've misread. But the words remain unchanged, bold black letters screaming up at me from the glossy page. Below the headline are several photos—candid shots. And in every single one is Chase. *My Chase.* With a stunning dark-haired woman I've never seen before.

My stomach lurches.

In the largest photo, she stands with her back to him, her head turned slightly to smile over her shoulder. His hands are at her neck, fastening what looks like a necklace.

My trembling fingers turn to the feature article,

scanning the text with growing horror. The words blur through my tears, but certain phrases burn themselves into my brain:

"...Sullivan heir spotted at Fairchild's Fine Jewelry with Celeste Astor, daughter of Ambrose's own media tycoon..."

"...sources confirm the pair have been dating for several weeks..."

"...appeared completely smitten as Sullivan helped Astor try on what appeared to be a diamond necklace..."

"...Astor family declined to comment on engagement rumors, but an anonymous source close to the family suggests an announcement may be forthcoming..."

The article continues, detailing their "obvious connection" and speculating about a "powerful union between two of Ambrose's oldest families."

The newspaper slips from my grasp, pages fluttering to the floor like broken butterfly wings. My breath comes in shallow gasps as the room spins around me.

Several weeks? He's been dating her for several weeks? The same weeks he's been with me?

A sob tears from my throat, raw and animal-like. I curl into myself, drawing my knees to my chest as if I could somehow contain the pain threatening to split me open. The physical discomfort of my illness fades into the background noise compared to this new agony.

How could he? After everything we've shared?

Not just lying. Living a double life—playing boyfriend to two different women.

My phone chimes with a text message. I reach for it blindly, my vision blurred with tears.

It's Olivia:

OMG, are you seeing this? Someone
delivered the newspaper to every dorm
room on campus. What the actual hell???

So she's seen it too. It's real. This isn't some fever dream born from my illness.

I clutch my stomach as a fresh wave of nausea hits, but this one has nothing to do with my hemochromatosis. This is pure, unfiltered betrayal, coursing through my veins like poison. I stumble to the bathroom, barely making it to the toilet before I'm violently sick. My body heaves until there's nothing left, and I collapse against the cool porcelain, shaking.

The physical pain in my abdomen intensifies, feeding off my emotional distress like some parasitic creature. I can't tell where one pain ends, and the other begins.

Chapter Thirty-One

CHASE

I BOUNCE through the revolving door of Sullivan Property Management with a grin on my face that even my father's corporate prison can't wipe away. The lobby's all glass and steel, exactly the kind of soulless architecture Dad loves—clean lines, no personality. Just like the suits who work here.

"Morning, Mr. Sullivan," the security guard says, handing me a visitor badge like I'm some stranger instead of the boss's son.

"Chase," I correct him, like I do every time. "Mr. Sullivan is my father."

I take the elevator to the fourteenth floor, nodding at the familiar faces who pretend not to know I'm only here because my father threatened to cut me off financially.

I check my phone. No texts from Daisy. I frown, tucking the phone back into my pocket. She looked so pale this morning, curled up in her bed, trying to hide how much pain she was in. Leaving her felt wrong, but she was trying to be tough, and I don't want her to think she isn't. But I'll go see her at lunch—maybe bring some more daisies like I did on our first date.

I toss my bag onto the desk in my cubicle and drop into my chair, spinning once before logging into the computer. Even the dull prospect of spreadsheets and market reports can't dampen my mood today.

I stare at the market analysis report on my screen without really seeing it, my mind drifting back to her sleepy smile this morning. *God, I'm in love with her.* I've known for weeks.

I want to tell her. As soon as she's feeling better, I'm going to take her somewhere special—maybe the butterfly garden at the botanical center. I'll buy her dinner afterwards, somewhere quiet where we can talk. I'll probably stumble over the words, make a complete idiot of myself, but I don't care.

My phone buzzes with a text notification. It's from my father:

My office, now.

I roll my eyes. Great—what now? Another lecture about responsibility? Another reminder that I'm wasting my potential? I consider ignoring it, but that would only make things worse. With a sigh, I push away from my desk and make the long walk down the corridor toward the corner office with its imposing double doors.

"You wanted to see me?" I ask, dropping into one of the leather chairs across from his desk.

Dad looks up from his computer, removing his reading glasses with that deliberate slowness he uses when he's about to deliver what he thinks is an important message. I brace myself for whatever criticism is coming.

"Chase," he says, folding his hands on the desk. "We need to talk."

Here it comes. I nod, trying to look attentive while mentally preparing my defense. Is this about being late yesterday? Or the Westridge proposal I half-assed?

"I've been watching you these past few weeks," he continues, his expression unreadable. "And I have to say, I'm impressed."

I blink, certain I've misheard him. My father doesn't do compliments.

"You've been handling your responsibilities here with more dedication than I expected," he says, studying me like I'm a puzzle he's trying to solve. "Your attendance has been consistent, your work has shown improvement, and I've received positive feedback from several department heads—including Luke."

I shift uncomfortably in my seat, not sure how to respond to praise from my father. It's like hearing a cat bark—something so unexpected my brain doesn't know how to process it.

"I know we've had our differences," he continues, his voice taking on an unusually gentle tone. "But I can see you're making an effort to turn things around."

"I am," I say cautiously, still waiting for the other shoe to drop.

He nods, looking almost... proud? "That's why I've decided to help you re-enroll at Dalton University next semester. Full tuition, books, housing—the works."

"Seriously?"

"Seriously," he confirms, the corner of his mouth twitching in what might actually be a smile. "You've shown me you're capable of commitment and hard work. I think you've earned another chance."

I'm speechless for a moment, my brain racing to catch up with what I'm hearing. "I... thank you. Seriously, Dad, thank you."

"Don't look so shocked," Dad says with a chuckle. "I'm not the villain you and your brothers make me out to be."

"I never said—"

"And I have to admit," he continues, leaning back in his chair, "seeing you with Celeste has shown me you're finally maturing. I knew all you two needed was a little push, and you'd hit it off."

Wait, what?

I blink, my momentary elation evaporating. "Dad, about Celeste... I was actually going to talk to you about that—"

"You don't need to explain," he interrupts, waving his hand dismissively. "Young love doesn't always follow the timeline parents expect. But I must say, jewelry shopping already? That's moving faster than even I expected."

My stomach drops. "Jewelry shopping? What are you—"

He reaches for something on his desk and tosses it toward me. It lands with a soft thud, pages rustling. The Ambrose Chronicle.

The headline leaps off the page at me:

CHASE SULLIVAN AND CELESTE ASTOR JEWELRY SHOPPING, IS IT LOVE?

Below the headline is a photo of me standing behind

Celeste, fastening the necklace around her neck. We look intimate, like a couple sharing a private moment. The photographer caught her looking over her shoulder at me with a smile that could easily be mistaken for adoration.

"Oh, God," I say, scanning the article. It's full of "insider sources" and speculation about our "budding romance" and "several intimate dates." Daisy," I whisper, my heart pounding in my chest.

"What was that?" Dad asks, his voice suddenly distant as panic closes in around me.

If Daisy sees this—if someone shows her—she'll think... God, she'll think exactly what the article suggests. That I've been dating Celeste behind her back.

"I have to go," I say, jumping to my feet so quickly that the chair nearly topples backward.

Dad's expression shifts from satisfaction to confusion. "What? Chase, we're in the middle of a conversation about your future—"

"I can't do this right now." I'm already backing toward the door. "I need to fix this."

I race through the office, ignoring the stares from coworkers as I sprint past cubicles toward the elevator. When it doesn't arrive immediately, I say screw it and bolt for the stairs, taking them two at a time, my heart hammering against my ribs.

Outside, I frantically wave down a taxi, nearly throwing myself in front of the car to get it to stop. The driver is startled when I yank open the door.

"Dalton University, Byrd Hall. It's an emergency," I say, breathless, as I slide into the backseat.

"That's across town, man. With this traffic, it'll take—"

I pull out my wallet, grab all the cash I have, and thrust a hundred-dollar bill over the seat. "I'll give you another hundred if you can get me there in fifteen minutes."

His money-hungry eyes widen at the sight of the cash. "That's breaking some serious traffic laws."

"Two hundred total," I say, desperate. "Please. My girlfriend—I need to get to her."

The driver gives me a long look through the rearview mirror, then nods, pulling away from the curb with a squeal of tires. I grip the door handle as he weaves through traffic, my mind racing faster than the car.

Please, please, please don't let her have seen it yet. Maybe she's still sleeping. Maybe her phone died. Maybe, by some miracle, the universe will give me fifteen minutes to explain before her world collapses.

When we finally screech to a halt outside Byrd Hall, I throw the promised cash at the driver and leap out before he can even thank me. I sprint across the quad, dodging students with backpacks who stare as I race past them like a madman.

I take the stairs three at a time, lungs burning, sweat beading on my forehead. Second floor. Third floor. My legs feel like lead by the fourth, but I push through, panic giving me energy I didn't know I had.

I skid to a halt in front of her door and pound my fist against the wood.

"Daisy!" I call out, my voice cracking with desperation

I hear footsteps approaching from the other side of the door, and relief floods through me. But when the door swings open, it's not Daisy standing there—it's Olivia, her eyes blazing with fury, arms crossed tightly over her chest.

Fuck—she's seen it.

"You've got some fucking nerve showing up here," she spits.

"Olivia, please—I need to explain—"

"Explain what exactly?" She steps into the hallway, pulling the door nearly closed behind her. "How you've been dating some rich girl the whole time you've been with my cousin? How you were out shopping for jewelry with her while Daisy was here suffering last night?"

"It's not what it looks like," I plead, running a hand through my hair. "That article is completely twisted. Celeste and I aren't together—we never were. It was all a setup by our parents."

Olivia laughs, but there's no humor in it. "Wow. That's the best you could come up with? A setup?" She shakes her head in disgust. "The photos don't lie, Chase. You were putting a necklace on another woman."

"It's not what you think. Please, let me talk to her," I beg, trying to see past Olivia into the room.

"She's not just sick, she's heartbroken," Olivia snaps, her voice cracking with emotion. "Do you have any idea what it's like to see those pictures when you're already feeling like your body's betraying you? She doesn't want to see you."

"I need to hear that from her," I insist, my desperation growing. "Please, Olivia. I love her."

"Oh, now you love her? That's rich—"

"Liv?"

My heart stops at the sound of Daisy's voice from inside the room. It's weak, strained, nothing like the sleepy warmth I heard this morning.

I try to push past Olivia, but she stands her ground, blocking the doorway with surprising strength.

"It's fine," Daisy's voice comes again.

Olivia turns, concern etched across her face. "Daisy, you don't have to—"

"It's okay," Daisy says.

Olivia hesitates, chewing her bottom lip before finally stepping aside. "I'll be right outside," she says, her voice low and threatening as she glares at me. "If you upset her more, I swear to God..."

She doesn't finish the threat. She doesn't have to.

I step inside, and the door clicks shut behind me. The room is dim, curtains drawn against the midday sun, casting everything in a muted glow.

The sight of Daisy knocks the wind out of my lungs. She's propped against her pillows in bed, knees drawn to her chest like a barrier between us. Her skin has taken on a sickly yellow pallor that signals her hemochromatosis is flaring badly. But it's her eyes that destroy me—red-rimmed and swollen, with dark circles underneath that weren't there this morning. Eyes that used to light up when they saw me, now dull with the pain I caused.

"Daisy," I whisper, taking a tentative step toward her bed.

Chapter Thirty-Two

DAISY

"Don't," I tell Chase as he steps closer to me.

He freezes mid-step, his hand still outstretched toward me. The look on his face is devastating—all earnest desperation and pleading eyes. I have to turn away.

I need him to stay over there, by the door, where I can't smell his cologne or feel the warmth radiating from his skin. If he gets any closer, I might crumble. That's the thing about Chase—his presence has always been overwhelming, like gravity pulling me in. Even now, with his betrayal burning through my veins, my traitorous body wants to lean into him, to let his arms wrap around me and believe whatever explanation he's about to offer.

"Please," I whisper, hating how my voice shakes. "Stay where you are."

"Daisy," he says, his voice breaking on my name. "Let me explain. What you saw in that paper—it's not what it looks like."

I wrap my arms tighter around my knees. My body aches from more than just my illness now. "I saw you with her," I interrupt, my voice steadier now, fueled by a flash of anger. "I saw you putting a necklace on another woman. A woman you've apparently been dating for weeks."

"None of that is true," he insists, taking another step despite my warning. "Daisy, remember when I told you about my dad? How he gave me conditions for getting back into school... One of them was dating his friend's daughter— Celeste. I told him I wasn't interested, but he insisted I take her out a few times and then let her down gently. On our first *fake*,"—he emphasises the word—fake, "date, she confessed she was in the same situation," Chase adds, his hands now shoved in his pockets like he doesn't trust himself to keep his distance otherwise.

I stare at him, trying to process this information through the fog of pain and betrayal clouding my mind. My head throbs with each heartbeat.

"So we made a deal," he continues, his voice softening. "We'd pretend to date for our fathers' sake, just enough to keep them off our backs. It was fake. All of it. Last night was supposed to be our last fake date before we told them it wasn't working out. It was all fake. Completely fake. I went on three —" he holds up three fingers "—three platonic outings with her while dating you."

I want to believe him. *God, how I want to believe him.* But the image of him with his hands on that beautiful woman's neck, fastening jewelry, is burned into my retinas.

"If it was fake, why were you buying her jewelry?" I ask.

"I wasn't," he says, running a hand through his hair in

frustration. "I swear to you, Daisy, I wasn't buying her anything. That article is full of lies."

I watch his face, searching for any sign of deception. His eyes—those deep brown eyes that have always looked at me with such honesty—hold mine steadily.

"What happened then?" I ask, my voice small but determined. I need to hear it all.

He takes a deep breath. "We were at the mall after this movie. Celeste wanted to look at an emerald ring she was planning to get her dad to buy her for her birthday. While she did that, I saw..." He pauses, looking almost embarrassed. "I saw this butterfly necklace in the display case. It was silver with tiny diamonds, and all I could think about was how perfect it would be for you."

My heart stutters painfully in my chest.

"A butterfly necklace?" I repeat, my voice small.

Chase nods, taking a tentative step closer. This time, I don't stop him. "I saw it and immediately thought of you. I was looking at it when the saleswoman came over. She assumed Celeste and I were together and asked if she wanted to try it on. Before I could explain, Celeste said yes." He shakes his head, looking frustrated at the memory.

I feel my walls crumbling at his explanation, but there's still something that doesn't add up. I take a deep breath, steadying myself against the pillows.

"If it was all so innocent, why didn't you just tell me about the condition from your dad in the beginning?" I question, my voice quiet but firm. "Why keep it a secret at all?"

He stands perfectly still, his mouth opening slightly but no words coming out. The silence stretches between us, growing heavier by the second. His eyes drop to the floor, then back to me, and in that moment, I have my answer.

"You knew it would hurt me," I say softly.

"Daisy—" he starts, then stops, sitting on the edge of my bed, careful to maintain some distance between us. "Yes. I was afraid you'd think exactly what you're thinking now—that it meant something when it didn't," he admits finally. "I'd just found you, and I didn't want anything to mess that up. I thought I could handle both situations without either affecting the other."

"But they did affect each other," I say, hugging my knees tighter. "They collided in the worst possible way," I finish. The pain in my abdomen sharpens as I shift position, making me wince.

He notices immediately. "Are you okay?"

I shake my head, not wanting his concern right now. I need clarity, *not* comfort.

"I should have asked more questions," I admit, looking down at my hands. "About your father, about his conditions. I knew something was going on that you weren't telling me, but I told myself it wasn't my place to pry—it was your family matter. *I trusted you.* Like with the black eye," I continue. "I never really asked what happened." I look at him, finding my courage. "The rumor is that your brother Luke did it. Is that true?"

Chase goes still, his expression shuttering slightly. "Yes."

"Why?" I press, watching his face carefully. "Why would your brother hit you?"

I can tell he doesn't want to answer. His jaw tightens, and for a moment I think he might make up some excuse or change the subject. But then his shoulders slump.

"The night before the camping trip," he says slowly, his voice barely above a whisper, "I was at this party. I was rolling on E, not thinking straight, and I..." He swallows hard. "I kissed his wife. Bebe."

My jaw drops. I stare at him, unable to process what I'm hearing. *Chase kissed his brother's wife? The same Chase who held me under the stars the next night and made me feel like the only girl in the world?*

"Wow," I manage to say, my voice strained.

"It's why I'm in therapy," he says suddenly, his voice cracking. His eyes lock with mine, filled with such raw vulnerability that I have to fight the urge to reach for him. "Two times a week. Not just because it was one of my dad's conditions for helping me get back into Dalton, but because I need it."

I stay silent, watching as he runs his hands through his hair, leaving it standing in messy spikes.

"I'm trying to fix everything I broke," he continues, desperation seeping into every word. "My relationship with Luke, my life... myself. I've been such a mess, Daisy. Depressed. The drugs, the drinking, the self-sabotage—" He shakes his head, looking away. "That night with Bebe was rock bottom. I lost my brother's trust. But then we went camping, and you gave me hope, Daisy—purpose. I was determined to come home from that trip and fix things even before I got kicked out of school and disappointed everyone who ever believed in me."

His voice breaks on the last word, and I see the shine of tears in his eyes that he quickly blinks away.

"I want to be better," he whispers. "I need to be better. For my family. For myself. And..." he hesitates, then meets my gaze directly, "for you. If you'll let me."

The intensity in his eyes makes my breath catch. I've never seen him this raw, this exposed. Part of me wants to comfort him, to tell him everything will be okay. But another part—the part that's still reeling from everything I've learned is still so fresh and raw—so I don't.

The room falls quiet, with just the sound of our breathing filling the space between us. I stare at the newspaper still lying on the floor where I'd dropped it; the photos mock me from across the room.

"I think you should go," I say quietly.

His face falls. "Please—"

"I remember what you told me that night at the lake," I continue, my voice barely above a whisper. "You said you ruin everything you touch." I swallow hard, hating myself for what I'm about to say but unable to stop the words. "I should have listened."

It's a low blow—cruel, even—but I'm hurt, angry and sick, and part of me wants him to feel as terrible as I do.

I see the pain flash across his face as my words hit their mark. For a moment, he just sits here, stunned, as if I've physically struck him. Then something shifts in his expression —a hardening of resolve, a gathering of courage.

He stands slowly. Then, instead of heading for the door like I expect, he moves closer to me. I want to hold my hands up to stop him, to create that barrier between us again, but my body won't cooperate. My arms feel like lead weights at my sides, useless against the gravity of him.

"Daisy," he whispers, and there's something in his voice

I've never heard before—a raw vulnerability that makes my throat tighten.

He kneels beside my bed, his face now level with mine. I close my eyes, unable to bear the intensity of his gaze. I feel his forehead press gently against mine, our noses brushing—a butterfly kiss, like the ones he's given me hundreds of times before. But this one is different. This one is wet.

He's crying.

I feel his tears against my skin, warm and devastating. My own eyes burn in response, but I keep them closed.

"I love you, Daisy," he whispers, his voice breaking. "I love you," he says again, more clearly this time.

He loves me. Chase Sullivan loves me. And I've just pushed him away.

His warmth vanishes as he rises to his feet, backing away from me with careful steps. I open my eyes to watch him retreat, every cell in my body screaming to call him back, to tell him I love him too. But I stay silent, frozen in my misery.

At the door, he pauses, his hand on the knob. "I'm sorry," he whispers, so softly I almost don't hear it.

And then he's gone.

Chapter Thirty-Three

CHASE

I CAN'T REMEMBER what legal precedent I'm supposed to be memorizing. The words on the page swim together, a jumbled mess of Latin phrases and judicial opinions that might as well be written in hieroglyphics. I've read the same paragraph twelve times. It doesn't matter—my brain refuses to absorb anything except memories of Daisy.

One week. Seven days. One hundred and sixty-eight hours since I walked out of her dorm room with her words echoing in my head: *I should have listened.*

I slam the law book shut and toss it onto my desk, where it lands with a satisfying thud. My bedroom at my parents' house feels like a time capsule—debate trophies, swim team medals. Everything exactly as I left it when I moved into the house with Wes and Luke. Before I ruined that too.

My phone sits dark and silent beside me. I've checked it a thousand times this week, hoping to see her name flash across the screen. No notifications. No missed calls. No texts.

The first few days, I called her constantly, each unanswered ring hollowing out another piece of me. Then I switched to texts—desperate at first, then apologetic, then finally pleading. When those went unanswered, I sent one last message—just three words: *I love you.* And that's when I discovered she'd blocked my number. She didn't even receive it. The message failed to deliver, a red exclamation point mocking my attempt.

I don't blame her. Not after what I did, keeping Celeste a secret.

Every time I close my eyes, I hear her words: *You said you ruin everything you touch. I should have listened.* She was right. I ruined everything. I ruined us before we even had a chance to become something real.

That's the worst part—knowing she regrets ever being with me. That she sees our entire relationship as a mistake. That if she could go back, she'd choose differently. Choose someone else. Someone who wouldn't hurt her.

My reflection in the mirror across the room shows a stranger—hollow-eyed, unshaven, wearing the same sweatshirt I've had on for three days. Dad's been eyeing me suspiciously at dinner, probably wondering if his son is spiraling again. Mom keeps asking if I'm "feeling alright," her voice dripping with that careful concern parents use.

I run my hands through my greasy hair and consider taking a shower. It's the bare minimum of human functionality, but even that feels like climbing Everest. Maybe tomorrow.

A knock on my door startles me out of my thoughts.

"Chase?" Luke's voice comes through the wood, hesitant but firm. "Are you in there?"

I consider pretending I'm asleep, but he'd probably just come in anyway. "Yeah," I call back, my voice rough from disuse. The door opens, and he steps in, surveying my room with a critical eye before his gaze lands on me.

"Jesus, you look like shit," he says, closing the door behind him.

"Thanks. It's always good to see you too." I turn away from him, not in the mood for company.

He walks over and sits on the edge of my bed. "I wanted to check on you. Make sure you weren't... you know, slipping back into old habits."

I understand immediately what he's asking. The weed. The pills. The escape routes I've taken before.

"I want to," I admit, staring at my hands. "God, I really want to. But I won't."

Luke studies me for a long moment, like he's trying to determine if I'm telling the truth. Finally, he nods. "Dad told me he's going to pay for Dalton next semester."

"Yeah, he mentioned that." I nod, remembering how excited I'd been about it just a week ago. How I'd imagined telling Daisy, seeing her face light up. Now it feels hollow.

"You should be happy about it," he says, watching me carefully. "Getting back into Dalton was what you wanted, right?"

"I am happy about that," I say automatically. I look away from his searching gaze, pretending to organize the mess of papers on my desk.

He sighs. "Have you heard from Daisy?"

I freeze, my hand hovering over a half-finished legal brief. "How do you know about her?" I ask, turning to face him. Then it clicks. "Wes told you."

He nods, looking slightly guilty. "We talked yesterday. He mentioned you'd been seeing her. Said it ended badly."

"No," I say, answering his original question. "I haven't heard from her. And I don't expect to." I swallow hard against the lump forming in my throat.

He winces. "That bad, huh?"

"Worse." I drop into my desk chair, suddenly exhausted. "I screwed up—like I do with everything lately."

Luke frowns. "You know what your problem is?"

"Please enlighten me," I mutter, not bothering to hide the sarcasm.

"You're so focused on what you've lost that you can't see what you still have." He leans forward, elbows on his knees. "Count your blessings, man. You've got a family that, despite everything, still cares about you. You've got your spot back at Dalton. You've got a future."

I scoff, turning away. "A future without her."

"Maybe that door will open again," he says quietly. "Or maybe there will be another door, another person—"

"I don't want anyone else," I cut him off, the words bursting out of me. "Just Daisy. There's no replacement for her, Luke. She's not... she's not interchangeable with some hypothetical future girlfriend."

He raises his eyebrows, clearly surprised by my vehemence.

"I've never felt this way about anyone," I continue, my voice dropping. "She was different from the second I met her. She made me want to be better."

His expression softens. "So what's your plan then?" he asks quietly.

I run my hand through my hair, letting out a long breath. "I'm going to give it time. Get back into Dalton next semester.

Focus on becoming the man she can actually trust again. I need to be better—for myself first, but also for her, if she gives me another chance." The words feel fragile as I speak them, but there's a solidness to them too—a foundation I can build on.

"That's a good plan, Chase," he says, nodding slowly. "Seriously."

"Yeah." I stare out the window at the darkening sky. "I just hope she doesn't find someone else while I'm getting my shit together." The thought makes my chest constrict painfully. "But then again, she deserves better than what I gave her."

Luke stands, clapping a hand on my shoulder. "Don't sell yourself short. You're not as bad as you think you are."

"Thanks for the ringing endorsement," I say with a weak laugh.

"I should get going. Got an early meeting tomorrow." He hesitates, studying my face. "You're gonna be okay."

As he reaches for the doorknob, something tightens in my chest. Dr. Mercer's suggestion from yesterday's therapy session echoes in my head. I've been turning it over in my mind since he mentioned it, weighing whether to bring it up at all.

"Luke, wait." The words tumble out before I can second-guess myself. He turns, eyebrows raised. "There's something I wanted to ask you."

He leans against the doorframe, arms crossed. "What's up?"

I clear my throat, suddenly nervous. "My therapist, Dr. Mercer—you know I've been seeing someone, right?"

He nods.

I take a deep breath. "He made a suggestion during our last session. You don't have to do it if you don't want to, but...

he recommended that you and Bebe come to a joint therapy session. He thinks it might help us work through what happened that night at the party." I swallow, feeling my heart race. "I'm not saying it would fix everything, but it's a start."

I brace myself for rejection, for him to tell me I've crossed a line even suggesting it.

"I want to fix this too," I say when the silence stretches too long. "What happened with... I know I can't take it back. But I miss my brother, Luke. I miss us."

"I'll talk to Bebe," he says finally. "See how she feels about it. I can't promise anything, but I'll let you know."

"Thanks," I say, relief washing over me. At least that's something. Luke could be yelling at me right now, telling me to go to hell for even suggesting she should have to see me again. Instead, he's standing here, considering it.

I want things to be the way they were before. Before the drugs, before the party, before I ruined everything again.

But what I can't shake is the realization that's been haunting me since I first kissed Daisy—I was never in love with Bebe. Not even close.

I lean back in my chair, staring at the ceiling as the truth settles over me. When Dr. Mercer asked me about Bebe during our second session, I couldn't articulate why I'd done it. Why I'd risked everything to kiss my brother's wife. He called it "misguided feelings" after I stumbled through an explanation.

"Sometimes we confuse admiration with attraction," he'd said, his voice calm and nonjudgmental. "Or we want what represents happiness rather than what would actually make us happy."

At the time, I'd nodded along, desperate for any explanation that made me sound less terrible. But now, having experienced actual love with Daisy, I understand what he meant.

What I felt for Bebe wasn't love. It was envy. Loneliness. A toxic cocktail of wanting what Luke had because his life seemed so much better than mine. Bebe represented everything I thought I was missing—stability, adoration, a future that made sense. Like what I've found with Daisy, even if I've lost it now.

I glance at the door Luke just closed and let out a breath I didn't know I was holding. The weight of everything settles on my chest—the mess with Luke and Bebe, the disaster with Daisy, my tentative return to Dalton. It's overwhelming when I think about it all at once.

But for the first time in months, I don't feel the urge to numb it all away with weed or alcohol. The pain is there, sharp and real, but it's mine. I need to *feel* it. To *learn* from it. To grow through it, like Dr. Mercer keeps saying.

I pick up my phone again, tapping the screen to life. My wallpaper is still her—Daisy laughing at the butterfly garden, sunlight in her hair, completely unaware I was taking her picture. The sight of her sends a fresh wave of ache through me, but I don't change it. I need a reminder of what I'm working toward.

Chapter Thirty-Four

CHASE

THE KNOCKING COMES like a ghost from an hour ago—three quick raps that make me wonder if Luke forgot something. I've been staring at the same paragraph in my property law textbook for twenty minutes, the words blurring together.

"Come in," I call, not bothering to look up. The door creaks open, and I catch a whiff of expensive perfume that definitely isn't my brother.

"Chase? Your mom said I could come in."

My head snaps up so fast I nearly give myself whiplash. Celeste stands in my doorway, her perfect dark hair falling in waves past her shoulders, wearing a cream-colored sweater that probably costs more than my textbooks. The last person I expected—*or wanted*—to see.

"Celeste. What are you doing here?"

She steps inside and closes the door behind her, which feels presumptuous in a way that makes my jaw clench.

"I wanted to check on you," she says, her eyes scanning my room, taking in the discarded clothes, empty coffee cups, and general disarray. "You haven't been answering my calls or texts."

"I'm fine," I say, sitting straighter in my chair and closing my textbook. "Studying. Trying to get back on track for Dalton."

The sight of her in my bedroom sends an uncomfortable prickle across my skin. I shouldn't care that she's here, but I do. Every second she stands in this space feels wrong, like I'm betraying Daisy all over again. Which is ridiculous because she and I aren't even together anymore, but the feeling persists.

She moves further into my room, her eyes taking in the details of my life. Without asking, she perches on the edge of my mattress, smoothing her skirt beneath her. Her knees are inches from mine, close enough that I instinctively roll my chair back a few inches.

"Your mom is nice," she says, filling the awkward silence. "She offered me tea."

"She does that," I mutter, running a hand through my hair. "Look, Celeste, I appreciate you checking in, but I've got a lot of studying to do."

"Your mom says you've barely left this room in days," she says, leaning forward. "Is this about that girl? How she saw the newspaper?"

I flinch at the mention of Daisy, even indirectly. "I don't want to talk about it."

She sighs, twisting a lock of hair around her finger. "I'm sorry about what happened with your girlfriend," she says, but her tone doesn't match her words. My gut tells me this apology is as fake as our dating arrangement was.

I study her face, searching for sincerity and finding none. Her eyes don't hold the right kind of remorse—they're calculating, assessing my reaction.

"Thanks," I say flatly, not bothering to hide my skepticism.

"But Chase," she continues, "if she couldn't understand after you told her the truth, then maybe..." She pauses. "Maybe she isn't right for you."

I blink, surprised. "What?"

"I'm just saying," She shrugs one elegant shoulder, "a girl who really cared about you would listen to your explanation. She'd trust you."

My mind races, trying to figure out where this conversation is going. Celeste has never shown a genuine interest in me before. Our "relationship" was purely transactional—a favor to our fathers.

Her hand suddenly moves to my knee. The touch jolts me like an electric shock. I stand up so fast my chair rolls backward and hits the wall.

"What are you doing?" I demand, backing away until I hit my desk.

She looks at me through her lashes, a practiced move that probably works on most guys. "I thought I could help you," she mentions, her voice dropping to a silky whisper. "If you'd let me, I could make you forget her."

The suggestion hangs in the air between us, loaded with implication. My stomach turns.

"I don't want to forget her," I say firmly, crossing my arms over my chest. "And I don't need your help."

Her expression shifts, the mask of sympathy falling away to reveal something harder underneath. And then it hits me—

a realization so obvious I can't believe I missed it. The timing, the convenient photographer, the detailed article when no one had bothered to follow us before.

"It was you," I say, my voice barely above a whisper. "You set that whole thing up. You made sure that the article and photos ended up in the paper."

Her face tightens slightly, her expression settling into something unreadable. Not denial. Not confirmation either.

Why now? Why would Celeste suddenly appear at my house, offering to "help" me get over her? The pieces click together with sickening clarity. She never wanted our arrangement to end—or rather, she wanted it to become real.

She takes a step toward me, her perfume invading my space. "Chase, you're being paranoid."

"Was this your plan the entire time?" My voice rises despite my efforts to stay calm. "Playing along with our fake dating scheme hoping I might fall for you?"

She doesn't flinch at my accusation. Instead, she takes another step closer, her eyes never leaving mine. "I think you're overthinking this," she says softly.

Someone had put it there. Someone had wanted her to see it.

"You had someone deliver it, didn't you? The newspapers. To every dorm. You made sure Daisy would see it."

Celeste's expression shifts, her mask slipping for just a moment before she recovers. That flicker of surprise tells me everything I need to know.

"I don't know what you're talking about," she says, but there's a new tension in her voice.

"Stop lying." My hands curl into fists at my sides. "You deliberately hurt someone I care about just to—what? Get me for yourself?"

She steps closer, reaching for my arm. "You're upset. I understand. But think about what's at stake here. Our fathers—"

I jerk away from her touch. "I don't give a damn about what our fathers want. And you know what? That's still no excuse for what I did—keeping our arrangement a secret from Daisy was wrong. But you—" I can barely get the words out through my clenched teeth. "You didn't have to hurt her like that."

"Chase—"

"Get out," I say, pointing to the door.

Instead of leaving, she steps closer, her hand reaching for my arm again. "Don't be like that. We both know you and I make more sense together. Our families, our backgrounds— we understand each other's worlds."

"Understand my world?" I laugh, and it's a harsh sound, nothing like my usual self. "You don't understand the first thing about me, Celeste."

Her expression hardens, that perfect mask finally cracking to reveal something ugly underneath. "I understand more than you think. I understand that girl was never going to fit into your life. Not really."

Something inside me snaps. All the pain, frustration, and self-loathing I've been drowning in for the past week crystallizes into cold clarity.

"Let me make something perfectly clear," I state, my voice steady and low. "I don't want you. I never will. Not today, not tomorrow, not ever."

A flicker of genuine shock replacing the calculated manipulation rippled over her face.

"If you think I'm your only chance at getting your

inheritance, or pleasing your father, or whatever this is really about—" I gesture between us, "—then I hope you live a very unfulfilling life, because that's exactly what you'll get if you're waiting for me."

"You don't mean that," she whispers, but I can see the first flicker of doubt in her eyes.

"Get. Out." I repeat, and this time my voice drops to a register I barely recognize—low and dangerous, vibrating with barely contained rage.

Celeste takes a half-step back. For a second, I glimpse what she really is—a spoiled, manipulative child who's never been told no.

Her face contorts with anger, tears of frustration gathering in her eyes. "You'll regret this," she spits, yanking the door open.

The door slams so hard my swim trophies rattle on their shelf. The sudden silence feels almost physical, pressing against my eardrums after the intensity of our confrontation.

I stand frozen in the middle of my room, heart hammering in my chest. I collapse into my desk chair, head in my hands. She deliberately sabotaged my relationship with Daisy.

The realization makes me sick to my stomach. I've been blaming myself entirely for the fallout, but she engineered this. She wanted Daisy out of the picture.

Not that it absolves me. I should have been honest with Daisy from the beginning about Celeste.

My phone blares suddenly from the desk, making me jump. I grab it without checking the screen, still reeling from the confrontation with Celeste.

"What?" I bark into the receiver.

The line is silent for a moment, and I pull the phone away to check who's calling. Unknown number. Great.

"Hello?" I try again, forcing my voice to sound somewhat normal. "Who is this?"

"Chase?" The voice is small, hesitant. My heart stops completely before thundering back to life at double speed.

"Daisy?" Her name comes out as barely more than a breath. I'm afraid if I speak too loudly, she'll vanish like a mirage.

"It's Olivia."

Chapter Thirty-Five

DAISY

"Is it... my liver?"

The doctor's face softens, her eyes meeting mine with that practiced clinical compassion they must teach in medical school. She pulls up a rolling stool and sits beside my bed, clipboard resting in her lap.

"Yes, Daisy. I'm afraid so." Her voice is gentle but direct. "Despite our best efforts to manage your hemochromatosis, your liver is failing. The iron overload has caused significant damage to the organ tissue. The bloodwork shows critical enzyme levels, and the imaging confirms extensive fibrosis." She gestures to the chart. "We're looking at end-stage liver disease."

The words hit me like a physical blow, though somewhere deep down I'd been expecting this. I've felt it in the increasing fatigue, the deepening pain, the way my body has been slowly betraying me more each day.

"So... what does that mean?" I ask, my mouth suddenly desert-dry.

"It means," Dr. Montgomery continues gently, "that we're moving toward the need for a liver transplant. We're starting the process of putting you at the top of the list. But you need to understand something, Daisy. The waiting list can be unpredictable, and it might not be quick enough."

The fluorescent lights above me are too bright, too harsh. I blink against them, trying to process what she's saying. "What do you mean, 'not quick enough'?"

"You're not at the top of the list yet," she says softly. "And even if you were, the waiting list could still take weeks, even months. You're a high priority now, but it depends on when a match becomes available. It's hard to predict."

My stomach drops. I feel like I'm sinking into the bed, my limbs suddenly too heavy to move. "So I just wait... hope?"

Dr. Montgomery exhales, her gaze softening. "Not exactly. You can help speed up the process. Have you considered community outreach? Finding a living donor?"

Living donor? The thought of asking someone to give up part of their liver, to risk their own life for me... it felt impossible. "You want me to... ask people? For a piece of their liver?"

"It's more common than you think," she says, her voice firm but kind. "A living donor could save months of waiting. We'd need to do some tests, but there are people out there who'd be willing to help, if you can reach them."

I stay silent for a moment, trying to wrap my head around the idea. I couldn't imagine asking anyone to go through something like that. A donor—someone who'd have to be healthy enough and willing enough to go through a major surgery for me.

But Dr. Montgomery continues. "You can reach out through social media, community groups, even friends and family. Your story might resonate with someone who will help."

I shake my head slowly. "I don't know if I can do that. I don't want to ask people to do something like that. It feels... wrong. Selfish."

She leans forward. "Daisy, I know this is overwhelming, but you have to understand—this is your life. A liver transplant can give you a second chance, but you need to be open to every option, including asking for help."

I meet her eyes, searching for some sign that this isn't as crazy as I feel. "How do I even start? How do I ask someone for something so big?"

"You don't have to do it alone," she says. "We'll help you. The transplant center has a team that can assist you with outreach. We'll provide you with the tools to make this manageable as possible."

I'm about to respond when a commotion erupts outside my door.

"You can't just barge in there!" Liv's voice cuts through the sterile hospital quiet like a siren. "She's with her doctor right now—"

"I need to see her!" The voice sends an electric jolt through my body. *Chase.*

My door swings open and Chase stands in the doorway, breathing hard like he's been running. His blond hair is disheveled, his eyes wild with something that looks like fear. Behind him, Olivia appears, her face flushed.

"I'm so sorry, Daisy," she says, glaring at him. "I tried to stop him."

Chase takes a step into the room, then freezes when he notices Dr. Montgomery. His confidence wavers for a split second, but his eyes find mine, locking on with an intensity that makes my heart stutter despite everything.

"Daisy?" he breathes my name like a question.

Dr. Montgomery turns to me, her expression carefully neutral. She doesn't say anything, but the question is clear in her eyes: *Do you want him here?*

I hesitate but nod.

Dr. Montgomery rises from her stool, her clipboard tucked against her chest. "I'll give you some time," she says, glancing between Chase and me. With a gentle gesture toward the stool, she offers him her place. "You can sit here if you'd like."

He nods gratefully, his eyes never leaving my face as he moves forward. The stool creaks under his weight when he sits next to my bed.

"I'll go start the paperwork," Dr. Montgomery adds, heading for the door. "We'll talk more about options when you're ready, Daisy."

Chase's hand reaches for mine, hesitant at first. I let him take it, feeling the familiar warmth of his fingers curling around mine. Despite everything, despite the anger and hurt that's still there beneath the surface, I can't deny the comfort his touch brings.

Olivia hovers in the doorway, her expression a mixture of concern and uncertainty. I give her a small nod, silently letting her know it's okay to leave us alone. She hesitates, then mouths, "Text me" before slipping out and closing the door behind her.

The silence hangs between us, heavy with all the things unsaid. His eyes search mine, full of questions and worry.

"How did you know I was here?" I finally ask, my voice barely above a whisper.

His thumb traces small circles on the back of my hand. "Olivia called me. She said you'd been admitted and..." his voice catches, "that it was serious."

A small, tired smile tugs at my lips. "I think she panicked and called the whole town."

I expect him to smile back, to share in this tiny moment of lightness, but his expression remains grave. The lines around his eyes deepen, and I can see now the shadows beneath them, the stubble on his jaw that speaks of sleepless nights.

"It's time, Chase," I say, the words coming out steadier than I expected. "I need the transplant now. Not later, not eventually."

He nods, squeezing my hand. "Then you'll get it. Whatever you need."

"It's not that simple. I'm on the list, but..." I swallow, the sterile hospital air suddenly thick in my lungs. "The waiting list could take too long. They don't think I have that time."

His face pales, fingers tightening around mine. "What are you saying?"

"I'm saying I might not get a liver in time." The words taste bitter as they leave my mouth. "Dr. Montgomery suggested community outreach—looking for a living donor. Someone who would..." I trail off, still struggling with the enormity of what I'd be asking.

"Someone who would donate part of their liver to you," he finishes.

I nod, feeling the hot sting of tears threatening. "She wants me to put out a call on social media, reach out to community groups, ask everyone I know." My voice cracks. "How do you ask someone for a piece of their body? How is that even fair?"

His expression shifts, determination replacing the fear in his eyes. "Then that's what we'll do," he says with such conviction. "We'll find you a donor. I'll help."

I look at Chase, his determined face inches from mine, and a wave of gratitude washes over me so strong it almost hurts. After everything we've been through—our fight, my pushing him away, his declaration of love—he's still here, still fighting for me. The thought makes my throat tighten.

"Thank you," I whisper, though the words feel wholly inadequate for what I'm feeling. I want to tell him how much it means, but I'm afraid to believe in this too completely. Hope is a dangerous thing when you've lived with disappointment for so long. I've had too many false starts with my health to trust that this will be different.

His eyes soften as he reads my face. He leans forward, closing the distance between us, and presses his forehead gently against mine. Our noses brush—a butterfly kiss. It's feather-light, barely there. This is his silent promise, his vow without words.

The gesture brings tears to my eyes. I close them, memorizing this feeling, storing it away for the hard days I know are coming.

He gives my hand one last squeeze before releasing it. "I'm going to start right now," he says, standing. There's a determined set to his jaw that I recognize. "I'll set up a website, social media accounts, everything. I know people who can help us reach the right communities."

"Chase, you don't have to do all this right this second."

"Yes, I do. Every second counts now."

The simple truth of his words silences any further protest. He's right. Every second does count.

Chapter Thirty-Six

CHASE

THEY SAY DESPERATION HAS A SMELL. If that's true, I've been reeking of it for seven days straight.

I stare at the spreadsheet on my laptop, the names and contact information of potential liver donors blurring together after hours of outreach. My bedroom has transformed into a command center—whiteboards with statistics and strategies, stacks of flyers waiting to be distributed, and empty coffee cups creating a caffeinated graveyard on my desk.

One week. That's how long it's been since I walked out of Daisy's hospital room with a mission burning in my chest. One week of barely sleeping, of calling in every favor, of learning more about liver transplantation than I ever wanted to know.

Every morning, I wake before dawn, my eyes burning as I check my phone for new donor applications, new shares of our social media posts, new anything that might bring us closer to finding someone who can save her.

"Living donor," I mutter to myself, scrolling through the latest batch of responses to our social media campaign. "Just need one perfect living donor."

My phone buzzes with a text from Olivia:

Any promising leads today?

I type back:

Two new people filled out the initial
screening form. Following up now.

It's become our daily check-in. Olivia handles things at Daisy's side while I work the outreach angle. We've developed an unexpected alliance, she and I. It's almost funny to think about, considering how much she must have wanted to kill me after I hurt Daisy. Hell, I would have let her. But somehow, faced with something bigger than both of us, we've found a way to work together.

I rub my eyes, thinking about how far we've come. We text daily, strategize together, and share the weight of this impossible situation. She still doesn't fully trust me—I can tell by the cautious way she phrases things—but there's respect there. Respect I never expected to earn back.

I look at the time—almost noon. I need to get moving.

Going to Dalton to hand out flyers.

I text her, already reaching for my jacket. Campus should be packed today with the fall festival happening.

No words needed. That's our rhythm now.

I grab the heavy box of flyers from beside my desk—five hundred copies hot off the printer this morning. Each one with Daisy's story, her blood type, and a QR code linking to our website with detailed information on living liver donation. The site tracks how many people visit our site and how many people fill out the screening forms. So far, we've had over three thousand hits, but only forty-seven people actually completed the donor questionnaire. The odds feel impossibly long, but I have to keep going.

I hoist the box into my arms and make my way downstairs, the weight of all those pieces of paper—all those potential chances to save her—making my biceps burn.

Mom is in the kitchen, chopping vegetables. Dad sits at the island, newspaper spread out in front of him. They both look up when I enter.

"Heading to campus," I announce, adjusting my grip on the box. "Going to hit the fall festival crowd. Should be tons of people there today."

Dad folds his newspaper carefully, his eyes tracking me with an intensity I've grown used to these past few weeks. Ever since I told them about Daisy's condition, he's been watching me differently—like he's seeing me for the first time.

"Wait a second," he says, sliding off the barstool. He disappears into the hallway without explanation, leaving me standing there awkwardly with the heavy box.

Mom gives me a worried look. "Have you eaten anything today, honey?"

"I grabbed a protein bar earlier," I lie. I can't remember if I actually ate it or just thought about eating it.

"Take my car," dad says, holding out his keys.

I blink, surprised. I'd been planning to call a rideshare.

"Chase, take it," he insists, jangling the keys.

I hesitate, caught off-guard by the gesture.

"Thanks," I say finally, shifting the box to one arm so I can take the keys. Our fingers brush during the exchange, and Dad doesn't immediately let go.

"I'm proud of you, Son," he says, his voice gruff but sincere. "What you're doing for this girl... it shows real character."

My throat tightens unexpectedly.

"I, uh—" I clear my throat. "Thanks, Dad."

He squeezes my shoulder. "Richard and I put the word out on The Keeper bulletin board yesterday. Got quite a response already. A bunch of the guys and their families are going to get tested next week."

I stare at him momentarily speechless. The thought that he's reached out to them on my behalf—without me even asking—leaves me momentarily stunned.

"I... don't know what to say." And I don't. After everything, after all the fighting and disappointment between us, this gesture feels monumental.

Mom appears at my side with a paper bag. "Sandwich and an apple. Eat them, please." Her tone leaves no room for argument.

Twenty minutes later, I'm navigating through the crowded campus quad, dad's luxury sedan safely parked in the visitor lot. The fall festival is in full swing—with tents and booths scattered across the green, music pumping from speakers near the student center, and the smell of food trucks wafting through the air. On any other day, this would be the perfect place to forget your troubles. Today, it's there's a sea of potential donors.

I position myself at the intersection of two main walkways, box at my feet, stack of flyers in my hands. The first few students approach, and I launch into my now-rehearsed pitch.

"Hi there. Do you have a minute to potentially save a life?" I hold out a flyer to a girl with a purple backpack. She takes the flyer with a slight smile. "I'll check it out," she says, tucking it into her folder. The next guy wearing massive headphones walks past without even acknowledging me. A potential match walking away. I watch him disappear into the crowd, wondering if his liver could have been the one to save Daisy.

"Hey, got one for me?" A bearded student in a biology department t-shirt reaches out.

"Yeah," I say, handing him a flyer. "The website has all the information if you're interested in getting tested."

He scans the QR code right there. "My cousin had a transplant last year. I know how important this is."

For a moment, hope flares in my chest. "Thank you."

The next twenty minutes continue like this—some people taking flyers with genuine interest, others grabbing them just to be polite, and many more walking past like I'm invisible. Each person who ignores me feels like a missed opportunity, a potential match slipping through my fingers. I try not to let it get to me, but the stakes are too high. Every person matters. Every single one could be the difference between life and death for Daisy.

I look at the stack in my hand, mechanically extending the

next flyer as a shadow falls across me. "Hi there. Do you have a minute to potentially——" When I raise my head, I'm startled to find Bebe standing there, her mismatched eyes meeting mine.

"Hey," I say, my voice catching with surprise.

She doesn't respond immediately, just holds the flyer between us. My eyes drift to her arm, where a small cotton ball is taped down with a Band-Aid at the crook of her elbow. It's similar to the one I had after I got tested to see if I'm a match for Daisy.

"You got tested," I whisper, unable to keep the emotion from my voice.

She nods, tucking a strand of reddish-brown hair behind her ear. "I don't know if I'll be a match, but..." She shrugs, letting the sentence hang between us.

I want to hug her, to thank her properly, but I don't know how Luke would feel about that—Bebe either. Instead, I just stare at her, overwhelmed by this unexpected act of kindness from someone who has every reason to hate me.

She reaches into the box and grabs a thick stack of flyers, and tucks them against her chest.

"You don't have to do that," I say, but she's already shaking her head.

"I know I don't have to. I want to." She moves to stand beside me, straightening her shoulders like she's preparing for battle. "So what's your pitch? The one that's working best."

For a moment, I watch her, this unexpected ally appearing when I least expected it. Bebe's presence feels like more than just practical help—it's a lifeline thrown across the wreckage of our friendship. I've missed her more than I realized.

"Usually I start with 'Do you have a minute to potentially

save a life?'" I tell her, watching as she nods and immediately turns to intercept a group of students walking our way.

As she launches into a surprisingly passionate version of my pitch, I feel something shift inside me. A tiny crack in the wall of isolation I've built around myself these past weeks. Having her here, helping with Daisy—someone who knew me before, who knows the worst parts of me and is still willing to support me—it means more than I can put into words.

Chapter Thirty-Seven

DAISY

The phone rings just as I'm half-dozing on the couch, watching a rom-com with Olivia, sunlight spilling across my dorm room. I fumble for it, assuming it's a telemarketer or another check-in from my mom, but when I see the clinic's number flash across the screen, my stomach lurches.

I stare at the phone, my thumb hovering over the screen as my heart pounds in my chest.

"Daisy," she says, nudging me with her elbow. "Answer it. You've been waiting for this call."

"What if it's bad news?" I whisper, the phone still vibrating in my palm.

"Then we'll deal with it together," she says firmly. "But you won't know until you answer."

I take a deep breath and swipe to accept the call, pressing the phone to my ear. "Hello?"

"Daisy? This is Dr. Montgomery." Her voice sounds different—lighter, almost buoyant.

"Hi, Dr. Montgomery," I manage, my fingers gripping the phone so tightly my knuckles turn white. Olivia reaches over and takes my free hand, squeezing it supportively.

"I have some news for you," she continues, and I can hear the smile in her voice. "The community outreach campaign has worked. You have a living donor match."

The world seems to stop spinning for a moment. I can't breathe, can't think, can't process what I'm hearing.

"A match?" I whisper, my voice trembling. "Are you sure?"

"Completely sure," Dr. Montgomery says. "We've run the compatibility tests twice to confirm. Blood type, tissue typing, cross-matching—everything looks excellent. The donor's liver function is perfect, and their anatomy is ideal for the procedure."

Her grip on my hand tightens as she watches my face, her eyes wide with anticipation.

"Who is it?" I ask, suddenly desperate to know who would do this for me.

"The donor has requested to remain anonymous," Dr. Montgomery explains gently. "But what matters is that our transplant team has thoroughly evaluated and cleared them. We've scheduled the surgery for Thursday morning at 6 AM. That's forty-eight hours from now, Daisy."

My free hand flies to my mouth as the first sob escapes. Forty-eight hours. After months of uncertainty, of watching my body deteriorate day by day, of preparing myself for the worst—I have a date. A real, concrete date when everything might change.

"We'll send you full instructions, but for now—rest,

hydrate, and let your support system know. We'll see you soon," she adds.

When the call ends, I stay frozen, phone pressed to my ear, heartbeat roaring. Then it hits me all at once—I'm not just waiting anymore. I'm going to get a second chance.

A sob bursts out of me, half laugh, half cry.

"Daisy! Oh my God!" Olivia launches herself at me, wrapping her arms around my shoulders so tightly I can barely breathe. But I don't care. I hug her back just as fiercely, our tears mingling as we rock back and forth on the couch.

"I can't believe it," I sob into her shoulder, my whole body trembling. "Someone's going to save my life."

"I knew it would happen," she says, her voice thick with emotion. She pulls back to look at my face, her eyes shining with tears. "Chase did it. He really did it." She nods, wiping tears from her cheeks. "He's been working nonstop on this campaign. I've never seen anyone so determined. Day and night, calling people, making flyers, building the website, managing the donor registry—he barely slept."

"I didn't know it was that intense," I whisper, my heart swelling with gratitude. "I mean, I knew he was helping, but…"

"Completely selfless," Olivia confirms, squeezing my hand again. "I was skeptical at first, you know, after everything that happened. But he proved me wrong. He's been organizing volunteers, managing the website, coordinating with the hospital."

"Do you think he knows about the donor yet? That they found a match?"

She shakes her head, tucking a strand of hair behind her ear. "I don't know. The hospital probably called him too, but..." She trails off, looking at my phone still clutched in my hand. "Maybe you should call him. Let him hear it from you." She stands, gathering our empty tea mugs. "And then you should call your parents."

I nod, my thumb already hovering over his contact. "You're right."

"I'll give you some privacy," she says, heading toward the kitchenette. "I'll be right over here if you need me."

Taking a long breath, I press the call button. My heart pounds as it rings once, twice, three times. No answer. My heart sinks a little as it goes to voicemail, Chase's voice filling my ear: "Hey, this is Chase. Leave a message and I'll get back to you."

"Chase, it's me. I just got the most amazing news—they found a match! Someone's going to donate part of their liver to me. The surgery is scheduled for Thursday morning." My voice catches, and I have to pause to collect myself. "I... I wanted to thank you. Olivia told me how hard you've been working on the campaign. I wouldn't have this second chance without you." I swallow past the lump in my throat. "Call me back when you can, okay? I'd like to talk to you."

I hang up and stare at the phone in my hand. It feels strange that he didn't answer. After everything Olivia just told me about how dedicated he's been, I would have thought he'd be waiting by his phone for news.

"He didn't answer?" Olivia asks, returning with fresh cups of tea.

I shake my head. "Went straight to voicemail."

"He's probably busy..."

The thought of Chase out there, still fighting for me even

now, makes my heart flutter. I wrap my hands around the warm mug, staring into the amber liquid as my thoughts drift.

He came through for me. When I needed him most—when my life literally depended on it—he showed up in ways I never could have imagined. Not with empty promises or hollow words, but with action.

"You're thinking about him," Olivia says, not a question but a statement. Her voice is gentle, without judgment.

I nod, unable to deny it. "He didn't have to do any of this. After how I pushed him away, he could have just... left. Given up."

"But he didn't," Olivia points out, settling back beside me.

"No," I whisper. "He didn't."

The realization hits me: I'm getting a second chance at life because Chase refused to give up on me. Even though I pushed him away, he was fighting for my future. The thought makes my breath catch.

"He loves me," I whisper.

"Yeah," she says softly. "He does."

I stare out the window, watching the way the sunlight filters through the trees. In forty-eight hours, I'll be in surgery. In forty-eight hours, my life will change forever. All because someone—a stranger—is willing to give me part of themselves. And because Chase moved heaven and earth to find them.

"I've been so unfair to him," I admit, my voice barely audible. "When I saw those photos with Celeste Astor, I just... I couldn't see past my hurt."

"You were scared," Olivia says, her hand finding mine again. "And sick—hurt. That's a lot for anyone to handle."

I continue, memories flooding back. "He came to my

room that day and poured his heart out, and I... I sent him away." I close my eyes.

The memory of that conversation floods back—me pushing him away, throwing his deepest insecurity back in his face. *You said you ruin everything you touch. I should have listened.* The cruelty of those words makes me wince now. Yet despite that knife-twist, he channeled all his energy into saving me.

"People deserve second chances when they earn them," she says quietly, studying my face.

Her words resonate in my chest, striking a chord I've been trying to ignore. If I'm getting a second chance at life— literally being given new tissue to replace what's failing—why am I clinging so tightly to old hurts?

I believe Chase about Celeste—that there was nothing romantic going on—it was a condition from his dad. *Should he have told me about her? Absolutely.* That secrecy hurt more than the act itself. I just hope he won't keep something like that from me again.

That kiss with Bebe—his brother's wife. He admitted he was high at a party, knew it was wrong and is in therapy to repair his relationships with his family.

But even that, I realize it happened before Chase and I were together. Just like I'd been so understanding about his breakup that had happened just a day before the camping trip. I'd known he was fresh out of a relationship when we began dating. None of that had mattered then.

Maybe he deserves a second chance too.

Chapter Thirty-Eight

DAISY

The night before the surgery...

I pull out the pale blue stationery from my bedside drawer, fingers lingering on the embossed butterflies along the border. Mom gave me this set for my sixteenth birthday for special occasions only.

If this doesn't qualify, nothing will.

The hospital room is quiet now. Mom and dad left an hour ago after helping me settle in for the night, their faces a complicated mix of hope and fear. The pre-surgery preparations start at 4 AM, which means I should sleep, but my mind won't stop racing.

I smooth the paper against the rolling tray table they've positioned over my bed and uncap my pen.

I tap the pen against the paper, searching for the right words. Somewhere in this hospital, there's another person—a complete stranger—who has agreed to undergo major surgery tomorrow to save me. They'll wake up with a scar and less of themselves than they had before. All for me. A person they've never met.

How do you thank someone for that?

I take a deep breath and let the pen move across the paper.

To the person who saved my life,

I don't know who you are or why you did this for me, but I need you to know what your gift means. Tomorrow, when they take part of your liver and place it inside me, you're not just giving me an organ. You're giving me birthdays I never thought I'd see. You're giving me the chance to graduate, finish college, and travel. You're giving me sunrises and laughter and all the ordinary moments I've been afraid to hope for.

I've spent so much time thinking about all the things I might lose—all the experiences I might miss out on. But because of you, I can start dreaming again. I can start planning a future instead of fearing I won't have one.

The doctors tell me I might never know your name, and I'll respect that choice if that's what you want. But I promise I won't waste this gift. I'll live fully enough for both of us. I'll honor what you've sacrificed. Your generosity and selflessness are beyond extraordinary, and I carry this gift with profound gratitude every single day.

Thank you,

Daisy Jacobs

I fold the letter carefully, sealing it in the matching envelope. I'm not sure when they'll deliver it to my donor, but I hope they know how much this means to me.

It's nearly dawn, the pale light just beginning to filter through the blinds. My pre-surgery prep must be starting.

"Come in," I call, slipping the letter under my pillow for safekeeping.

A nurse enters, clipboard in hand, followed by a man in scrubs and a white coat. He can't be much older than thirty, with neatly trimmed dark hair and rectangular glasses that make him look more like a grad student than a surgeon.

"Good morning, Daisy. I'm Dr. Chen," he says, extending his hand. His smile is warm but professional. "I'll be performing your transplant today."

I shake his hand, trying to hide my surprise. "You're my surgeon?" The question slips out before I can stop it.

He chuckles, clearly used to this reaction. "Yes, I am. Board certified in transplant surgery with a specialization in living donor procedures. I've performed over seventy liver transplants in the past three years." He continues, his voice reassuring despite my obvious skepticism.

I feel my cheeks flush with embarrassment. "I'm sorry. It's just..."

"That I look like I should be doing my residency instead of leading the transplant team?" He finishes for me, his eyes crinkling with good humor. "I get that a lot. But I promise, your liver and you are in good hands."

I nod, still uncertain but too exhausted to worry about it now. At this point, I'd let Dr. Dolittle operate if it meant getting my second chance.

"So, Daisy," Dr. Chen says, pulling up a stool beside my bed, "let me walk you through exactly what's going to happen today."

He explains the procedure step by step—how they'll make an incision below my rib cage, remove my damaged liver, place the donor portion inside me, and connect all the blood vessels and bile ducts. He uses his hands to illustrate as he speaks; his movements are precise and confident.

"The surgery will take approximately six to eight hours."

"Your family will see you in recovery," he adds as he finishes his explanation. "The first twenty-four hours are critical, but I'm optimistic about your prognosis."

A knock at the door interrupts us, and my parents enter, both dressed in clothes that look slept in. Mom's hair is pulled back in a messy ponytail, and Dad's wearing the same sweater from yesterday. They've been camping out in the hospital waiting room since I was admitted.

"We'll meet you in the recovery room, sweetheart," Mom says as she leans down to kiss my forehead.

Dad squeezes my hand. "You've got this, kiddo," he whispers, and I catch the shimmer of tears in his eyes before he blinks them away.

Behind them, Olivia appears in the doorway, clutching a small stuffed butterfly. "I'll be waiting too," she promises, placing the plush toy beside me on the bed. "For good luck."

I scan the doorway behind Olivia, searching for one more face I desperately want to see. My heart sinks when I don't find it.

"Has Chase called?" I ask, trying to keep my voice casual. "Is he in the waiting room?"

Olivia's face falls instantly, her excitement dimming. She shifts the stuffed butterfly on my bed, avoiding my eyes for a moment.

"No, sweetie," she says finally. "He's not here. I haven't heard from him."

"He never called me back," I say, feeling a heaviness settle in my chest. "After I left that voicemail about finding a match."

"I'm sure he'll be here when you wake up," Olivia says, her voice taking on that forced brightness people use when they're trying to be reassuring but don't quite believe what they're saying.

My parents exchange a look I can't quite interpret, but I see the concern in their eyes.

"I could try calling him again," Olivia offers, already reaching for her phone. "Maybe he just—"

"No, it's okay," I interrupt, forcing a smile that feels brittle on my face. "I'm sure he has his reasons."

"It's time, Daisy," the nurse says, appearing with a second staff member. "We need to take you to pre-op now."

I clutch the stuffed butterfly in my hand as they unlock the wheels on my bed. My parents and Olivia step back, their faces blurring slightly as tears fill my eyes. The nurses wheel me toward the door, and I can't help scanning the hallway one more time, hoping to see Chase rushing toward us, breathless with apologies for being late. At this point I'd forgive him because I just really need to see his face.

But the corridor is empty except for hospital staff and other patients.

"We love you," Mom calls after me. "We'll be right here waiting."

As the nurses push my bed down the long, sterile hallway, a hollow feeling spreads through my chest. After everything—after the campaign, after all his work to find me a donor—Chase isn't here.

Chapter Thirty-Nine

DAISY

BEEPING machines fade in and out like distant stars as I drift through darkness, floating somewhere between consciousness and oblivion. The pain is there, but muted, as if it belongs to someone else's body.

I'm aware of tubes and bandages, the clinical smell of antiseptic, and then—something different. Something familiar.

"Daisy, I love you." His voice is so faint I might have imagined it. "I'd do it all over again."

Chase. I try to open my eyes, but they're too heavy, weighted with anesthesia and exhaustion. I can't see him, but I know he's here. His presence fills the surrounding space—that warmth that belongs only to him. And his scent, that mixture of laundry detergent and something distinctly Chase—cuts through the sterile hospital air.

I want to respond, to tell him I'm listening, but my body

refuses to cooperate. I'm trapped in this half-conscious state, aware but unable to reach back through the veil separating us.

I feel his breath against my skin, then the gentle brush of eyelashes against my cheek—soft as butterfly wings. *Our kiss.* The one we'd made our own, intimate and secret. My heart monitor beeps a little faster, and I try to reach for him, but my arms won't move. The dark tugs at me again, pulling me back into its embrace. I try to whisper, but the word stays trapped inside my mind as consciousness slips away.

When I finally open my eyes, sunlight streams through half-drawn blinds. I blink rapidly, trying to orient myself. Recovery room. Surgery. Liver transplant. The memories come back in fragments as a nurse in blue scrubs notices I'm awake and approaches my bed.

"Welcome back, Daisy," she says, checking the monitors beside me. "Surgery went beautifully. How are you feeling?"

I blink, trying to clear the fog from my mind. "Chase?" My voice comes out as a rasp.

The nurses exchange a glance. "There's no Chase here," the younger one says. "But your family is waiting right outside."

Was it a dream? The memory of his voice feels so real, yet already it's slipping away like water through my fingers.

My throat feels like sandpaper. "Water," I croak.

She helps me take small sips through a straw, then checks my vitals and surgical dressing. The ache is there now, a dull throbbing beneath the medication.

"Your family will be in shortly," she tells me. "The doctor wants to see you first."

As she leaves, I try to piece together my foggy memories. Chase's voice, his butterfly kiss, the words he whispered—it felt so real. But as consciousness fully returns, doubt creeps in. Maybe it was a dream, my mind creating what I wanted most.

Dr. Montgomery enters, clipboard in hand, smiling as she approaches my bed. I try to focus on her face, but my attention drifts to something behind her—a splash of color on the windowsill that wasn't there before.

"Your vitals are looking excellent," she says, but her voice fades into background noise as I strain to see past her.

There, bathed in morning light, sits a simple glass vase filled with white daisies and purple wildflowers—exactly like the ones Chase brought me on our first date. My heart skips, and the monitor beside me beeps erratically, drawing Dr. Montgomery's attention.

"Are you alright?" she asks, concern furrowing her brow.

"Those flowers," I whisper, pointing with a trembling finger. "Who brought those?"

She glances over her shoulder. "They were here when I came in. Maybe your parents?"

But I know better. Mom would have brought roses—she always does. And the wildflowers are too specific, too meaningful to be a coincidence. The butterfly kiss, his whispered words—they weren't a dream. *Chase was here.*

"He was real," I murmur, more to myself than to Dr. Montgomery.

But where is he? Why wasn't he here beside me when I woke up?

I scan the room again, as if he might materialize from

behind a curtain or emerge from the bathroom. The room is painfully empty except for Dr. Montgomery and her clipboard. My heart sinks, and the device beside me reflects the change in my pulse.

"Daisy?" Dr. Montgomery is looking at me with concern. "Are you in pain? I can adjust your medication."

"No," I whisper, though the incision site throbs beneath my hospital gown. "I just thought... someone would be here."

She pats my arm gently. "Your family has been taking shifts in the waiting room since your surgery. They're eager to see you."

And I love them for it, but they're not who I'm looking for.

"The transplant itself is just the beginning," Dr. Montgomery says, shifting into what I've come to recognize as her professional explanation mode. "You'll need to stay with us for at least another week, possibly two, depending on how your recovery progresses."

I nod, trying to pay attention to her words rather than the questions about Chase swirling in my mind.

"We'll start you on immunosuppressants immediately— you'll be on them for the rest of your life," she continues, making a note on her clipboard. "These medications prevent your body from rejecting the new liver tissue. The first few months are the most critical period, but I want to emphasize that everything looks excellent so far."

"So my body could still reject it?" I ask, suddenly anxious. All this—Chase's campaign, the donor's sacrifice, my family's hope—could be for nothing?

Dr. Montgomery's expression softens. "That's always a technical possibility with any transplant, but I have no reason to believe it will happen in your case. The match is exceptional, and your initial bloodwork is promising. We'll monitor you closely, adjust medications as needed, but you're looking at a quick, straightforward recovery."

I feel a moment of relief in her words.

"Your donor is recovering well too," she adds, checking something on her clipboard. "The procedure went exactly as planned."

My anonymous donor. The person who gave me part of their liver. The person Chase found through his relentless campaign.

"Have they—" I suddenly remember, struggling to sit up straighter despite the pain flaring across my abdomen. "Did you give my donor the letter I wrote?"

"Yes, we did. It was placed on their bedside table for when they regained consciousness."

Relief washes over me. "Thank you," I whisper, sinking back against the pillows. "I really wanted them to know how much this means to me."

"I'm sure they'll appreciate it," she says with a gentle smile. "I'll go get your family."

She slips out, and moments later the door bursts open. Mom rushes in first, her eyes red-rimmed but her smile radiant. Dad follows close behind, his normally stoic face crumpling with emotion. Olivia trails after them, clutching a small gift bag and beaming through tears.

"Oh, sweetheart," Mom breathes, reaching for my hand and squeezing it gently, careful not to disturb any of the tubes or monitors.

Dad stands on my other side, his large hand engulfing mine. "You did great, kiddo," he says. "My girl," Dad adds, his voice cracking with emotion. "My strong, brave girl."

As they surround me with love and relieved chatter, I can't help but glance around the room again. The flowers on the windowsill—likely a silent confirmation that Chase was here. That he came when I needed him most, even if he's gone now.

And suddenly, it hits me with perfect clarity—I'm alive. Really alive. Not just existing in the limbo of waiting for a miracle or preparing for the worst. The donor liver inside me is already working, already becoming part of me, already giving me what I've been desperate for—*time*.

Today is officially day one of my second chance.

Chapter Forty

DAISY

One month later...

The sunlight streaming through my dorm room window feels different now—warmer somehow, more precious. I trace my fingers along the healing scar across my abdomen, a permanent reminder of my second chance. The doctors say I'm recovering remarkably well.

I should feel nothing but gratitude. And I do, most days.

But today, as I sit cross-legged on my bed surrounded by the get-well cards that still arrive occasionally, I stare at my phone. No messages from Chase. No calls. Nothing since that night in the hospital when I thought I felt his butterfly kiss against my cheek.

Jason says that Chase has been distant from him too but assures him that he's okay.

I pick up the small stuffed butterfly Olivia brought me— the one that sat beside me through surgery. Its wings are slightly crushed from where I've held it too tightly on the hardest nights.

My fingers find the photo tucked under my pillow—Chase and me at the botanical gardens, his arm around my shoulders, both of us laughing at something I can't even remember now.

I trace our smiles in the photo, feeling a hollowness expand in my chest. The weight of his absence hits me all at once—not just his physical presence, but everything he was. The way he'd draw tiny butterflies on my coffee cups. His ridiculous toothpaste faces in the mirror. The gentle way his fingers would find my hair while we read.

My throat tightens as memories flood back—his laughter during our rain-soaked kiss, the warmth of his lap beneath my head, the steady rhythm of his breathing as we studied side by side. Each memory carves a deeper hole in me.

I clutch the photo tighter, my vision blurring. It wasn't just the grand gestures or even the way he rallied for my donor. It was the thousands of tiny moments that made up us—the ordinary magic we created together. The safe harbor of his arms. The quiet understanding in his eyes.

"Where did you go?" I whisper to his frozen smile.

I set the photo down with trembling fingers and wrap my arms around myself, trying to hold the pieces together. The enormity of what I've lost crashes over me like a wave. Not just a boyfriend—but the person who saw me.

God, I miss him so much it hurts to breathe sometimes.

My gaze drifts to the wall where his catastrophe of a "Starry Night" hangs crookedly by my desk. That painting—all chaotic swirls and misplaced stars, looking more like a kindergartner's finger painting than Van Gogh. I laugh out loud and it catches me by surprise as I remember him dramatically bowing to nonexistent applause, declaring himself "clearly Van Gogh reincarnated" with such mock seriousness.

The sound of my laughter startles me. It feels foreign after so many quiet, empty days.

I stand, walking closer to examine his artistic disaster. My fingers trace the lumpy paint strokes where he'd gotten too enthusiastic with the blue. "Your boyfriend painted it," he'd said, testing the word between us for the first time.

Something shifts inside me as I stare at those messy swirls. This ridiculous painting is proof—proof that what we had was real, that Chase Sullivan existed in my life as more than just some beautiful dream my mind conjured during my illness.

A decision crystallizes with startling clarity. This limbo is worse than any rejection could be. *I need answers.* I need to know why he hasn't come to see me, why he's disappeared from my life.

Is it possible he thinks I don't want him around? The thought makes my stomach twist. Or maybe finding the donor was just obligation or guilt—his ultimate act before walking away.

But what if he's hurting too? What if something happened that I don't understand?

The question hits me with sudden force—could we work this out if I just found him? Does he still want to be with me at all?

I grab my phone without giving myself time to second-guess. I scroll past Chase's name—no point trying that again after weeks of unanswered texts and calls—and tap Olivia's contact instead.

She answers on the third ring. I don't even bother with hello.

"Liv, how can I find Chase?"

Chapter Forty-One

CHASE

My life fits into cardboard boxes much easier than I expected. It's almost insulting how little space a life takes up.

I toss another handful of t-shirts into the box labeled "CLOTHES" in my hasty scrawl, not bothering to fold them.

I'm grabbing an armful of sweatshirts from my closet when a movement in my peripheral vision makes me spin around, the clothes tumbling from my arms.

"Jesus!" I gasp, my heart hammering against my ribs.

Daisy stands in my doorway, one hand resting lightly on the frame, wearing a simple white sundress that makes her skin glow. Her hair is longer than when I last saw her, falling in soft waves past her shoulders. She looks healthy—vibrant in a way I never expected to see again. For a moment, I wonder if my mind is playing tricks on me—conjuring her from sheer longing and exhaustion.

"Sorry," she says softly. "I didn't mean to startle you. Your mom let me in."

Of course she did. Mom needs to stop doing that—just letting people into the house without warning. Though in this case, I can't bring myself to be truly annoyed. My heart is still racing, but now for entirely different reasons.

"You look good," I manage to say, the words feeling inadequate compared to what I really want to tell her. *Healthy. Beautiful. Alive.*

She gives me a small smile, not quite meeting my eyes. "Thanks. I feel good."

Her gaze drifts past me, landing on the far wall of my bedroom to what Luke had called my "beautiful mind" setup —the chaotic collage of donor information, medical research, contact lists, and hospital data I'd assembled during those desperate weeks searching for her match.

She steps fully into my room, drawn to the wall. She moves closer to the charts, her fingers hovering over the web of information I'd meticulously assembled. I stand frozen, watching her take it all in—the medical terms highlighted in different colors, the spreadsheets tracking potential donors, the timelines and statistics I'd obsessed over for weeks.

"This is..." she whispers, her eyes wide as they scan the wall. "This is incredibly thorough." Her fingers trace a path between connected notes, following my logic. "All of this... this saved my life."

I can't speak. My throat feels like I've swallowed sand. All I can do is stand there and look at her—alive, breathing. The miracle I worked so hard for stands before me, examining the physical evidence of my desperation.

"You did all this work," she continues, turning to face me. "You orchestrated this entire campaign to save me. And yet you weren't there before my surgery. You weren't there when I woke up. Why?"

"I was there," I whisper, the words escaping before I can stop them.

Her expression shifts, confusion replacing wonder. "What?"

"I was there," I say again.

Her brow furrows. "What do you mean you were there? I never saw you."

I run a hand through my hair, trying to find the right words. "I was in the hospital, Daisy."

"Then why didn't I see you?" she questions, her voice rising. She takes a step toward me, arms crossing over her chest. "If you were there, why didn't you wait until I woke up? Did you think I wouldn't want you there?" Her eyes search mine, looking for answers. "Or was it more about obligation? You found the donor, checked that box, and then what? Your—"

I open my mouth to respond, but her questions stop abruptly. Her gaze has shifted to something behind me. I turn to follow her line of sight, and my stomach drops.

Fuck.

The letter—*her letter*—is sitting on my desk, unfolded and exposed. The pale blue stationery with its butterfly border is unmistakable.

Before I can move, she walks over and picks it up. Her fingers trace the embossed butterflies, her eyes growing wider with each word she reads. Finally, she looks up at me; her face a mixture of confusion and dawning realization.

"Why do you have this?" she asks, her voice barely above a whisper. "This was for my donor."

I swallow hard. I hadn't wanted her to find out.

"Chase," she says, her voice stronger now, more insistent. "Why do you have my letter?"

My mouth opens, but no words come out.

How do I explain something this enormous? Something that changed everything?

Her eyes narrow, and I can see pieces clicking together in her mind. She looks from the letter to me, then back to the letter again. "Lift your shirt," she blurts.

"Daisy—" I try, but she cuts me off.

"Lift your shirt, Chase."

She wants to see the scar. The matching one to hers.

I hesitate for a moment, caught between the truth and something more complicated. With a deep breath, I grasp the hem of my shirt and slowly lift, revealing my stomach.

She believes I'm her anonymous donor, that I gave her part of my liver, that I've been hiding this secret from her.

Her eyes drop, searching frantically for a surgical scar—*one that isn't there*—just smooth, unmarked skin. I watch as confusion replaces certainty in her expression, followed by what looks like disappointment. The hope draining from her face makes my chest ache.

"I don't understand," she whispers, her fingertips hovering inches from my unmarked skin. "If you're not... then who?"

"Daisy," I say her name softly, like it might break in my mouth.

She stares at me, eyes glistening with unshed tears. "Who is it, Chase? You must know."

I swallow hard, the name sticking in my throat.

"It doesn't matter who it was," I say, my voice hoarse. "What matters is that you're alive."

She steps closer, her hand still clutching the letter. "It matters to me," she whispers. Tears begin to spill down her cheeks. "Please. After everything we've been through, don't I deserve the truth? Please," she says again, her voice breaking.

Something inside me cracks.

"Celeste Astor," I say, the name falling between us like a stone.

Her jaw drops. She steps back as if I've physically pushed her. "Celeste? As in the woman you fake dated? That Celeste?"

I nod, unable to find words as I watch the shock ripple across her face.

"This is unbelievable," she says, shaking her head.

Her eyes flare with suspicion, hardening as she takes another step back, the letter now crumpled slightly in her tightening grip. "Were you lying to me all along about her? About your relationship?" Her voice rises with each word. "Because why would someone who's just your fake date suddenly donate part of her organ to save my life?"

The accusation hangs between us, sharp and unavoidable.

"No, I wasn't lying about our relationship," I say firmly, meeting her gaze. "Everything I told you about her was true. We never dated."

"Then explain this," she demands, waving the letter. "Normal people don't just hand over vital organs to complete strangers, Chase."

I take a deep breath, the weight of the truth pressing down on me like a physical thing. There's no easy way to say this.

"She set me up, Daisy. Celeste arranged everything—the photographer at the mall, the newspaper article. She even paid a freshman to deliver a paper outside every dorm room."

"What are you talking about?"

"She was playing me the whole time." The words taste bitter as they leave my mouth. "She wasn't just going along with our fathers' arrangement—she actually wanted it to be real. She wanted me to fall for her."

She sinks onto the edge of my bed, still holding the letter. Her knuckles have gone white. "That's... that's insane."

"I know." I move cautiously toward her, afraid she'll bolt if I get too close. "I was furious when I figured it out."

"But that doesn't explain this," she says, holding the crumpled letter. "What does any of that have to do with her giving me part of her liver?"

I run my fingers through my hair, the words I've been dreading to say finally forcing their way out.

"She'd seen all the social media posts, the flyers—everything, and got tested. She was a perfect match, Daisy. Her blood type, tissue compatibility—everything the doctors were looking for."

"I don't understand," she whispers, shaking her head. "Why would she do that after you rejected her?"

I draw a deep breath. "She said she'd only do it if I did something for her in return."

Her eyes lock with mine, a flicker of understanding already darkening her expression. "What did she want?"

"Marry her. She wanted me to marry her so that she could get her inheritance."

Daisy stares at me, her complexion draining of color. "What?" she whispers, the single word barely audible.

"Celeste would be your donor if I married her. That was her condition."

"Are you..." Her voice trembles. "Are you going to marry her?"

"Oh, Daisy," My throat tightens, tears pooling in my eyes. "I already did."

The words hang in the air between us, heavy and final. I watch as understanding crashes over her face—first disbelief, then shock, and finally a devastation so raw it makes me physically ache. It's like watching her heart break all over again, right in front of me.

Her hand flies to her mouth, stifling whatever sound was about to escape. Tears fill her eyes, spilling over and tracking down her cheeks.

"She wouldn't have signed the donor papers or gone through with it if I hadn't," I say.

With the letter clutched in her trembling hands and I can't bear to see her like this. I drop to my knees in front of her, gently taking her hands in mine.

"None of this matters," I tell her, my voice breaking with emotion. "I'd do it all over again if it meant saving your life. Every single part of it. I'd marry her a hundred times if that's what it took."

Her eyes light with recognition flashing across her tear-streaked face. "You said that before," she whispers. "In the hospital. 'I'd do it all over again.' That was you. You were there."

I nod, squeezing her hands. "I came when you were still under anesthesia. I couldn't... I couldn't face you when you were awake. Not knowing what I'd done. But this is your second chance, Daisy," I continue, my throat tight. "You can finish college now. Study your butterflies. You can find someone, someone to love you the way you deserve," I press, the words cutting through me like glass. "Someone tall, handsome. Worthy."

My voice breaks on the last word. I need her to believe this, to see the future that's possible for her now. *If she doesn't embrace this second chance at life, then what was it all for?* The sacrifice, the marriage, all of it would be meaningless.

"You're going to graduate, become a brilliant entomologist, travel the world studying your butterflies. You'll fall in love, Daisy."

"No," she chokes out, her voice raw with emotion. "No. I don't want someone else."

"You have to," I whisper, my own vision blurring. "Please, Daisy. I need to know that you'll be happy. That's the only way any of this makes sense."

"How can you say that?" she demands, suddenly gripping my hands so tightly her nails dig into my skin. "How can you just tell me to move on?" Daisy cries, her face flushed with anger and tears. "After everything you've sacrificed for me? You married someone you don't love—someone who manipulated you—just so I could live." She releases my hands to wipe roughly at her tears. "And now you expect me to walk away and pretend none of this happened? Pretend we never happened?"

I can't look at her. Every tear that falls from her eyes is like a knife to my chest. I stand and walk to the window, needing distance between us before I crumble.

"I did what I had to do," I state, my voice steadier than I feel. "And yes, I'm asking you to move on. To live the life you've been given."

"But why?" she demands, rising from the bed. "Why can't that life include you?"

I turn to face her, forcing myself to meet her gaze. "Because I'm married."

Chapter Forty-Two

CHASE

I'VE BEEN MARRIED to Celeste for a little over a month and I'm already plotting her murder. Not literally—I'm not that far gone—but the fantasy of her vanishing provides a certain comfort as I trudge up the stairs to her—*our*—apartment.

I stare at the door for three full minutes before I can make myself put the key in the lock. The fact that I'm calling this place "home" now feels like swallowing glass.

The key sticks in the lock like it's trying to warn me. *Go away. Run.* But I twist harder, and the door swings open to reveal the luxury apartment in all its sterile perfection. Everything is white or cream or that particular shade of beige that rich people think looks expensive. Nothing out of place. Nothing with personality. Everything in this place screams money—from the marble countertops to the floor-to-ceiling windows overlooking downtown Ambrose.

"I'm back," I call out. The smell of something cooking fills the air—garlic, herbs and wine. For a second, I almost feel like

I'm walking into a normal home, but then Celeste appears in the kitchen doorway, spatula in hand.

"That's it?" she asks, her perfect eyebrows arching in disappointment. "Just 'I'm back'?"

I stare at her, momentarily confused. "What else would I say?"

She sighs dramatically, like I've failed some fundamental test. "I don't know, Chase. Maybe 'honey, I'm home' like a normal husband?"

I can't help the laugh that escapes me—short, harsh, and completely humorless. "That's never going to happen."

"You're late," she says. "I expected you an hour ago."

"Had to finish a paper," I mutter, leaning against the doorframe. I have no desire to step fully into what she's created here—this parody of domestic bliss.

She turns to face me, her expression a practiced pout. "And you didn't think to text? Dinner's getting cold." She gestures toward the elaborately set table—candles, wine glasses, the works. "I made your favorite."

I almost laugh. She has no idea what my favorite anything is.

"I don't have a favorite dish," I say, the words coming out harsher than I intended. "And I already ate on campus."

The lie slips out easily. I grabbed a coffee, but that's it. My stomach growls traitorously, but I ignore it. The thought of sitting across from Celeste, pretending we're a normal couple sharing a meal, makes me want to puke more than my hunger makes me want to eat.

She's completely delusional if she thinks playing house will somehow transform our legal contract into an actual marriage. Like I'll suddenly forget how we got here—how she used Daisy's life as leverage to trap me.

In a year, once the prenup conditions are satisfied, we'll divorce, and I'll never have to see her perfect face again.

I turn and head down the hallway toward my bedroom—the guest room she grudgingly cleared out when I refused to share her bed.

"Chase," she huffs, following behind me. Her heels click against the hardwood floors. "This would be easier for both of us if you'd just try to be happy."

I don't slow down. "I'm not interested in easy, Celeste. Or happy. Not with you."

She catches up with me as I reach my door. "You're being childish. We made a deal."

"Yeah, we did." I swing the door open. "The deal was marriage. Not love, not happiness, not playing house. Just marriage."

I slam my door in her face and drop my backpack onto the bed. The room is sparse—just a queen mattress, a cheap dresser, and a desk I bought secondhand. It's the only space in this entire apartment that feels remotely mine, even if it is just four walls in her gilded cage.

The door opens without warning, and Celeste barges in like she owns the place. Which, technically, she does.

I don't turn around.

"You forgot something today," Celeste says, her voice artificially sweet.

When I finally face her, she's fishing around in her apron pocket. She pulls out my wedding ring—the platinum band that feels like a shackle every time I put it on.

"I didn't forget it," I tell her flatly. "I left it here on purpose."

Her expression shifts instantly, that practiced smile hardening into something cold and calculated. "The prenup clearly states you must wear this in public at all times, Chase. And if anyone asks—"

"I know what it says," I cut her off. "I have to tell them I'm happily married."

"Exactly." She takes a step closer, the ring balanced between her perfectly manicured fingers. "So put it on."

"I'll wear it when I need to," I say. "Campus doesn't count."

Her face goes stern, all pretense of warmth vanishing. "Campus absolutely counts. What if you run into someone who knows my father? Or yours?"

I don't answer. I'm too tired for this argument. *Again.*

She'll get her inheritance in three months, but since appearances are important to the Astors, she wants to keep this facade going for a year so society doesn't believe that she married me just to get her money.

She tosses the ring at me with a flick of her wrist.

I don't even try to catch it. The platinum band hits the hardwood floor with a metallic ping, then rolls in a lazy circle before settling against the baseboard.

"I don't have time for this," Celeste hisses, her face contorting with rage. "I've been cooking for hours, trying to make this work, and you can't even pretend to appreciate it."

She storms toward the door, pausing only to glare at me over her shoulder. "When you decide to stop being such an ungrateful asshole, your dinner will be in the microwave." With that, she slams the door so hard the walls shake.

I collapse onto my bed, burying my face in my hands. The silence that follows her exit is a blessing, but it doesn't ease the crushing weight on my chest. I peek through my fingers at the ring gleaming on the floor, taunting me with its permanence, with what it represents.

One year. Just one year of this hell, and then I'm free.

I lean back against the headboard, my eyes burning with exhaustion. *Was it worth it? Trading my freedom for Daisy's life?* The question barely forms before the answer comes—*yes. A thousand times yes.* I'd marry Celeste a hundred more times if it meant Daisy could live.

I close my eyes; the image of Daisy's face when I told her to move on still haunts me. The raw pain in her eyes, the way her lips trembled as she tried not to cry—and failed. Each tear cut through me like a serrated blade.

The memory makes me feel hollow, scraped out from the inside. *But what choice did I have? What choice do I still have?* This marriage is a prison sentence with a release date. One year. But I can't ask Daisy to put her life on pause for me. To wait around while I fulfill my legal obligation to a woman I despise. That wouldn't be fair to her.

She deserves better than stolen moments and whispered promises of "someday." She deserves better than me.

I've hurt her enough. First with Celeste, then by marrying her. Making her believe, even for a second, that there could still be an "us" would be the cruelest thing I could do.

I reach for my phone, pulling up the last photo I have of her—taken at the butterfly garden during those few perfect weeks we had together. Her face is tilted toward a blue morpho that had landed on a nearby flower. Her smile is radiant, carefree—everything I'd ever wanted for her. Everything I *still* want.

How can I move on from this? Not just getting through each day without her, but actually finding happiness again? The thought seems impossible. A part of me wonders if I even deserve to move on, to find joy after everything I've done.

Maybe this is exactly what I deserve. The cosmic balance for all my mistakes. From stealing that candy bar from the 7-11 when I was five years old, to spying in the girls' locker room with my brothers in middle school. For kissing Bebe. For failing college. For lying to Daisy about Celeste. For all the ways I've hurt people I claim to care about.

What if this is my penance? The guy who kissed his brother's wife, who hurt the only girl he ever truly loved—he doesn't get a happy ending. He gets Celeste.

Perhaps she is my perfect match after all—not because we belong together, but because we deserve each other. Her manipulation, my self-destruction. *A match made in hell.*

I laugh bitterly at the thought, the sound hollow in my empty room. My stomach growls again, reminding me I haven't eaten. With a sigh, I pull myself up from the bed and walk over to retrieve the wedding ring from where it rolled against the wall. The metal feels cold and heavy as I slip it onto my finger.

I stare at it for a long moment. This small circle of platinum represents everything I've lost and everything I've saved. Daisy's alive *because* of this ring. *Because* of this marriage. *That has to be worth something, doesn't it?*

With a deep breath, I open the door and head out to the kitchen, my footsteps heavy against the hardwood floor. The smell of food hits me harder now, making my stomach clench with hunger.

Celeste sits perched on one of the expensive bar stools at the kitchen island, fork in hand, pushing food around her plate. Her back straightens as I approach.

I pull out the stool across from her, the metal legs scraping against the floor. The sound feels too loud in the tense quiet. She stares at me blankly for a long moment, her eyes cold and evaluating, before pushing the casserole dish across the granite counter toward me.

"Thank you," I say, the words feeling strange in my mouth.

She doesn't respond, just takes a bite of her food. The casserole looks good—some kind of chicken and pasta dish with a golden crust of cheese on top. Steam rises from where she's already served herself a portion. Despite everything, my mouth waters.

I reach for a clean plate from the stack she's set out and serve myself a generous portion. The first bite is frustratingly delicious. I hate that she's good at this—that she can cook a meal that makes me close my eyes involuntarily at how good it tastes. It feels like another manipulation, another way she's trying to make me forget why we're here.

And it's working.

Chapter Forty-Three

DAISY

4 MONTHS LATER...

I fold another t-shirt and place it in the box labeled "SUMMER," marveling at how much stuff I've accumulated over the past year. Sophomore year is almost over, and while part of me can't wait for the freedom of our new apartment, another part will miss the simplicity of dorm life.

It's been five months of recovery, of regaining strength, of trying to focus on classes while pretending my heart isn't shattered.

"Do you want to keep these?" Liv holds up a string of fairy lights that hung above my bed all year.

"Definitely. They'll look perfect in our new living room."

The apartment we signed for is small but charming—two bedrooms, one bathroom, and a kitchen-living room combo that gets amazing morning light. A proper home, not just a temporary dorm room.

"Have you seen my butterfly field guide?" I call to Olivia, who's sorting through a pile of textbooks on my bed.

"Check under your pillow," she says without looking up. "That's where you always leave it."

She's right, of course. I lift my pillow, and there it is, worn and dog-eared from constant use. I run my fingers over the cover, smiling at the familiar iridescent blue morpho butterfly. This book has been my constant companion through some of the darkest and brightest moments of my life.

Three sharp knocks on our door interrupt my packing rhythm. I sigh, placing the field guide in my "ESSENTIALS" box before crossing the small room.

"If that's Jen wanting to borrow your printer again, tell her it's already packed," Olivia mutters.

I pull open the door and freeze, my greeting dying in my throat.

I've only seen her in pictures—from the newspaper and Google searches—but I'm pretty sure Celeste Astor is standing in my doorway, looking like she just stepped out of a luxury fashion catalog. Her dark hair falls in perfect waves past her shoulders, and her cream-colored dress hugs her slender frame in a way that makes my t-shirt and jeans feel childish by comparison. The small scar near her ribcage is hidden beneath expensive fabric, but I know it's there—a permanent mark that connects us.

"Hello, Daisy," she says, her voice as polished as her appearance.

I hear a crash behind me and turn to see Olivia has dropped the box of clothes she was carrying, my socks and shirts now scattered across the floor. Her mouth hangs open in shock, eyes darting between me and the woman at our door.

"I hope I'm not interrupting," Celeste says, but she's already stepping forward, gently pushing past me into our room before I can even respond.

The scent of her expensive perfume fills the small dorm room, somehow making the space feel even more cramped. I remain frozen by the door, my brain struggling to process that Chase's wife is standing in the middle of my half-packed dorm room, examining my belongings like she's browsing items at a yard sale.

Who am I kidding? This woman would never shop at a yard sale.

"What are you doing here?" Olivia's voice cuts through the tension, sharp and protective. She's moved to stand slightly in front of me, her posture rigid.

Celeste turns, her perfectly manicured hand still touching the edge of my desk. "I wanted to talk to Daisy," she says simply, as if dropping by unannounced is the most natural thing in the world. "Privately, if possible."

"Why?" Olivia demands, crossing her arms. "Haven't you done enough?"

I'm grateful for Liv's fierce protection when my own voice seems trapped somewhere deep in my chest. The woman standing before us literally gave me life—and simultaneously took away any chance at happiness with Chase. The contradiction leaves me speechless, caught between gratitude and resentment.

Olivia turns to me, her eyes asking a silent question: *Do you want me to kick her out?* I can read the offer in her expression, the willingness to be the bad guy if that's what I need.

I take a deep breath and nod. "It's okay, Liv. I'll talk to her."

Olivia's eyebrows shoot up, but she doesn't argue. "If you're sure..." She grabs her keys off the small table by the door. "I'll go grab more moving boxes from the car. Text me if you need me to come back sooner."

The door closes behind her with a soft click, leaving me alone with the woman who saved my life and stole my future in one calculated move. The silence stretches between us like a taut wire.

I cross my arms over my chest, suddenly self-conscious about my faded university t-shirt and messy ponytail compared to her polished appearance.

"I wanted to thank you," she says as she glances around my half-packed room. "I know it's strange for me to show up like this, but I needed to tell you that the transplant changed my life in ways I never expected."

"Thank me?" I repeat, confusion washing over me. "I should be thanking you. You're the one who—"

"No," she interrupts, shaking her head. "You don't understand. Because of this—" she gestures vaguely toward her abdomen where her scar must be, "—I've found the love of my life."

My stomach drops. The room suddenly feels airless, like all the oxygen has been sucked out in an instant. *They're in love now?* After everything, they've actually fallen in love. The forced marriage has become real, and the thought kills me more effectively than my failing liver ever could.

"He's the most attentive, kind, and brilliant man I've ever known," she continues, absently twisting her wedding ring. "I never expected to find someone like him, especially not through something as unusual as an organ donation."

I struggle to breathe normally, to keep my face composed while my heart shatters all over again.

I suddenly realize what this visit is really about. She didn't come to check on me—she came to gloat. To rub it in my face that she won. *That she got Chase, the marriage, money apparently, everything, while I got... what? A piece of her liver and a lifetime of immunosuppressants?*

"I'm pregnant," she announces, her hand moving to rest on her still-flat stomach.

The room spins. I stumble backward until my legs hit my desk chair, and I collapse into it, my knees suddenly too weak to support me. *Pregnant.* Chase is going to be a father.

"Two months along," she continues, her voice distant through the roaring in my ears.

I can't breathe. Can't think. Chase with a baby—Chase holding his child, Chase pushing a stroller, Chase building a life with Celeste. The images flash through my mind like a cruel slideshow, each one cutting deeper than the last.

I'm about to tell her to leave when she reaches into her purse and pulls out a folded piece of paper. Not just any paper —I recognize the pale blue stationery with butterfly borders immediately. *My letter.* The one I wrote to my donor the night before surgery.

"I've read this so many times," she says, her voice softer now, almost reverent as she unfolds it carefully. "It changed everything for me."

I look at her completely lost. "I don't understand."

"This surgery," she continues, running her finger along the edge of the paper, "it taught me what it means to truly love

335

someone. And I realized it wasn't Chase." She extends the letter toward me. "It never was."

I take the letter with trembling fingers, my mind spinning as I try to process her words. "What are you saying?"

Celeste sighs, perching on the side of my desk. "I forced Chase to marry me so I could get my inheritance. My grandfather's will had this ridiculous clause—no need to bore you with the details..." She shakes her head. "This all led to Alan," she adds, a soft smile playing at her lips.

"Alan?" I stare at her blankly. The name means nothing to me.

"Dr. Chen," she clarifies, her cheeks flushing pink.

"Dr. Chen?" I repeat, stunned. Absolutely stunned. "The doctor who did our surgeries?"

She nods, and her entire expression shifts, lighting up in a new way. The transformation is startling—her features softening, her eyes brightening with genuine emotion. This isn't the calculated, polished woman who manipulated Chase into marriage. This is someone else entirely.

"We had this... spark from the very first pre-op consultation," she explains, her voice taking on a dreamy quality. "He checked on me every day during my recovery, far more than was medically necessary." She laughs softly. "At first I thought he was just being thorough, but then he started bringing me small gifts—trinkets. We'd talk for hours about everything—his work, my childhood, books we'd both read."

She touches her stomach again, but now I see the gesture differently. "I love him," she says, her eyes gleaming with genuine joy. "I've never felt this way about anyone."

I gaze at her, struggling to make sense of what she's telling me. My brain feels like it's trying to solve a complicated puzzle with half the pieces missing.

"Wait," I say, holding up my hand. "You're... not in love with Chase? And the baby—it's not—?"

Celeste scoffs, the sound sharp and dismissive. "God, no. Chase has never touched me—wouldn't even kiss me when we got married." She twists her wedding ring, looking at it with a strange mix of emotions. "He made it very clear from the beginning that it would be a loveless and passionless marriage so I can get my money. A business arrangement, nothing more."

My heart stutters in my chest, hope flaring so suddenly it's almost painful.

"I'm only his wife on paper," she adds, meeting my eyes directly. "Chase slept in the guest room. We barely see each other. He's been taking extra classes so he can graduate on time. Anyway," she says, straightening her shoulders with newfound resolve. "I filed the divorce papers today. He's been moved out of my apartment for the last week." She nods at the letter still clutched in my hand. "He should be the one to have that. Not me."

I stare at the pale blue paper. "But you're the donor. You saved my life."

Celeste shakes her head. "No, Daisy. Chase saved your life —not me. I may have given you part of my liver in the literal sense, but it was for all the wrong reasons. I was selfish and manipulative. I used your life as leverage to get what I wanted. And I did. I got my inheritance. Our prenup was supposed to be for a year, but I amended it—I'm letting him go."

My mind is spinning, trying to process everything she's telling me.

Chase is free.

The marriage is ending.

He's not in love with her.

He never was.

"You did the right thing," I say, my voice stronger than I expected.

She glances at her watch and makes a small sound of surprise. "I need to go." She grabs her purse off one of my moving boxes, her movements suddenly hurried. "I'm meeting Alan and our parents to discuss wedding plans—a real one this time." She smiles, a genuine expression that transforms her face. "We're combining it with a baby shower."

"Congratulations," I manage to say, the word coming out more sincerely than I expected. Despite everything, I can't help but feel a strange sense of gratitude toward her. Not just for the liver, but for this unexpected gift of truth.

"Thank you," she says, pausing at the door. "And Daisy? He never stopped loving you. Not for a single day."

Celeste reaches for the door handle just as it swings open. Olivia stands there, arms loaded with flattened cardboard boxes, her eyes widening in surprise at nearly colliding with Celeste.

"Oh!" Olivia exclaims, stepping back awkwardly.

"Perfect timing," Celeste says with a polite smile, holding the door open wider. "I was just leaving."

Olivia hesitates, clearly torn between her protective instincts and basic courtesy, before slipping past Celeste into my room. Her eyes immediately find mine, scanning my face for signs of distress.

"I'll see myself out," Celeste says, her hand unconsciously drifting to her stomach again. "Take care."

Olivia drops the boxes on my bed and rushes to my side. "Are you okay? What did she want? Did she upset you?"

But I can't stop smiling. The relief flooding through me is so intense it makes me light-headed.

"Daisy?" she presses, her concern deepening. "What happened?"

"He's free," I whisper. "Chase and Celeste are getting divorced. She's pregnant with someone else's baby."

Her jaw drops. "What? Are you serious?"

I nod, clutching the letter to my chest. The hope blooming inside me feels almost dangerous in its intensity. "She told me everything. The marriage was never real. Just a business arrangement so she could get her inheritance."

But then something cold seeps into my joy, freezing it mid-bloom.

"What's wrong?" Olivia asks.

"If he's free..." My voice catches. "If he left the apartment a week ago, why hasn't he reached out? Why hasn't he come to see me?"

The silence that follows feels heavy with possibilities, none of them comforting. I remember the last time I saw Chase, the desperation in his eyes as he told me to move on with my life, to find someone else.

What do I do now?

Chapter Forty-Four

CHASE

THE WEIGHT of the diploma in my hand feels too light for something that cost so much. Not just money—though God knows there was plenty of that—but time, sweat, mistakes, regrets. Lives altered. Hearts broken.

I stand on the field of Dalton University's stadium, surrounded by a sea of identical blue caps and gowns, trying to process that it's finally over. The dean had just called my name. "Chase Sullivan." Two simple words that somehow sound different now that I've earned them, now that I've crossed that stage and shaken his hand. Now that I'm a college graduate.

"Chase!" My mom's voice cuts through the crowd noise, and I turn to see my family pushing toward me. Mom's already crying, mascara smudged beneath her eyes as she waves frantically. Dad follows behind her, his face set in that proud expression I've spent most of my life chasing. Wes towers over both of them, his NFL-sized frame parting the crowd like

Moses at the Red Sea, Amelia holding his arm and beaming at me, while pushing a stroller—my niece and nephew in tow.

And then there are Luke and Bebe. My chest tightens at the sight of them together—not with jealousy anymore but with relief. We've come a long way in the past few months, the three of us. Therapy sessions, hard conversations, forgiveness that didn't come easy. They're smiling at me now, genuine and warm.

Mom reaches me first, wrapping me in a tearful hug that threatens to knock my cap off.

"My baby," she sobs into my shoulder, squeezing me so tight I can barely breathe. "My last baby has graduated college!"

"Mom," I laugh, patting her back. "I'm hardly a baby. I'm twenty-one."

She pulls back, cupping my face in her hands. "You'll always be my baby though."

Dad steps forward next, his hand extended formally, but I pull him into a hug instead. He stiffens for a second before returning it, patting my back with unexpected tenderness.

"Well done, Son," he says when we separate. Then, with a solemnity that makes my breath catch, he reaches into his pocket and pulls out a small velvet box. The sight of it makes my heart skip. I know what's inside before he even opens it. "It's time," he says, his voice carrying a weight of tradition I've witnessed twice before with my brothers. He opens the box to reveal the Keeper ring—platinum band with the engraved crest.

The ring glints in the sunlight as I take it from the velvet box, a physical symbol of everything the Sullivan name represents. The platinum band feels heavier than it looks, the engraved crest catching the light as I slide it onto my right hand.

"Thank you, Dad," I say, my voice thick with emotion I didn't expect to feel. For the past year, I resented this tradition, seeing it as another expectation I couldn't live up to. Now, having earned it on my own terms, it feels different. Like acceptance rather than obligation.

Dad clasps my shoulder, a rare display of physical affection. "You've earned it, Son. I'm proud of you."

Before I can respond, I spot Jason making his way through the crowd, his parents and Olivia following. His face is flushed with excitement beneath his graduation cap, diploma clutched in one hand while the other is firmly intertwined with Olivia's.

My eyes instinctively scan the crowd behind Olivia, searching for the familiar flash of blonde hair, the butterfly-patterned accessories she always wears. Where Olivia is, Daisy is usually close by. But she's not here.

A hollow feeling opens up in my chest. I shouldn't be surprised—we haven't spoken in months. I'm not sure if she's heard I'm divorced.

I thought I'd convinced myself I'd made peace with our ending. But the reality of not seeing her hits harder than I expected.

"Congratulations, Chase!" Jason pulls me into a back-slapping hug, breaking my train of thought. "We did it, man."

"Never doubted us for a second," I lie, returning his embrace.

My dad turns, his expression brightening when he sees Jason. "Congratulations, Jason."

"Thank you, Mr. Sullivan," he says, reaching out to shake my father's hand.

LULU HART

Dad doesn't just shake his hand—he pulls out another small velvet box identical to mine.

"Jason," my father says, his voice conveying the same ceremonial weight, "you've earned your place among us."

Jason smiles as dad opens the box to unveil another Keeper ring.

Jason takes the ring with trembling fingers, sliding it onto his right hand.

"Thank you, Sir. This means... everything," Jason says.

I notice Olivia beaming at Jason, her eyes shining with pride and something else—knowledge. She catches my gaze and gives me a subtle nod, as if we're sharing a secret. And suddenly it hits me: *she knows.* She knows exactly what the Keeper ring means, what it represents beyond just a graduation gift. She understands the significance of the secret society that's been part of Dalton U.

The realization that she knows—and appears completely comfortable with it—feels significant. The Keepers are a lifelong commitment, a brotherhood with connections that stretch across industries and generations. And she's accepted it as part of who Jason is.

My thoughts drift back to Daisy, a pang of longing hitting me.

I wonder if she would have been as accepting of The Keepers as Olivia clearly is. *Would she have understood what this ring means, what being part of this brotherhood entails?* Probably. She always had a way of seeing through facades to what mattered. But I guess I'll never know for sure now.

"Hey," Jason says, clapping me on the shoulder. "You ready for our guys' camping weekend? Just what we need after four years of academic torture."

I nod, pushing thoughts of Daisy aside. "Yeah, definitely."

Olivia steps forward with a smile. "And that's my cue to exit. You boys have fun." She kisses Jason on the cheek, then surprises me by giving me a quick hug. "Congratulations on your graduation, Chase."

There's something in her eyes—a knowing look that makes me wonder if she's heard about the divorce. News travels fast in our circle. But she says nothing else, just squeezes my arm once before stepping back.

I turn to Wes and Luke. "You guys sure you don't want to join us?" I ask again. I had first asked them to join when Jason came to me with the camping trip idea. "It's just a few guys from Dalton. Nothing crazy."

Wes exchanges a quick glance with Amelia before shaking his head. "Wish I could, man, but I have a thing... a football thing."

"Right," I nod, though something about his answer feels rehearsed.

Luke shifts his weight, clearing his throat. "And I promised Bebe we'd go look at wedding venues. You know how it is...."

Bebe smiles a little too brightly beside him. "The perfect venues book fast!"

There's something off about both their excuses—a certain tension in their postures, the way they're not quite meeting my eyes. But I decide not to push it.

"No worries," I say, adjusting my cap.

I pull my family into one last group hug. It's a strange feeling—standing here surrounded by the people who've shaped me, wearing this ridiculous outfit that symbolizes the end of one chapter and the beginning of another. I wasn't sure I'd make it to this point.

"Be careful driving up there," Mom says, wiping at her eyes. "The mountain roads can be dangerous."

"We'll be fine, Mrs. Sullivan," Jason assures her with his most responsible smile.

I roll my eyes but appreciate the way it makes my mom relax. With one last round of hugs and handshakes, we finally break away from the family crowd and head toward the parking lot.

"You ready for this?" he asks as we weave through clusters of graduates taking photos.

"More than ready," I tell him, feeling a surge of anticipation. A weekend with the guys is exactly what I need right now—cold beers, stupid jokes, no responsibilities. Just a few days to forget about everything: graduation, the future, my messy personal life.

The truth is, I need the distraction. Every minute I spend in this town is another minute I might run into Daisy. Another minute I might crack and call her, even though I promised myself I wouldn't. She deserves her space, her chance to move on without me.

The sooner we get there, the better.

Chapter Forty-Five

CHASE

I GRIP the dashboard as the car lurches to yet another unscheduled stop; the tires crunching on gravel. I could strangle him right now. My patience, already worn tissue-thin after five detours, finally tears.

"Seriously, Jason? Another one?" I can't keep the exasperation from my voice as he kills the engine beside a weathered farm stand overflowing with produce. Wooden crates of vegetables and fruits are arranged in neat rows, like some rustic Pinterest fantasy come to life.

He flashes that annoying grin of his. "Come on, Chase. Look at this place! It's charming."

"Charming isn't getting us to the campsite before nightfall," I mutter, but he's already out of the car, the door slamming behind him.

I check my phone: 5:47 PM. The sun is already sinking, painting the sky in warning shades of orange. We should have been setting up tents by now, not browsing for—I squint through the windshield—strawberries.

With a resigned sigh, I drag myself out of the passenger seat. I slam the car door harder than necessary and trudge over; the gravel crunching under my boots.

"We're burning daylight," I mutter, but Jason doesn't seem to care.

"Where are these grown?" he asks the weathered old man behind the stand.

I glare at him. *Is he serious?* We're already two hours behind schedule because he had to see a world-famous beef jerky stand I'd never heard of and an abandoned gas station he read about on some obscure travel blog.

"Jason," I say, trying to keep my voice level, "what time are the guys supposed to be at the campsite again?"

He barely glances at me, too engrossed in a conversation about soil quality with the old farmer. "Later," is all he says with a dismissive wave of his hand.

I clench my jaw so hard I'm surprised my teeth don't crack. *Later.* As if that's an actual time. As if we don't have five other people waiting for us with all the cooking supplies.

He picks up a bright orange fruit, turning it over in his hands with exaggerated fascination. I watch in disbelief as he picks up a peculiarly mottled orange, examining it with the focused attention of a jeweler appraising a rare gem. "Is this one of those crossbred types? The color is incredible."

The farmer launches into a detailed explanation about hybrid citrus varieties while I check my watch for what feels like the hundredth this afternoon. The second hand ticks mockingly. Six o'clock now. We're officially late.

I pace behind Jason, shooting him meaningful looks that

he expertly ignores. He moves on to examining a display of heirloom tomatoes, asking about growing seasons and watering schedules like he's suddenly developed a passionate interest in agriculture.

"The purple ones have the best flavor profile," the farmer says.

By the time he finally purchases three heirloom tomatoes, two strange-looking oranges, and a basket of strawberries that "we absolutely need for breakfast," I've mentally packed up our friendship along with the camping gear.

"Are you done?" I ask, not bothering to hide my irritation.

"Yeah, yeah." He pays the farmer, who wraps everything carefully in brown paper.

We finally pull back onto the road, the sun hanging dangerously low on the horizon. I slouch in my seat, arms crossed, while Jason hums contentedly beside me, as if we're on some leisurely Sunday drive instead of running hours behind schedule.

Not even ten minutes pass before his voice cuts through my brooding silence.

"Oh, Chase, look!" He points excitedly at an approaching roadside sign. "A mineshaft! We can dig for gold! We have to check it out!"

His hand hovers near the turn signal.

"Jason, I swear to God, if you turn this car, I will strangle you with your own hiking bootlaces."

His hand drops from the turn signal, and he lets out a dramatic sigh. "Fine. You win. Campsite it is."

The rest of the drive passes in relative peace, though his pouting is almost as irritating as his detours. By the time we finally turn onto the familiar dirt road leading to our usual camping spot, darkness has fully settled in. The headlights cut through the night, illuminating pine trees.

"We're here," he announces unnecessarily as we pull into the clearing. "Only... three hours later than planned."

I'm about to unleash a well-deserved "I told you so" when something catches my eye. There's an orange glow coming from our campsite. Not just any glow—a fully built, crackling campfire.

"Do you see that?" I ask.

"The fire? Yeah." Jason slows the car to a crawl. "Maybe the guys got tired of waiting and started without us?"

But as we pull closer, I can make out something else: standing tall and pristine, is what looks like a fancy bell tent— the kind you see in glamping photoshoots. Nothing about this scene matches our usual setup of pop-up tents and camp chairs.

"Jason, double-check your permit, would you?" I say slowly, unease crawling up my spine. "Are you sure this is our spot?"

He fumbles for his phone, the blue light illuminating as he scrolls through his emails. "This is definitely it, Chase. Spot 17, same as always." He looks up, squinting at the campsite number post barely visible in our headlights. "See? Seventeen."

"Then who set up that fancy tent in our spot?" I nod toward the bell tent.

He kills the engine, and suddenly we're enveloped in the sounds of the forest—crickets, the distant hoot of an owl, and the soft crackle of the fire that someone else built. In *our* spot.

"Only one way to find out," he says, reaching for his door handle.

We climb out of the car, the night air colder than I

expected. Our boots crunch on the pine needles as we approach the bell tent. It's even more impressive up close— canvas the color of sand, with some kind of intricate pattern stitched around the edges. The firepit in front of it has a perfect arrangement of logs, burning steadily.

Jason steps ahead of me, clearing his throat. "Hello, is anybody home?" He calls out in a strange, singsong voice that doesn't match the tension of the moment. His tone is almost playful, like he's calling out to a friend during hide-and-seek rather than confronting potential strangers who've taken our campsite.

No response comes from the glowing tent. The fire crackles, sending sparks into the night sky.

"I'm going to check the facilities, see if anyone's around." He gestures vaguely toward the campground's main area. "Why don't you head to the lake? Maybe whoever set this up went for a night swim."

Something feels off, but I can't place it. Still, checking the lake makes more sense than standing here staring at an empty tent. "Fine," I mutter.

I start down the familiar path that winds through the pines to the water's edge. The moon is nearly full tonight, casting enough silvery light that I don't need my flashlight. The path dips and curves, and I can smell the lake before I see it—that distinctive blend of wet stones and algae.

When I emerge from the tree line, the lake stretches before me, a dark mirror reflecting the night sky. And there, perched on the flat rocks that jut into the water—I see a figure. The silhouette is small against the vast darkness of the lake, just sitting there with knees pulled up to chest. Something about the posture makes my heart skip. The curve of those shoulders, the way the head tilts slightly to the right.

It reminds me of Daisy.

My feet slow as a memory surfaces—finding her here last time, perched on this same rock.

I blink, trying to clear the memory away. It can't be her.

But as I get closer, the figure shifts, and moonlight reveals the familiar profile that I've traced with my fingertips many times. My heart hammers against my ribs.

It is Daisy.

I stop dead in my tracks, breath caught in my throat. She hasn't noticed me yet, still gazing out at the water, her blonde hair lifts occasionally by the breeze.

"Daisy?" My voice comes as I step on a twig and it snaps beneath my boot.

The figure turns, enough for me to catch her profile, and my suspicions solidify into certainty. It is her.

"Chase?" Her voice carries across the small distance between us, soft but unmistakable.

My heart pounds against my ribs as I take a tentative step closer. "What are you doing here?"

She scoots over on the rock, making room for me.

"I'm supposed to be camping with the guys," I say, my voice sounding strange to my own ears. "Graduation celebration weekend."

"Right." She nods slowly. "With Jason."

Something in her tone makes me pause. There's a knowing edge to it, like she's in on a joke I don't understand. Before I can ask what she means, a sound from behind me— footsteps on the path—makes me turn.

Jason and Olivia stand at the top of the path, watching us.

They're holding hands and wearing matching expressions—a mixture of smugness.

And just like that, all the pieces click into place. The detours. The delays. The mysterious tent. The way my brothers declined to join us with those flimsy excuses.

This isn't a guys' camping trip. This was planned.

Chapter Forty-Six

CHASE

I CATCH Olivia's wink before she and Jason disappear up the path, and suddenly we're alone—me and Daisy, just like that first night months ago.

When I turn back to her, the moonlight catches in her hair, turning the blonde strands silver. She looks ethereal, like something from a dream I've had a thousand times since we parted.

"So," I say, still standing awkwardly by the edge of the rock, my voice rough with emotion, "you did this?"

"Surprise," she whispers, the word hanging between us like a question. Her eyes search mine, uncertain and vulnerable in a way that makes my chest ache. She doesn't know if I'm happy about this ambush—this miracle.

I slide onto the rock beside her, close enough that our shoulders almost touch. The lake stretches before us, a perfect mirror of the star-filled sky.

I can't help myself. I reach out, my fingertips grazing her cheek, feeling the softness of her skin beneath my touch. She leans into my hand, her eyes fluttering closed for just a moment, and it's like the past six months dissolve into nothing.

"I wanted to bring you back here," she admits softly, "where it all began." Her voice trembles slightly as she meets my eyes. "I know what you told me—that I should move on and find someone else. But I couldn't, Chase. I haven't even tried."

My heart hammers against my ribs.

"After I found out about the divorce..." She takes a shaky breath. "I wanted to reach out, or you to, but I was afraid you'd already taken your own advice. That you'd moved on."

I shake my head, unable to find words for a moment. "Never," I finally say. "Not for a single day."

She shifts closer, her knee brushing against mine. "I kept thinking about this place. About when everything changed." Her fingers find mine in the darkness, tentative at first, then intertwining with certainty. "I thought maybe if we came back here..."

"A second chance," I whisper, completing her thought.

"Is that crazy?" she asks, vulnerability etched across her features. "To think we could start over?"

I lift our joined hands, pressing my lips to her knuckles. "Not crazy at all," I say, my voice thick with emotion.

Her eyes shine in the moonlight, and I watch as she takes a deep breath, like she's gathering courage. Her fingers tighten around mine.

"Chase," she whispers, "I need to tell you something I should have said sooner." She pauses, her gaze never leaving mine. "I love you. I've loved you since the first night on this rock. I never stopped, not even when I thought I'd lost you forever."

The words hit me like a physical force, stealing my breath. For months, I've dreamed of hearing her say those words, convinced it would never happen.

"Daisy," I manage, my voice breaking on her name. "I love you too. God, I love you so much it hurts." I cup her face in my hands, needing her to understand. "Every day without you has been torture. I thought I was doing the right thing letting you go, but it was killing me."

She leans forward, closing the distance between us, and when her lips finally meet mine, everything else disappears. Her taste, her scent, the soft warmth of her mouth against mine—it's exactly as I remember, yet somehow even better. My hands slide into her hair as I pull her closer, deepening the kiss with a hunger that's been building for months.

She makes a small sound in the back of her throat—half sigh, half moan—and it sends my senses ablaze. Her tongue slides against mine growing confidence as her arms wrap around my neck.

I lose myself in her, in the perfect rhythm we find together. It's like we were never apart, like our bodies remember exactly how to move together, and I groan against her mouth.

"I've missed you," I whisper against her lips, unable to pull away even to speak. "So much."

She responds by kissing me harder, more urgently, her body shifting until she's practically in my lap. I wrap my arms around her waist, steadying her on the uneven surface of the rock, drawing her closer until I can feel her heartbeat against my chest.

We break apart just long enough to catch our breath before I'm pulling her back to me, unable to bear even that small distance. Her body presses against mine as I trail kisses along her jaw, down the column of her throat, feeling her pulse race beneath my lips.

"Chase, I need you," she breathes against my mouth, her words igniting something primal inside me.

I don't hesitate. Taking her hand, I lead her up the path toward the campsite, toward that mysterious bell tent that now makes perfect sense. We move quickly through the darkness, guided by moonlight and desperation.

When we reach the tent, I hold the canvas flap open for her. Inside, it's like stepping into another world. Someone— Olivia and Daisy, I'm guessing—has transformed the space into something magical. Lanterns hang from the center pole, casting a warm, golden glow over a proper mattress covered in soft blankets. There are pillows scattered across it, and flowers in small vases on a low table beside the bed.

Daisy steps inside ahead of me, her silhouette beautiful against the soft light. She turns to face me as I secure the tent flap behind us.

"Too bright?" she asks, her voice soft as she reaches for the lantern.

I nod, suddenly feeling overwhelmed by the moment, by her presence after so many months apart. She turns the dimmer, and the tent fills with a softer glow.

I close the space between us in two strides, unable to wait another second. My mouth finds hers with desperate hunger, my hands sliding under her flannel shirt to feel the warm skin beneath. She gasps against my lips as my fingertips trace the curve of her waist, then higher to brush the underside of her breast.

"I've thought about this every night," I whisper, tugging at the buttons of her shirt. "Dreamed about touching you again."

Her fingers work at my belt buckle, fumbling slightly in her eagerness. "Me too," she breathes. "I couldn't stop remembering how you felt against me."

We undress each other between fevered kisses, clothes falling to the floor in a careless trail. When her shirt finally falls open, revealing a simple cotton bra beneath, I have to pause just to look at her. The lantern light bathes her skin in gold, highlighting every curve I've missed so desperately.

"You're even more beautiful than I remembered," I state, my voice thick with emotion.

A flush spreads across her chest as she reaches behind to unhook her bra. It falls away, and I can't help but stare at her perfect breasts, remembering how they felt in my hands, against my mouth. She pulls me closer, and I feel the heat of her skin against mine as we tumble onto the mattress together.

I hover over her, my weight supported on my forearms as I kiss her deeply. Her fingers trace patterns on my back, waking up every nerve ending in my body. I break the kiss to observe her face—her flushed cheeks, her eyes dark with desire, her lips swollen from my kisses.

"I need to taste you," I whisper, trailing kisses down her neck to her collarbone. "Every inch of you."

She arches beneath me as I move lower, my lips finding her breast. I take her nipple into my mouth, circling it with my tongue until she gasps my name. Her fingers tangle in my hair, holding me closer as I lavish attention on first one breast, then the other.

I continue my journey downward, pressing kisses along the soft skin of her stomach, dipping my tongue into her navel. Her breathing quickens. I shift lower, settling between her thighs, kissing my way down until my mouth finds her center. I part her pussy with my tongue, savoring that first taste of her. A groan escapes me—she's so wet, so ready for me. I lick along her slit before circling her clit, drinking her in like a man who's been wandering the desert for months. *In many ways, I have been.*

"Chase," she gasps, her fingers tangling in my hair as I explore her with my tongue.

I take my time, relearning every inch of her, savoring each gasp and shudder. I lick and suck, alternating between gentle strokes and deeper pressure.

Her thighs tremble on either side of my head as I circle her most sensitive spot with my tongue. I slide my hands beneath her, lifting her hips for better access, and she cries out when I slip a finger inside her while still working with my mouth.

"Oh God," she moans, her back arching off the mattress. "Chase, please..."

She's getting close, her muscles tightening around my finger.

"Chase, please," she moans, her voice thick with need. "I want you inside me. Now."

The urgency in her voice sends heat rushing through me. I sit up and wipe my mouth with the back of my hand, savoring the taste of her on my lips one last time before moving up her body. Her legs fall open for me as I position myself between them, my cock hard and aching. I take a moment to look at her—flushed skin, parted lips—and I can hardly believe we're here again after everything.

I grasp her thighs, guiding them wider. The first touch of her wet heat against the head of my cock nearly undoes me. I press forward slowly, watching as I disappear inside her inch by inch. The sight is mesmerizing—her body accepting me, taking me in, welcoming me home.

Chapter Forty-Seven

DAISY

HE FILLS ME COMPLETELY, stretching me in a way that makes my breath catch and my mind go blank. I feel him everywhere—not just where our bodies join, but in every cell, every nerve ending suddenly alive and singing.

"Oh my God," I gasp as he pushes deeper, my body yielding to him. My fingernails dig into his shoulders, anchoring me as the sensation overwhelms me.

He pauses when he's fully sheathed, his forehead pressed against mine, our ragged breathing mingling in the small space between us.

"Daisy," he whispers, my name a prayer on his lips. "You feel incredible."

I wrap my legs around his waist, pulling him impossibly closer. The fullness is exquisite—like a missing piece slotting back into place.

"Move," I breathe against his mouth. "Please."

I can't form words, I can only moan as he slides almost all

the way out before pushing back in. The friction is exquisite, sending ripples of pleasure radiating through me. His body covers mine, solid and warm, his weight pressing me into the mattress in the most comforting way.

I lift my hips to meet his thrusts. Our bodies move together as if they've never forgotten each other, as if the months apart were merely seconds.

"Yes," I whisper against his lips, "just like that."

This isn't just sex—it's making love. The difference is in the tenderness of his touch, the way his eyes never leave mine. I've missed this connection that transcends the physical, this feeling of being completely seen and cherished.

Chase captures my mouth in another kiss while he keeps moving inside me. Our breaths mingle, quick and shallow, punctuated by soft gasps when he hits that perfect spot. I can taste the salt on his skin as I trail kisses along his jaw, feel the vibration of his moan against my lips.

"I love you," he murmurs, his voice breaking as his pace quickens.

I cradle his face between my hands, bringing his forehead to rest against mine. "I love you too," I whisper back, the words flowing from my heart with absolute certainty. "So much."

His movements slow as emotion flashes across his face. In one fluid motion, he wraps his arms around my waist and rolls us over without breaking our connection. Suddenly I'm straddling him, feeling him impossibly deeper from this new angle.

"Oh!" I gasp.

Before I can lean forward, he sits up to meet me, his arms encircling my back. Our chests press together, my breasts against the hard plane of his torso. Our faces are so close I can feel his breath on my lips.

"Like this," he murmurs, guiding my hips into a slow, rocking motion.

We're completely intertwined—legs wrapped around each other, arms holding tight, bodies joined at our most intimate places. The position is intensely intimate, allowing almost no space between us. Every part of me is touching some part of him.

I rock against him, finding a new rhythm that's less about thrusting and more about grinding, feeling him deep inside me. His hands slides down to cup my ass, guiding me in a deeper grind. I feel him twitch inside me as I roll my hips in a circular motion.

"I love being this close to you," he whispers against my ear, his voice thick with emotion.

The fervor of his words matches the intensity of our connection. I've never felt so completely joined with another person—physically, emotionally, spiritually. It's overwhelming in the best possible way.

I capture his mouth with mine, kissing him, my tongue sliding against his in a dance as intimate as our bodies. My fingers tangle in his hair, holding him close as our movements become more urgent. The pressure builds low in my belly, a familiar tightening that grows with each rock of my hips.

"Chase," I gasp against his mouth, "I'm close."

His hands hold my hips firmly, guiding me into a faster rhythm as one of his hands slides between our bodies. His thumb finds my sensitive bundle of nerves, circling with just the right pressure.

"Let go," he urges, his eyes locked on mine. "I want to watch you come apart."

The intensity of his gaze pushes me over the edge. My orgasm crashes through me like a wave, starting where we're joined and radiating outward until even my fingertips tingle with it. I cry out, a small, broken sound that echoes through the tent. I clench around him, my inner walls pulsing with each wave of pleasure. His breath hitches, rhythm faltering as he watches me come undone above him.

"You're so beautiful," he says, his voice strained as he continues to move beneath me.

Still riding the aftershocks of my release, I rock against him more deliberately now, tightening around him with each downward motion. I want to feel him lose control, and want to cause his undoing.

"Come for me," I breathe against his ear, nipping gently at his earlobe.

Chase's hands grip my hips harder, his fingers digging into my flesh as he thrusts up into me with increasing urgency. His movements grow erratic, his breathing ragged against my neck. I feel the exact moment when he reaches the edge—his entire body tenses beneath me, his arms tightening around my waist.

"Daisy," he groans, burying his face in my neck as he pulses inside me, filling me with his cum. I hold him through it, my arms wrapped around his waist, my lips pressed against his shoulder.

We stay locked together, our bodies still joined, foreheads pressed against each other as we catch our breath. I can feel his heart thundering against my chest, matching the wild rhythm of my own. Sweat cools on our skin, making us stick together.

I don't want to move. I want to preserve this perfect

moment of reunion, to memorize every sensation—the weight of him inside me, the heat of his skin against mine, the slight tickle of his eyelashes when he blinks. After months apart, after everything we've been through, this connection feels sacred.

His hands slide up my back, one coming to rest at the nape of my neck. His thumb traces gentle circles against my skin.

"I thought I'd lost this forever," he whispers, his voice raw with emotion. "Lost you. There were days I couldn't breathe thinking about it."

I pull back just enough to look into his eyes, finding them bright with unshed tears. The vulnerability there makes my throat tighten. I cup his face; my thumbs brush his jawline.

"I never stopped loving you," I tell him, running my fingers through his hair. "Not for a single day."

Chase's eyes hold mine as he leans in, but instead of pressing his lips to mine, he brushes his eyelashes against my cheek in the gentlest caress. The flutter of his lashes tickles my skin; time seems to shiver and still. A butterfly kiss—so delicate, so intimate, *so us.*

"I love you," he whispers, his breath warm against my skin as his eyelashes flutter against my cheek again.

My heart swells until I think it might burst from my chest. In this simple gesture, I feel everything—his tenderness, his devotion, his promise.

"I love your butterfly kisses," I whisper, emotion making my voice catch. I picture us years from now, decades even, his hair gray at the temples, lines of laughter etched around his eyes, still giving me these gentle touches that speak volumes without words. I imagine us old and weathered by time but still finding this connection, still making each other's hearts race with something as simple as the brush of eyelashes against skin.

"I hope you never stop giving me these," I tell him, running my fingers through his hair. "Even when we're old and gray," I whisper, the thought emerging unbidden. I surprise myself with how certain I am that I want a future—want him—for the rest of my life.

Chase pulls back, his expression serious. "I promise," he says, his eyes never leaving mine. "I'll be giving you butterfly kisses when we're ninety years old, sitting on our porch swing watching our grandchildren play in the yard."

My breath catches at the certainty in his voice, the absolute conviction that we have a future—not just tomorrow or next year, but decades from now.

"You see us with grandchildren?" I whisper, unable to keep the wonder from my voice.

"I see everything with you, Daisy," he says, brushing a strand of hair from my face.

Tears prick at the corners of my eyes, overwhelmed by the depth of his certainty, his love. This isn't just passion or reconciliation—it's a promise.

Epilogue

CHASE

4 YEARS LATER...

I crouch behind the fallen log, adjusting my mask while trying to steady my breathing. Wes and Luke are huddled beside me, their paintball guns clutched tightly in gloved hands. Wes's expression is deadly serious as he sketches a quick diagram in the dirt with a stick.

"Chase, you flank left through those trees," he whispers, pointing to a dense patch of pines. "Luke, you go right. I'll provide cover fire from here."

"They're expecting us to split up," Luke argues, peering over the log before ducking back down. "We should stick together, overwhelm one position."

I nod, checking the hopper on my gun. "Luke's right. They've got the high ground at the ridge. If we split up, they'll pick us off one by one."

Wes considers this, his competitive nature clear in the tight set of his jaw. Even in a friendly game of paintball, my oldest brother treats strategy with military precision. Some things never change.

"Fine," he concedes. "We move together toward the eastern ridge, then—"

The shrill blast of a horn cuts through the forest, signaling the start of the game.

Luke nods seriously, his jaw set with determination. "Remember, no mercy. Not even for Bebe."

"Especially not for Daisy," I add, thinking of my wife's competitive streak. "She's been practicing at the range all month."

Wes tightens the strap on his tactical vest. "Amelia's deadly accurate. Don't underestimate her."

We bump fists, a ritual before battle. The morning sun filters through the trees, highlighting dust particles in the air.

"For Sullivan honor," Luke whispers, and we share a last nod before leaping up from our cover.

We've barely taken three steps when the air fills with the distinctive pop-pop-pop of paintball fire. A bright blue splatter explodes against the tree inches from my head, bark fragments spraying my cheek. Another whizzes past Wes's shoulder, close enough that I hear him suck in a sharp breath.

"Down!" I shout, diving behind a fallen oak. Luke tumbles in beside me, while Wes rolls behind a nearby boulder. My heart hammers against my ribs as feminine giggles echo through the trees.

"They knew exactly where we were," I hiss, wiping sweat from my forehead. "How do they always know?"

Luke peeks around the edge of our log before quickly

withdrawing as another paintball whizzes past. "Bebe's got us pinned," he mutters, a reluctant smile tugging at his lips. "My wife is still too good at this."

"Your wife has actual combat training," I counter, checking my ammunition.

More giggles float down from the ridge, closer now. I recognize Daisy's laugh instantly—that bright, musical sound that still makes my heart skip even after two years of marriage. We tied the knot right after her college graduation, which coincided perfectly with my law school commencement. The timing couldn't have been better—both of us starting our careers together, building our life in a little apartment before buying our first home last year.

"They're moving to the west ridge," Wes whispers, interrupting my thoughts. "We need to reposition."

I nod, refocusing on the battle at hand. It's funny how the mighty Sullivan brothers have fallen. Back in the day we were undefeated in these woods—paintball legends in our own minds. But since we started playing husbands versus wives, we haven't won a single match. Not one. Our tactical superiority means nothing against the uncanny coordination of the women in our lives.

"On three," Luke mouths, holding up his fingers to count down.

Before he reaches two, a barrage of paintballs rain down on our position. I flatten myself against the ground as colors splatter all around us, the distinct purple of Daisy's ammunition landing inches from my boot.

"Retreat!" Wes yells, but a volley of paintballs cuts off his command.

"Come out, come out, wherever you are!" Daisy's voice rings through the trees, sweet but menacing.

"Quit hiding like little girls!" Amelia's taunting follows, her usually gentle voice surprisingly intimidating when she's holding a paintball gun.

"Yeah, Sullivan boys! We thought you guys were supposed to be good at this?" Bebe's voice joins the chorus, coming from somewhere to our right.

I exchange glances with my brothers, Wes's face splattered with a mixture of determination and sweat, Luke looking increasingly worried.

"They're trying to psych us out," I whisper. "We need a new strategy."

The women's laughter echoes through the forest, followed by another barrage of paintballs hitting the surrounding trees.

"I say we each take one," I suggest, checking my ammo. "Wes, you go after Amelia. I'll handle Daisy. Luke, you take Bebe."

Wes nods firmly, his eyes narrowing with competitive focus. "Divide and conquer. I like it."

Luke, however, shakes his head, looking genuinely concerned. "I don't know, man. My wife is scary. Last time she got me, I had bruises for a week."

"Aww, is little Lukey afraid of his wife?" Wes teases.

"Man up, Luke," I tease, giving him a shove. "We can't let them win again."

"Fine," Luke mutters.

"On three," Wes raises his hand to count down. "One... two... three!"

We break apart, scrambling in different directions. I sprint toward where I last heard Daisy's voice, my boots crunching on fallen leaves. Adrenaline courses through my veins as I duck behind trees, moving in a zigzag pattern to make myself a harder target.

I spot a flash of blonde hair through the foliage and drop behind a large rock. Pressing my back against the cool surface, I ready my gun and listen. The forest is suspiciously quiet now —no giggles, no taunting calls. Just the rustle of leaves in the breeze and my heartbeat pounding in my ears.

I peek along the edge of the rock, scanning the trees. Nothing.

That's when I feel it—the unmistakable presence of someone behind me. Before I can turn, a paintball explodes against my back, the impact making me jolt forward. I whirl around to find Daisy standing there, her paintball gun casually resting on her shoulder, a triumphant smile lighting up her face.

She throws her head back, laughing with pure delight. Her blonde hair catches the sunlight filtering through the leaves, creating a halo effect that makes her look angelic—despite having just shot her husband.

"You should see your face right now," she says between giggles, her eyes sparkling with mischief.

I stare at her in disbelief, my mouth hanging open. "You shot me! You actually shot me in the back!"

"That's four games in a row now," she quips, twirling her gun with surprising dexterity. Her grin widens as she takes in my paint-splattered back. "You boys are getting predictable."

I shake my head, unable to keep the smile from tugging at my lips despite my defeat. She's so beautiful when she's victorious—cheeks flushed, eyes bright with excitement.

She steps closer, reaching out to tap my chest with her finger. "Maybe next time—"

I don't let her finish. In one fluid motion, I raise my gun and fire, catching her squarely in the stomach with a blue splatter. Her mouth drops open in shock as she looks down at the paint spreading across her camo vest.

"That's not fair!" she pouts, her victorious expression replaced by indignation. "I already got you. You're out!" she exclaims, pointing at my blue-splattered back.

"If I'm going down, you're going with me," I declare, closing the distance between us. "Romeo and Juliet style."

She rolls her eyes, an adorable little wrinkle forming between her brows. "You need to re-read the book, Chase. That's not how it went. They both died alone, at separate times. It was tragic, not romantic."

"Always the scholar," I say, stepping closer to her.

I reach out and gently pull off her protective mask, revealing her flushed face beneath. Her blonde hair is slightly matted from the mask, a few strands sticking to her forehead with sweat. She's never looked more beautiful. I remove my own mask and toss it aside, not caring where it lands.

"You know what they did do, though?" I murmur, my voice dropping low as I pull her against me, paint splatters and all.

"What's that?" she whispers, her mock annoyance already melting away.

"This," I angle down toward her lips, capturing them with mine, tasting the salt of sweat on her lips. She melts into the kiss, her paintball gun dropping to the forest floor with a soft thud as her arms wrap around my neck. The world narrows to just us—her body pressed against mine, the softness of her lips, the small sigh she makes as I deepen the kiss.

"Get a room, you two!" Wes's voice interrupts our moment, followed by the sound of his heavy footsteps approaching through the underbrush.

I reluctantly break the kiss but keep my arms around Daisy's waist, turning to see both my brothers trudging toward us. Luke's entire front is splattered with bright pink paint, while Wes's helmet sports a perfect yellow bullseye on the forehead.

"Game's over anyway," Luke grumbles, wiping ineffectually at the paint on his chest. "We all got eliminated. The girls won. *Again*."

"Bebe got you good," I observe, struggling to keep the amusement from my voice as I take in Luke's paint-covered form.

"Like I said, she's scary," Luke replies, dabbing at a particularly large splatter on his shoulder with a grimace.

The savory aroma of smoked meat fills the air as I slide into the booth beside Daisy. Smokey's, the local BBQ joint down the road from the paintball range, has become our traditional post-game spot. The rustic wooden tables are already sticky with sauce, and country music plays softly in the background.

"I ordered the family platter," Wes announces, gesturing to the waitress who's approaching with a tray so massive it requires both arms to carry. "With extra burnt ends for the champions."

Amelia elbows him playfully. "You mean for us wives?"

The waitress sets down a wooden board overflowing with brisket, ribs, pulled pork, and all the fixings. Steam rises from the meat, carrying the scent of hickory and spices. My mouth waters as I reach for a rib.

"Before we demolish this feast," I say, raising my beer bottle, "I want to thank all of you for coming out this week. It means everything to have our family together for this milestone. The butterfly sanctuary opens Monday, and we wouldn't want to celebrate with anyone else."

Daisy squeezes my thigh under the table, her eyes sparkling with excitement. "We already have a few elementary schools lined up for field trips in the fall," she adds, her voice brimming with pride. "The response has been incredible."

Wes shakes his head, a bemused smile playing across his lips. "Never in a million years did I see my little brother becoming an environmental lawyer and co-running a butterfly sanctuary." He raises his beer in salute. "But it suits you, Chase. It really does."

"They're definitely in love," Bebe says, leaning against Luke's shoulder. "Not just with each other, but with those butterflies too."

"To Chase and Daisy," Luke raises his glass. "And to their butterfly sanctuary!"

"To the butterflies!" everyone echoes, clinking glasses around the table.

We all dig into the feast before us, passing plates and trading stories between bites of smoky brisket and tangy ribs. I watch them all—my family—and feel a wave of gratitude so intense it nearly takes my breath away.

How did we get here?

It started with Bebe—her moving into our house after a simple classified ad. "Roommate wanted, male preferred. Private room in a house with three brothers. Walking distance to the university." We were just looking to make some extra cash by renting out the spare bedroom in our house. I remember how shocked we were when she showed up at our door. We had no idea we were inviting a member of one of the most powerful crime families into our home. But it worked out for Luke: A mafia princess and a secret society prince.

Then there's Wes and Amelia—my NFL star brother fell for our career-driven next-door neighbor after she lost her husband. He happily traded college parties and women for her. Wes is raising her daughter as his own, and they have a baby boy of their own—making me a proud uncle of two.

And me? I was the most broken of all of us. After everything with Luke and Bebe, after the spiraling and the self-destruction, I never thought I'd find my way back. Let alone find someone who would look at me the way Daisy does—like I'm whole, worthy and enough.

I remember how certain I was that I'd ruined any chance with her when I married Celeste. How I'd convinced myself I didn't deserve happiness after everything I'd done. Yet here we are, two years married, building something meaningful together. Something that matters.

As conversation flows around us, I can't help but marvel at how perfectly everything has fallen into place. Each of us finding our match, our purpose. The Sullivan brothers, once so lost in our own ways, are now anchored by the extraordinary women who chose us.

I press my lips to Daisy's temple, breathing in the familiar scent of her shampoo mixed with the day's adventures— sunshine, forest, and now barbecue. She turns to me, her eyes crinkling at the corners with a smile that's meant just for me.

"What was that for?" she whispers.

"Because I can," I murmur back, feeling my heart swell with an emotion too vast to name.

I want to spend every day of my life with this woman. Building our sanctuary, watching monarchs migrate each year, growing old together.

I lean in closer, my face near hers, and instead of kissing her lips, I flutter my eyelashes against her cheek in the softest butterfly kiss. She immediately recognizes the gesture, her breath catching as she turns to meet my eyes.

Without a word, she leans forward and returns the gesture, her eyelashes fluttering delicately against my skin.

"Oh look, they're doing it again," Amelia's voice cuts through our intimate moment, her tone a mixture of amusement and affection.

I hear Bebe release a soft "Awww" from across the table, followed by Amelia joining in with her own cooing sound.

But I don't pull away. Neither does Daisy. We stay locked in our private ritual, her eyelashes still fluttering against my cheek like butterfly wings. In this moment, there's only us— the gentle tickle of her lashes, the warmth of her breath on my skin.

When we finally separate, her eyes meet mine with a warmth that makes the rest of the restaurant fade away. She doesn't appear embarrassed by our audience. If anything, there's a quiet pride in her expression, a contentment that matches the fullness in my chest.

"You guys..." Luke says with a good-natured eye roll, but I can see the genuine smile beneath his teasing. "It's sickeningly cute."

"I think it's adorable," Bebe counters, leaning forward.

It amazes me how that simple touch—eyelashes against skin—can convey more love than words ever could. Our own private language, born that night by the lake—*butterfly kisses*.

The end.

About the Author

Lulu Hart

Lulu Hart is a passionate storyteller who has been fascinated by the written word since childhood. From the whimsical worlds of Disney and Dr. Seuss to the thrilling adventures of Goosebumps and Sweet Valley High and the literary classics studied in high school. While in college, she dabbled in poetry, eventually publishing a collection that captured her creative spirit.

Lulu decided to bring her own love stories to life and share them with the world. Her debut novel, *Punches & Pirouettes*, marks the beginning of an exciting chapter in her writing journey. With its emotional depth, unforgettable characters, and engaging storytelling, this love story will keep lovers of contemporary romance captivated and yearning for more.

Lulu is a full-time professional in administrative healthcare and lives in Las Vegas, Nevada, with her loving husband and adorable daughter. In her free time, she finds fulfillment in watching horror movies, reading romance novels, and celebrating the joy of the holidays—Christmas being her favorite.

Also by Lulu Hart

The Fitzpatrick Clan

Punches & Pirouettes

Whiskey & Wine

Interludes with Insects

The Killer Bee

Ladybug Designs

Butterfly Kisses